Land of Madness

The Tales of Drendil
Fallen Stars
The Collapse of Madira
Dark Magic
Raven's Requiem
The Manticore
Murder
The Basilisk
Minotaur

The Drendil Saga
Land of Madness
Siege of Shemont (Coming Soon)
Downfall
Road to Ruin
Scapegoat (Coming Soon)

Land of

Madness

B T Litell

RAVENSTEEL
PUBLISHING

This is a work of fiction, and the views expressed herein are the sole responsibility of the author. Likewise, characters, places, and incidents are the product of the author's imagination, and any resemblance to actual persons, living or dead, or actual events or locales, is entirely coincidental.

Cover art by Cherie Fox @ fiver.com
Edited by Megan Hundley

First edition published 2020 independently
Second edition published 2022 by Ravensteel Publishing, LLC

Visit https://btlitellauthor.com for more information about the author and his projects

ISBN: 978-1-7379624-1-0
Kindle ASIN: B09Q95NYHY

Write to:
Ravensteel Publishing, LLC
PO Box 274
Canal Winchester, OH 43110

*For anyone who ever uprooted themselves
from the only life you knew to start fresh in a
land you knew nothing about. If you are in
the process of doing this, know that things
get better and there will be peace eventually.*

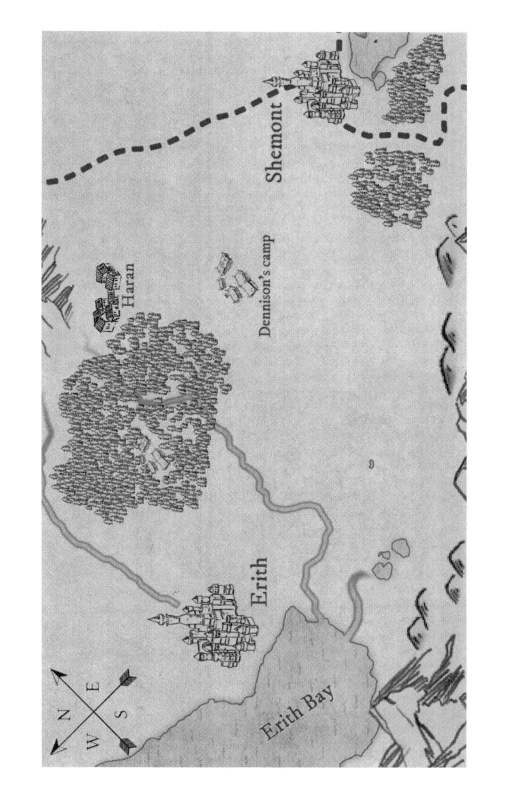

Table of Contents

Prologue

arkness clung to the city like a damp shirt. This was the impenetrable darkness of a moonless, overcast night. Even the colors which would splash the sky and herald the coming sunrise were hours away, but in this darkness, it felt like that would take a lifetime to arrive. *Ting. Ting. Ting.* A heavy, hollow ringing sound echoed through the city like dozens of various-sized, bronze bells sprouted up under key points in the city overnight. This sound was new and unwelcome. This sound, disturbing the eerie tranquility that normally came with night watches, continued, reminding all who were awake of something ominous to come. The sound caused the city to stir earlier than it should have; concerned citizens peeked their heads out of their doors or windows to see if they could find the source of the ringing sound to no avail.

Michael despised patrolling the streets, especially at night. No matter what, once the sun went down, he felt like a thousand eyes watched him no matter where he moved. Tonight, with the *ting*-ing sound coming from under his feet, that sensation worsened and only added to the uncomfortable feeling of night watch. Without stopping, Michael periodically turned around to get a good look at his surroundings. Most guards carried a torch or lantern during their night patrols, but Michael wanted his eyes adjusted to the darkness as much as possible. He turned, the stiff leather soles of his shoes whispering faintly against the cobblestone beneath him, and scanned the street behind him, looking for any kind of threat he could possibly see. *I have to get to the guardhouse,* he thought. *Someone there will know what to do.* Even if no one *did* know what to do, they could at least form a plan for dealing with this noise.

Not wanting to waste any time, Michael took off running toward the nearest guardhouse. As he ran, the stiff leather armor he wore creaked and moaned, the sound soothing him slightly. His longsword swung at his hip and the shield on his back flapped like a singular wing, trying its hardest to achieve flight. The armor he wore, including his shield, bore the same crimson and gold colors as every other guard who walked the streets. On his chest showed a rampant griffin, the sigil of the king. The same griffin flew on every pennant and tapestry in the city and anywhere someone wanted to show allegiance to the king. The only person in the army who wore anything different was the Master General who wore shoulder boards bearing six stars in the shape of Deja, the phoenix constellation many travelers used for navigation as it was always found in the northern part of the sky no matter the time of year.

Rounding a corner onto a larger street, Michael nearly bumped into Týr, another guard also assigned to night watches. Týr always reminded Michael of a hunting wolf with the way he walked, never letting his eyes stay in one place long. One of Týr's hands remained on the hilt of the knife he wore, and he repeatedly moved it out of the sheath enough to know the blade was free before slamming it back. The knife, not issued by the armory, was something he carried as a memento for his sister who died a couple of years before. She owned the wickedly curved blade and now it belonged to Týr. Many stories, some possibly true and others likely exaggerated, revolved around that knife and what the man could do with it.

"I loathe this sound, Michael," Týr said. "This ringing almost sounds like a song which will be in my head for a few nights at least."

"I'm on my way to the guardhouse to speak with the captain about it. Come with me?"

"You know the captain will pitch a fit about me leaving my post, even though investigating this noise should be more important than a *lieutenant* patrolling the streets. Do you know how many thieves would be out during this noise? None. *I* certainly don't want to be out during this, but here I am."

"Are you coming with me then?" Michael asked.

Týr nodded and spun on the balls of his feet before starting to run toward the guardhouse. Michael did the same, trying his best to keep up with the former thief. Even when he ran, his hand stayed on the knife hanging on his belt. Michael never could understand the obsession he had with the knife, but Michael was an only child. Some things were not meant to be understood, he decided. Together they ran a few blocks until Týr stopped, looked down an alley, and called to someone.

"Joshua, come with us! We may need some help talking sense into the captain."

"That sounds better than trying to find the source of this noise," the Mage said before exiting the alley and joining them.

Together the trio ran a few more blocks, changing direction a few times as they approached the guardhouse. When they arrived a few minutes later, the captain stood on the porch barking orders at a gaggle of guards who already gathered concerning the noise. The captain was a stout man with an overpowering persona and a wavering sense of decision-making. Once the trio came within view, the man's face flushed red with a vein popping out in his forehead and neck. Thankfully, Michael realized that was just his normal reaction to seeing Týr. Týr should have been promoted to Guard-Captain, but an incident between him and the now-promoted captain stopped that from happening. Michael didn't know nearly enough of the details about that and chose not to ask to maintain his ignorance of the subject. He disliked rumor-mongering.

"Lieutenant, take your sentries to the southeast corner of the city to see what you can learn about this noise. Report back any findings you have," the captain said, waving a hand toward Týr, Michael, and Joshua.

"I'm sorry, but I'm not a sentry," Joshua said firmly.

"Give me lip again and the Supreme Warlock will hear about you being openly insubordinate to a senior officer," the captain threatened.

Joshua took a few moments to think about his next words before sighing and speaking resignedly. "Yes, sir."

"That's better, Mage," the captain said with a sly grin on his face. "Now, move along you three. I don't want to hear any more excuses. Report back at the next bell."

Michael, Týr, and Joshua clapped their right hands to their chests and took off, running toward the southeast corner of the city. As they ran, the ringing sound grew louder. The loud noise caused the city to stir, and terror flooded every face Michael saw looking through the windows and doorways of their houses as the three men ran down the streets. He tried to stop and reassure a family but couldn't fall behind his comrades who didn't break from their fast pace. His heart ached for the people of the city.

As they came within sight of the city's southeastern wall, the ground shook and the wall collapsed. The trio fell to the ground as a cloud of dust and stone pieces showered down on them from where the wall stood not even ten seconds before. The cloud of dust that rushed into the streets blocked everything more than a couple of meters from view. The ground trembled again, and something else came tumbling down, but with the dust from the first eruption blocking their vision, there was no way to know what exactly collapsed. More dust filled the streets, bringing less visibility. Michael and Joshua coughed as they both got back to their feet. Týr remained on the ground not moving, his left hand tucked under his stomach. Michael grabbed the shield off his back and held it over his head as more stone continued to rain down on them. Joshua, seeing this, cast a spell and a protective bubble formed around the trio which even cleared some of the dust out of their way. Chunks of stone *flumph*-ed off the top of the bubble and clattered against the cobblestone road at the edge of the spell.

Michael went to check Týr to make sure he was alive and, as he stepped toward his comrade, he saw looming shapes emerge through the dust cloud. The shapes, clearly not human, stood roughly three meters tall and more than one across at what Michael thought looked like shoulders. Michael quickly touched Týr's neck to make sure he was still alive and, feeling his heartbeat, shook the man gently to try and wake him up. Joshua came over quickly and cast a spell that brought Týr back to consciousness. He gasped loudly and rolled onto his back before struggling briefly to stand. Michael helped him to his feet, his eyes locked on the approaching shapes the entire time.

"We have company," Michael whispered to Týr.

"Shit!" Týr muttered under his breath.

"State your intentions!" Michael shouted, following protocol. He released Týr and his hand shot for his sword hilt.

The only response to Michael's challenge that came through the dust was the *clip-clop* of hooves and labored breathing that sounded much like a bull. Michael, confused by the upright nature of the shadows and the sounds he heard, wracked his brain for possibilities but only came up with myths and other impossibilities. *It can't be a minotaur. Those don't exist,* he thought as the clacking of hooves continued coming closer. As the one shadow approached, Michael saw several others behind it, all moving together.

Before anyone could speak again, a tree branch swung through the bubble spell Joshua cast earlier, catching Michael directly in the chest. Air rushed from his lungs and an ache more severe than anything he felt before accompanied the *crunch* sound as the branch made contact. The force of the blow knocked him off his feet and into the nearest building. He slammed into the building's façade and felt something shift inside his body followed by agonizing pain. His vision blurred and the world swirled around him as he sat against the ground unable to move without great amounts of pain shooting up his back and through his ribs. Michael fought the encroaching darkness as he watched Týr and Joshua fight off a pack of minotaurs. As two fell, a figure in a shadowy robe cut through the group of monsters and began fighting with Týr and Joshua. Those shadowy robes didn't move as the mysterious, new arrival walked, and the newcomer looked as if he floated along the ground. Michael's eyes closed involuntarily as a shower of sparks flashed from an impossibly dark sword the shadowy figure wielded. Everything around Michael faded into impregnable blackness. A void. A darkness that consumed everything.

Chapter One

Michael's eyes snapped open, and his breath came in ragged gasps. Despite spring's expected nighttime chill invading his room through the open window, he felt sweat cover his entire body. He whipped his blanket off himself and sat up, still trying to catch his breath. Within a few moments, his heart stopped racing and his breathing calmed down. He stood and walked to his dressing table, poured some water into the basin, and grabbed a wash rag. He dipped the rag into the cold water and wrung it out before wiping the sweat from his bare chest, neck, and face. His chest felt tight with the cold water, but he welcomed the cold after another unpleasant nightmare about the unknown city under siege by minotaurs and a black-robed figure. He didn't know why

1

these dreams kept happening, or why they grew more frequent as the days went by. In the past week, he experienced the same dream five times. He wracked his brain trying to learn what he could from the dream, but every time he tried to analyze it, memories of the dream slipped through his mental grasp like smoke. What he did know was the city was not Feldring. Actually, he knew he wasn't anywhere on Prikea, based solely on the livery he and the other guards wore. No city in Prikea wore crimson and gold. The king's court in Safdin wore tan with black ravens while Feldring's soldiers bore black tabards with yellow lilies on their chests.

Regardless, he tried to analyze the dreams when they came to him, but he never got far with that task. Instead of trudging through the dissipating memories of his nightmare, this time he decided to try and relax his mind some. He looked out his bedroom window and cursed under his breath seeing how dark the night sky was. Though he didn't have to work for Master Gamel in the morning, he would only have a few more hours to sleep before he needed to attend to house chores. Instead of fretting over the loss of sleep, he stoked the fire in his hearth and added another log to the dying embers to ensure the flames would at least have something to take hold of again. After prodding the embers, flames sparked back to life, and he sat on a nearby stool and grabbed his pipe and its accompanying pouch of tobacco leaves.

He skillfully packed the leaves into his pipe and grabbed a piece of kindling, placing it in the embers only long enough to get the end lit. He used the burning stick to light his pipe, blowing smoke out the sides of his mouth as he puffed at the mouthpiece held firmly

2

between his teeth. The pipe lit quickly, and he tossed the burning stick back into the hearth. He stretched his legs toward the fire and let the heat warm his chilly feet. The heat from the waxing flames felt nice against the soles of his feet, a welcome relief from the cold, wooden floors of his bedroom.

Despite telling himself he wouldn't analyze his dream, Michael found himself staring into the growing flames trying to pick apart everything he could remember. By this time, he should have his dreams memorized. They were always the same: he and two others patrolled the streets in a city he didn't know right before an attack. Every dream ended the same way too. A tree branch struck him in the chest, throwing him into a nearby building while the other two fought off a horde of minotaurs and a black-cloaked figure with an impossibly dark sword. He never dreamed any further than that, though he sometimes wished he could just to see what would happen. These dreams felt like premonitions, but he knew such things were merely the stuff of stories. No one could tell the future or even inklings of it. It was all just nonsense that old women with nothing better to do would sell to you in hopes for more of your coins.

Michael, nearly finished with his pipe, grabbed his kettle, and filled it halfway with water before placing it over the fire to heat. He didn't need a full boil to make tea but at least wanted the water warmed enough to make a pleasant drink. With the kettle over the fire, Michael finished smoking his pipe. Before he could clean the tobacco out of the bowl, he heard the faintest knock on his front door. *Tap. Tap. Tap.* The knocking sounded thrice then stopped and was just faint enough he almost thought it was only in his head.

Michael tapped his pipe vigorously onto the hearth, set it on his stool, and went down his stairs to the front door. He attempted to look through the windows beside the door to see who was knocking but saw nothing. Finding this odd, he cautiously opened the door just wide enough to see a man wearing tan, hooded robes with black accents. His heart started beating faster, and he opened the door all the way. He looked beyond the stranger at his door and saw no one else. *Why is someone from the king's court here?* Michael wondered.

"Good morning. I'm sorry for the intrusion, but I am here because you are having recurring dreams of the future. May I come in?" the man asked with little room in his voice for Michael to refuse his request.

"How do you know about the dreams?" Michael asked, taken aback by the thought of a stranger showing up like this.

"The Order of Ravens knows of many things which threaten the world."

"Well that hardly tells me anything," Michael protested.

"I promise all will be explained in due time. May I come in?" the stranger asked again.

Michael hesitated for a moment, thinking of the implications this before sighing. "Of course. Come in. I have a kettle upstairs if you would like some tea. I can't promise the water is quite ready yet, though."

The man stepped into Michael's front room and lowered his hood, revealing a shaved head, dark green eyes, dark eyebrows, and a strong jawline with a cleft chin. As his hands came down, Michael saw a black raven tattooed into the back of the man's right hand. The tattoo was black with shimmering silver accents that almost looked like they moved as if the raven were flying on the back of the stranger's hand. Everything about the man seemed normal except the color of his robes and the strange marking he bore on his right hand. Michael also wondered about the emblem he wore on his chest. *This man has traveled here all the way from Safdin?*

"Thank you for the offered tea, but I am fine for now. If you want some, please don't let me keep you, Michael."

"You know a lot about me, yet I know hardly anything about you, stranger," Michael said, looking at the man for a moment before sitting in one of the chairs.

"I apologize for my lack of manners. My name is Joshua and I'm a priest with the Order of Ravens here on Prikea. I was sent here to discuss the dreams you're having and see if you would come with me to speak with the others in my Order. I know this is a daunting request, but we need you to help us figure out what we can do to save the world. Your dreams have a connection to a great darkness in this world which the priesthood wishes to snuff out like a candle. While many stories call these dreams premonitions, we think of them as loose prophecy."

"You said your name is Joshua?" Michael asked, thinking of the Mage in his dreams. *It can't just be a coincidence, can it?*

"Correct. You seem more concerned about this revelation than I expected."

Michael inhaled sharply. "Considering what you know about me and these dreams, I'm just concerned that you don't see the coincidence in bearing the same name as someone from my dreams. Won't you admit that's at least convenient?"

"I'm not schooled in the ways of prophecy, sadly. I was merely told what I needed to know before heading here. As for the name, it is fairly common, so it's hard to say."

Michael thought about his options for a moment. "How long do I have to decide if I want to come with you? I would have to leave everything behind and that is something that takes time to consider."

"I can remain here in Feldring for a short time while you consider your choices. If you need to find me, I will be praying at the temple. Take the time you need to make this decision, but I will not remain here long. Tomorrow evening, I will make my way back to Safdin as duties require my attention there," Joshua said. "I want you to know that your dreams may mean something beyond grave is happening within the world. You may be the only person we know of having these nightmares."

"That's encouraging," Michael said, trying not to sound sarcastic. "No pressure at all."

"I don't want to put any burden on you, but the fate of the world could be at stake. I know this is a lot of pressure on you, but please take your time and take this into consideration carefully. I understand if you don't want to come with me, but please consider the weight of this decision."

Michael stared at the floor in front of his feet while he considered. "Do you know how long I would be gone?"

"That I don't know, but I can't imagine it would be very long. It takes two days to ride to Safdin by horse, and I would imagine it would take some time to get your dreams sorted out with the other Ravens. I think you should expect to be gone for at least a week," Joshua replied. "If anything would keep you longer, would it be a problem?"

"No, it won't be a problem if I'm gone longer than a week. Master Gamel will understand if this is something that concerns the safety of the world," Michael said. "Is there anything else that I can do for you at the moment?"

"I have nothing else. Please find me in the temple when you have made your decision," Joshua replied, walking toward the door, and pulling his hood up as he reached the threshold.

"I will see you again once I make my decision," Michael said.

Joshua nodded once and turned to walk down the street, not looking back at Michael as he moved silently. Michael watched the priest walk for a few moments before closing the door, setting the lock, and walking back upstairs. Once in his room, he removed the kettle from the hook over the fire and poured water into a cup before adding his tea leaves. While the tea steeped, he filled his pipe with more tobacco and lit that with another piece of kindling from the fireplace. He puffed at the pipe again and drank his tea as he considered what the priest said. *It's only a week*, he thought. *What's the harm in that?* Not much would happen at the store in a week, and Master Gamel would be fine with any of the work that arrived in that time. Michael wasn't the carpenter's only apprentice anyway. Everything would be fine. It's not like he would be leaving for good, never to come back. That would be a different decision to make. He shifted on his stool as he thought about the prospects of being away for even a week or so. This was a tough decision.

Michael looked through his bedroom window at the Feldring skyline. The city, built into the side of a few mountains, overlooked the plains that approached the Gilded Mountains, a range that split the continent of Prikea into two large pieces. On the north of the mountain range stood one kingdom and to the south another, where Michael lived. The two kingdoms coexisted peacefully enough in the past and traded goods between themselves often. Most of those goods traveled through Feldring on their way to their destinations because a major river started high in the mountains and flowed east toward the sea. Michael looked at the tops of buildings as the sky began to change from a deep black to a lighter grey, verging on blue. The sun would rise in due time; Michael estimated that in about an hour and a half until there would be enough light to walk through the house without a candle or lamp lit. Feldring's skyline was the only thing he knew in this life. How could he leave all this behind, even for a week's journey to the capital city? What if he preferred the other city more? Would it be possible to uproot his life and live there for the foreseeable future? He didn't have answers to these questions, though he knew they were trivial at best. He knew plenty of people who traveled outside of Feldring, but they always came back. Perhaps that should be enough to make this decision for him.

Michael finished drinking his cup of tea and smoking his pipe, then stood to get dressed. He needed to see to a few things before making his way to the temple to relay his decision to the priest. He pulled on his trousers and a shirt then made his way downstairs to his desk where parchment, a quill, inkwell, and sealing wax sat ready to use. He drafted a letter for Master Gamel and explained the entire situation from the dreams to the visit from the priest from the Order of Ravens. He omitted no details as he knew Master Gamel would ask many questions if anything were left out. He read through the letter after he finished writing, made sure everything at least made sense, then blew on the ink to ensure it dried fully before folding the letter and heating the end of the sealing wax. He placed a glob of the wax on the letter's opening and pressed his seal, a simple sunrise with his name around the edge, into the wax. There would be no mistaking the origins of the letter when Master Gamel opened it in a couple of hours when the shop opened.

With his mind made up, and his letter to Master Gamel written, Michael went upstairs and packed what he would need for the journey with Joshua to the capital city. He placed his knapsack on his bed and threw some clothes into the bottom followed by a pouch of his favorite pipe tobacco which he just purchased the day before. He was originally against the idea of cherry-flavored tobacco but decided he would rather have that than no tobacco and it quickly became a favorite of his. Michael placed the pouch containing his pipe and the tobacco on top of everything within his sack then closed it and slung it over his shoulder. Before leaving his room, he ensured the fire in the hearth was out and any additional wood wasn't left there for stray embers to take hold of. Finally, he grabbed his thick, wool coat and slung it over his arm just in case he needed it. Spring was still cold in the mornings in the mountains, and he figured he might need it. *Better to have it and not need it than need it and not have it,* his father's words bounced into his head as he opened his front door and stepped into the street.

At this hour of the morning, few people other than the city watch walked the streets. Michael found himself among those few as he walked toward the temple where he would find Joshua meditating. Michael passed a pair of guards patrolling the street. One carried a torch which cast dancing shadows on their faces as they walked. Michael nodded and smiled at the guards as they passed, but they didn't pay him any mind as they were focused on their duties. Michael turned his attention from the guards as they walked past him and once again focused on his task at hand. He needed to stop at the shop on his way to the temple to leave the letter for Master Gamel. While not entirely on the way to the temple, the workshop also wasn't out of the way. He simply had to go a few blocks away before making his way down the main street within the city where the temple stood.

Michael reached the shop within a few minutes and used his key to unlock the front door. Everything in the store was exactly as he expected it: immaculate. Master Gamel ran a tight woodshop and tolerated very little when it came to errors. Samples of what they could make were placed in the front of the shop with simple tags that stated the type of wood, the price, and how long it would take to make the product. Michael always enjoyed making the rocking chairs or parts of them. Master Gamel, as a master carpenter, could make everything in the shop but generally stuck with the more complicated tasks or with just running the shop. Jordan, one of the other apprentices, did great carving, but she felt too self-conscious making anything other than the intricate engravings that acted as finishes to most of the products. Michael thought she did fine work with the lathe, but sometimes a person is their hardest critic and that could be difficult to get around. Michael personally disliked carvings and would do the rest of the work, then pass the project on to Jordan for finishing. She seemed to enjoy that arrangement as she got more time with the intricacies.

Michael shook his head and walked to the counter where Master Gamel would sit with the ledger and the catalog of everything else they could make. Knowing Master Gamel would only open the ledger as necessary, Michael opted to put his sealed letter neatly atop the ledger to ensure Master Gamel would see it right away when he came into the shop. Michael, with nothing else tying him to the shop for the week, Michael walked out the door and relocked it before continuing down the street to return to Feldring's main street. He knew there were only a few blocks until he reached the temple and simply walked in that direction, watching the city as it started stirring as the sky grew lighter with each passing minute until, finally, full-blown sunlight blasted between the buildings and lit the streets. Something about the waking city seemed so peaceful, but Michael knew that tranquility wouldn't last long as wagons would soon pour into the city to gather supplies to take elsewhere on the continent.

Michael reached the temple quickly and stopped to admire the marble façade and the carved double doors before opening one of the arched doors and walking inside. Inside the vestibule, Michael noted the six seraphs who guarded the Allfather carved into the marble walls, three on each side of the entrance. In the middle of the vestibule stood a small pedestal with a bowl resting atop which contained clean water. Not being an overly religious person, Michael simply walked around the holy water but did stop at the bank of partially lit candles. He grabbed one of the burning sticks left on the table, lit it with one of the other candles, then touched the fire to the unlit wick of another candle. He said a prayer for those he wished to remember and then put out the flame on the stick. He turned to the front of the temple's sanctuary and saw Joshua kneeling at the altar with his hood pulled down and his shaved head bowed reverently. Not wanting to disturb the priest's meditation, Michael walked as silently as he could and sat in one of the chairs set up in the temple, placing his knapsack in the chair beside him. He sat for only a few moments before Joshua raised his head and spoke to Michael without turning around.

"What decision have you made?" he asked.

"I will come with you. A week or maybe more is hardly any time at all. Life will still be here in Feldring after that," Michael said.

"I appreciate your decision. You should know the world will be safer with this choice," Joshua said as he stood and turned toward Michael. The raven on the back of his hand shimmered more than it had earlier this morning, but Michael figured it might be from the light coming into the temple through the stained-glass windows showing various saints and other religious figures.

"When do we leave for the capital?" Michael asked, grabbing his knapsack, then wondering why he asked the question when he was ready to leave right away.

"Do you need time before we leave? I have two horses in the stable, but they are covered until tomorrow. If you need more time, you can have another day," Joshua said.

Michael took a moment to think about this but quickly pushed the notion of staying another day in Feldring out of his mind. "We can leave now. There's no point delaying this any, right? I am feeling some doubts, though."

"Doubt is a normal emotion in life. The Allfather may have chosen you for this, but your doubt shows that you are more than a carpenter's apprentice."

"What else does it make me?"

"Alive. It's not important why the Allfather chooses us. What matters is our willingness to hear the call and follow. You shouldn't feel shame for experiencing doubts in this, Michael," Joshua said as he walked toward the entrance of the temple. Michael followed closely behind.

When he reached the stoup with the clean water, Joshua dipped his fingers just barely into the water and touched his forehead then his heart and mouthed something as he did so. Unsure what the priest said, Michael once again avoided using the stoup and instead walked around it toward the door waiting for Joshua who only took another moment. Michael pushed the door open by walking backward

13

carefully, then waited for Joshua to lead the way to the stables. Together they walked toward the main gate of the city in silence. They avoided wagons and carts that bustled through the city streets on their way to the markets and the mines until Michael and Joshua reached the stables outside the gate.

Joshua walked in and spoke with the hand who seemed to immediately recognize him and nodded many times before rushing off toward two stalls. He whistled loudly toward the other two hands who rushed over and helped with retrieving the horses. The horses, one solid black except for a white splotch centered between its eyes, and the other solid white, walked resolutely behind the hand leading them by the reins. The young man handed the reins to Joshua who handed back a pouch that Michael assumed contained coins. The hands all bowed many times and helped Joshua and Michael both mount their horses. Joshua climbed into the black horse's saddle with an ease that seemed almost natural. Michael, on the other hand, having only ridden a horse a few times in his life, struggled and needed help from the hands getting into his saddle. With what he hoped was a minimal effort, Michael finally situated himself in the saddle and grabbed the reins from the hands. Based on their size and how little they moved, Michael wondered if the horses were once war horses.

Seeing Michael settled in his saddle, Joshua tugged on his horse's reins, and it started walking gracefully. Michael did nothing, but his horse started following the other by instinct it seemed. Michael grabbed the pommel on his saddle for dear life and hoped they wouldn't be galloping soon as he feared falling off his horse going much faster than their current trot.

"Are you fine in the saddle, Michael?" Joshua asked, turning his head to look at his travel companion.

"It has been a while since I've ridden a horse. If we go much faster than this I will need some help, I think," Michael replied, looking dead ahead as the road crested a hill and dropped gently toward the plains which butted up against the Gilded Mountains.

"We can slow down if you would like," Joshua suggested.

"At least for now," Michael said.

Joshua nodded and pulled his reins straight backward, pulling his horse in. Michael's followed without any direction from its rider. They walked the horses along the road until Michael felt comfortable enough to trot again. Together, Michael and Joshua rode in near silence for about an hour until they came up to a small forest which the road split in half. Joshua snapped his reins as they reached the edge of the woods and his horse sped up slightly into a canter. Michael followed and his horse soon sped up to follow Joshua's. Back in the groove of riding a horse, Michael felt more at ease and loosened his grip on the saddle's pommel. He kept one hand on it but not tight enough for his knuckles to turn white again.

The trees they rode through showed signs of spring's arrival. Buds blossomed on branches and birds sang their songs throughout the branches as Michael and Joshua rode through the woods. Michael even dared to take his gaze from the trail and look to his right as they rode, and he could see the scurrying of the rabbits and squirrels as they searched for fresh food after the long dead of winter. He quickly shot his gaze back to the road but smiled at the thought of life returning to the world after months of bitter chill and snow. He wanted to look back at the mountains to see if the snow was receding from the city like a middle-aged man's hairline, but he dared not try that just yet. It was too early in his riding experience for that, especially while they were moving quicker than before.

The trees that formed the woods thickened, blocking out some of the sunlight. Michael saw a patch of light beams shoot through the canopy of leaves overhead and illuminate some moss-covered stone fragments. The pieces of stone looked to resemble a house or other such structure, but the pieces were scattered all around and the walls seemed to stand haphazardly. Michael stopped his horse to get a better look at the structure. Joshua stopped his horse as well and turned it around to return to Michael who already left the saddle and walked on foot toward the ruins. Joshua watched for a moment, dismounted, raised his hood, and walked over to join Michael at the side of the road. Getting a closer look, Michael saw patches of vines and ferns beginning to reclaim the profane structures of men that they left behind as a scar within nature. Joshua looked briefly, then turned to Michael with his hand stretched toward the ruins.

"These are the outskirts of what once was a kingdom here in Prikea. The name of this kingdom, and the cause of its demise, have long since faded from our history books, but these structures remain as the only remnants. This society collapsed long before our ancestors arrived on this continent, their history already nearly forgotten even then," Joshua explained.

"Interesting. How long ago do you think anyone lived here?" Michael asked.

Joshua looked at the ruins and sighed. "A few hundred years. Maybe someday these ruins won't even exist, and nature will thrive here again. We should only have about an hour or so left in these woods. Would you be against riding faster to get through them?"

"Not against going faster. I think I'm getting more comfortable in the saddle. My legs are a bit sore though."

"We will be stopping for the night soon. Do you need a rest now before we head off again?" Joshua asked with a concerned look on the part of his face that Michael could see.

"If we could rest briefly, I'd appreciate that," Michael said.

"Very well. Let's take a few minutes and regain our strength," Joshua said.

After a few minutes, Michaela and Joshua climbed back into their saddles and made their way through the remainder of the woods. As they rode, the wind picked up and the branches around them shook and clattered together. Some branches further into the woods broke under the force of the winds and fell to the ground, tumbling as they landed. Joshua motioned something to Michael and snapped his reins and leaned forward as his horse sped up. Michael followed Joshua's lead, though he didn't lean as far forward as the priest did. They rode like this for some time, until eventually the wind calmed down and the clouds over the top of the woods broke, letting sunlight once again filter through the leaves. Joshua slowed his horse to a trot and sat up as it slowed down. Michael again followed Joshua's lead, pulling straight back on the reins to slow his beast.

"Not sure what that was about, but I hope it's over," Michael said.

"It should be, judging by the sky," Joshua said, looking around.

They continued their ride in silence until they reached the edge of the woods and a fork in the road. One path continued south, while the other turned left, heading east. Joshua motioned toward the road that branched off, and Michael moved his reins so the horse would turn left. Not far after the fork in the road, Joshua stopped and dismounted from his saddle. He led the horse off the road a few meters and let the reins go. Michael also released his and watched as Joshua set up everything they would need for a campsite. Joshua removed two bedrolls from his saddle and some kindling from a saddlebag. With a few rocks from around their campsite, he soon had a ring set up and stacked the kindling and tinder for a fire. Michael offered to grab some fuel from the woods, and Joshua said he would get everything else set up in Michael's absence. Michael returned about ten minutes later with plenty of wood for their stay and found Joshua meditating again. Michael looked as inconspicuously as he could at the raven on the back of the priest's hand to see if it was shimmering again as it had been in the temple. Sadly, he could see nothing different about the raven this time and assumed the shimmering must have been from the light coming through the stained-glass windows.

"You're curious about my talisman," Joshua said, startling Michael who was setting up the logs on the fire.

"Your what?" Michael asked, not sure what the priest meant.

"The raven on my hand. It's a mark all priests in my order wear. It's a gift from the Allfather that we earn during our trials leading toward priesthood. It is harmless and does little for us besides allowing us to identify other priests. It may seem alive at times when I commune with the Allfather, but that's about all it will do," Joshua explained.

"It's quite interesting. Earlier, in the temple, I thought I saw it shimmering," Michael admitted. "Did you feel it when you received the talisman?"

"Not at all. Unlike a tattoo, this never was a wound in my flesh. The best way to think of it is that it exists between our realm and the Allfather's. It's not actually on my hand if that helps explain it," Joshua explained as he leaned forward and worked at lighting the fire. "Feel free to make yourself comfortable, Michael."

Michael unfurled his bedroll and a blanket he found tied to his saddle. He spread everything out on the ground as the fire crackled to life amid the kindling and the wood pieces Michael brought from the woods. With his bed established, Michael reached into his knapsack and removed his pipe and the pouch of tobacco, his third pipeful of tobacco that day. To Michael's surprise, Joshua also removed a pipe from a pouch sitting next to him and filled its simple bowl with his own dried leaves. Michael watched but said nothing before fetching a burning stick from the fire to light his pipe. He handed the stick to Joshua who did the same thing before returning the stick to the fire.

"Most people would have something to say about a priest smoking a pipe, Michael," Joshua said, a curious look on his face as he puffed gently at his mouthpiece.

"I have no reason to judge another person's life choices," Michael said, trying to make a smoke ring but failing. "Especially as I smoke my own pipe."

"Our life would be easier if more people followed that same mindset. You're quite wise to practice that, Michael," Joshua said before he successfully blew a smoke ring toward the fire then blew a smaller one inside the first.

Michael laughed and continued his attempts at blowing a smoke ring until there was no more smoke to pull through his pipe. After cleaning out his pipe and putting it back in its pouch, Michael laid down, looked up at the night sky, and contemplated the stars that he saw and how far away they might be. He wondered if anyone spent time and figured that out or if the scholars spent their time studying the world in which they lived instead. Michael felt his eyes growing heavy and gave in to sleep as he considered the stars. As he drifted off, another dream captured his mind, showing him images of terrible things that may come. Destructive beasts more evil than he thought could possibly exist waded through the churning river of his subconscious.

Chapter Two

A fierce wind howled across the tundra and picked up loose, powdery snow as it raced across the open landscape. Everything was frozen which was not unusual for this tundra at this time of the year. Winter had not fully ended this far north and with it being this cold still, there was little hope that the weather would grow warmer in the next couple of months. There was snow as far as the eye could see. The snow and ice created a desolate land, uninhabitable to anything but animals with large fat reserves and resilient evergreen plants that clung to the hope the sun once brought. There was only snow and ice. And blood. Too much blood for the mangled, frozen carcass laying atop the snow to have been killed by wolves. Wolves had certainly found the carcass, but they had not killed the creature. It looked like it might have been a caribou or elk, but too little was left for the hunter to know for sure.

Looking up from the carcass, the hunter adjusted his coat and mask to protect his face from the bitter wind. Only his eyes could be seen above the top of his mask. The fur on his heavy coat waved with the brutal gusts of wind. The cold alone could kill a man in a few hours up here. The wind would kill a human quick without any shelter. Out in the tundra, there was often no such thing as shelter. The hunter dug a shelter in the snowbank upwind from the carcass to block the wind.

The wind picked up and grew colder as the hunter looked up from the carcass again. The icy wind stung his eyes, making them water instantly. He had to get inside soon or there would be problems. But the traps *had* to be set. The hunter stood, taking one last glance at the mangled remains of the animal, its form seeming to merge with the ice of the tundra. Flesh and muscle, torn from the body in sheets, showed extensive fang marks. Those were likely left from the wolves. In the snow, he found several sets of bloody paw prints that led east away from the carcass, toward the woods with his settlement. *Probably a hunting party, too few sets of tracks to be the whole pack*, the hunter thought, counting four, maybe five, sets of tracks.

Two sets of footprints went north from the carcass. These tracks were deeper and larger than the wolf tracks, but too much snow pushed by the wind covered the prints and stopped him from identifying the species. The shape of these footprints still resembled a wolf, but they were far too large. Unless there was a wolf out here that was at least four feet tall at the shoulders. The only other predator the hunter encountered that was larger than a wolf, at least in this tundra, were bears. A few wolves couldn't have chased off a single bear. Not that easily. The hunter had seen enough wolf carcasses torn through by bears to know that. These tracks weren't from a bear, that much was clear. Bears have a very wide foot with five toes along the top and long claws marks above their tracks. After examining one of the prints in the snow as closely as he could, these were narrower without the distinct claw mark. They really did look like unnaturally large wolf tracks.

With the next gust of wind, howls rushed across the tundra. *Wolves*, he thought to himself. *Spent too much time at the carcass.* He still had to set a trap before going back. Something else was likely to come back to eat what remained of the frozen carcass, and whatever that was, it would have meat. The hunter quickly set his trap in the snow near the carcass, covering the edges of the trap with loose snow, made sure it wasn't easily visible, and then headed south-southwest. No sense going directly back to the settlement, leading whatever predators were out here back home. They had defenses, but precautions still needed to be taken. The settlement was only a couple of kilometers away, and even with the wind, he could make it back before freezing. Moving would keep his body temperature up. If he stayed still, he *would* freeze.

Half a kilometer south of the carcass, the hunter found a spinney buried in a deep bank of snow. He had used these trees as a landmark for the past two decades, when he started hunting the tundra. Continuing south from there, a small river ran through the tundra,

23

somehow not frozen solid in the cold. Much like the water, the hunter had to keep moving. This river ran east-west then banked south toward a lake a few leagues away. The hunter crossed the river, his feet instantly feeling the cold through his boots. He trudged westward through the snow toward the settlement. Walking through the water broke the trail of his scent, in case the wolves followed him. On the other bank, he continued his arduous trudging through the knee-deep snow. Without the snow, this trek should have taken an hour, maybe a little more, but it was closer to three hours with the snow. The hunter found himself lost in thoughts of warming beside a fire and the sizzling of some meat. Their reserves still held meat, for now. He could imagine the warm tinge of whiskey as it ran down his throat.

About a kilometer from the settlement, the hunter reached a tree line, the edge of the forest they had claimed as home. The forest was thick with tall trees, so less snow covered the ground, allowing the hunter to walk easier. The wind broke a bit on the trees, which kept the icy gusts off his back. Being in the woods this close to home was a welcome change in scenery from even a few minutes before. His legs burned from all his work getting back to the woods.

Twigs snapped nearby and the hunter stopped and reached for his bow. Perhaps it was a caribou seeking the forest's shelter from the wind and snow. That amount of meat would feed the village for a while. They wouldn't even need to dip into the stores. Leaning out from behind a nearby tree, the hunter set an arrow on his bowstring. There was no caribou. He saw no signs of any animal that snapped the twigs but decided to hunt momentarily before heading home. He would be late, but if he returned with something his delay would be forgiven. Surely, they would forgive tardiness if he brought a fresh kill.

Within a few minutes, the hunter found the broken twigs. As he knelt to examine the twigs, branches overhead rustled, like when a squirrel runs through the trees. It was too cold for squirrels to be out. It was too cold for *him* to be out, but here he was. Ignoring the rustling overhead, the hunter continued to examine the twigs. They were broken cleanly, as they were older twigs. The ground was too frozen to leave any prints in the dirt, but rubbings against the tree showed a possible path a deer could take through the forest. This path led northeast to southwest, and the hunter started heading southwest in the hope of finding his prey.

Mindful of his footing, the hunter stalked the path and looked for fresh signs of a deer. He promised himself that if he didn't find anything in the next twenty minutes he would make his way back to the settlement. He saw no sense getting lost on the trail for animals that might not even be there. Branches overhead rustled again, but the hunter dismissed the sound. Squirrels had followed him in the woods before; they were curious critters. It was likely no more than squirrels in the trees. To test his thought, the hunter stopped and looked down the deer path, as he longed for any signs of an animal. The rustling continued briefly, then stopped. *Just a squirrel following me. Nothing to worry about*, the hunter said to himself.

He took a few more steps down the path when a sharp pain struck his leg. The wound burned, and the hunter groaned, despite his desire to make no sounds. He looked down and found the branches of a pesky thorn bush stuck to his leg, a handful of long thorns snaggled into his leg. The thorns were large enough to go through his fur pants. With one hand, he reached down and removed the thorn from his leg, watching some blood soak into the fur. The wound was minor, but could still become infected, especially with that burning, throbbing sensation he felt. It was beyond time to head home. The deer he heard didn't run this way. That much was clear now.

When the hunter turned, he immediately stopped. A wave of fear crashed over him like waves crashing against rocks near the shore. A few meters down the path stood a monster. This was the beast who killed that caribou, he did not doubt it. Tall, dark, and furry, its back hunched toward the top. Some of its features resembled a wolf, but it walked on two feet like a man, with hands that ended in large, sharp talons. The beast's mouth was filled with sharp teeth, with protruding fangs in the front, much like a wolf.

The hunter tried to pull his arrow back, but his arms felt locked at his side. He opened his mouth to yell at the beast, hoping to scare it, like a coyote, but he felt only dryness in his throat as if he swallowed sand. His eyelids refused to blink, and his feet wouldn't move. The beast took a step forward and the wave of fear formed into a tsunami. A lump formed high in his throat, which he tried to swallow but couldn't. His heart pounded in his chest, threatening to break through his rib cage and fall onto the ground. The beast took another step closer. Its large feet made little to no impression on the icy ground. Its feet look like a wolf's but *much* larger, confirming his idea that this was the beast he saw signs of. *But I saw two sets of tracks leaving the carcass*, he thought right as branches overhead rustled again.

Something heavy and sharp grasped the hunter by his shoulder and his vision grew dark. He was forced to the ground, where he laid on his back, unable to move. As his vision went dark, he saw a second beast that fought with the first. Claws sliced flesh, snarls and howls sounded from both, the echoes resounded through the trees. The hunter felt the comfort of warmth embrace him like he was sitting beside a fire. Suddenly, a chill colder than the gusts of tundra wind sank all the way to his bones.

*   *   *

A shimmering, wavy doorway opened not far from two werewolves fighting over the carcass of a dying man. A dark man appeared in the doorway which vanished a moment later. The man had a sinister aura around him, and he stood right in front of the doorway, watching as the beasts eventually set aside their differences and began to devour the body of a man unfortunate enough to venture into these woods. And without any silver weapons, it appeared. Few signs pointed to who the man was or why he came into these woods to begin with, but his body being in this place was a sign that no matter who he was, the man had been a fool. The dark-robed man approached the feeding monsters slowly, as he knew how volatile they could be. They would likely attack if he interrupted their meal.

That was the very volatility that he needed at this particular moment. Their supposed savagery was unmatched among other specimens that the humans called 'monsters.' *Such a derogatory term*, the dark man thought to himself.

As he observed the beasts, he noticed they were large, especially for their species, roughly two meters from end to end. They did stand on their hind legs like the men they used to be and should be measured as such, after all. They had long arms that ended in claws at the end of human-like hands. Their faces resembled a man's face with wolfish features. The ears belonged to a wolf, pointed and furry, and the fangs replaced the teeth that would normally occupy the mouth. Thick fur covered most of the body with patchy tufts covering the legs, arms, back, and neck. The fur on their backs was raised in a ridge that went about halfway down their spines. One of them bled from fresh claw marks cut into the flesh on the left side of the ribcage. The blood glistened black as it seeped from the wound.

The dark-robed man stepped closer to the beasts, and one looked up from the mostly devoured body and lunged without hesitation. The man cast a spell and caught the beast in the air and lifted the other off the ground. He brought both monsters close and spoke to them softly, though his voice still possessed great command.

"I'm forming an army to destroy this world. You will fight for me and bring chaos to this land. Gather the other werewolves when I command it and I shall give you anything you wish. Do you accept this arrangement?"

The first werewolf snarled and snapped its jaws at the man. With a quick motion, the spell that held the beast in the air swirled and snapped its thick neck. As the body went limp, the spell released and dropped the dead werewolf onto the trail they had formed in the woods. The other werewolf whimpered, its ears pulling back as the man turned his gaze, hidden in his hood, to the monster.

"What about you? Are there any objections to my proposal?" the man inquired again.

The monster's mouth worked to form words that eventually came to her. "I accept your offer," she said in a smooth but guttural voice.

"Very good." The dark man released his spell and set the werewolf on the ground gently. "Now, find more of your kind and bring them to me."

The werewolf took a few skittish steps backward away from the man then lifted her wolfish snout to the air and released a long, hollow howl toward the sky. The forest came alive with the sound of responding howls. First one. Then a few more. Then dozens at a time joined the cries. Whoever the foolish man had been, he never was going to make it out of these woods, the dark-robed man knew that much.

Chapter Three

Michael bounced in his saddle as he and Joshua rode the horses through the streets approaching the city of Safdin at a canter. Michael needed to focus really hard between riding around people, trying not to fall out of the saddle, and getting a good look at everything around him. Riding a horse was not how he imagined his first time visiting the Prikean capital. Thankfully, the roads changed as they approached the city, going from packed dirt to scattered stones and finally cobblestone swatches cut through the landscape. The horse walked more smoothly on the cobblestone than it did on the packed dirt but only just. As they rode along, Joshua pointed out various landmarks and provided a bit of history to them. Michael paid as much attention as he could and nodded along politely but couldn't recall even the last fifteen minutes of the geography lesson he had received. He felt bad, but the ground would feel worse if he stopped paying attention. Not long after arriving in the outskirts of the city, they slowed the horses to a walk, and Michael took a better look at his surroundings.

As they grew closer to the city, the smell of briny salt grew heavier in the air, something which Michael did not enjoy but figured he could get used to. After all, he was only going to be here for a week. Once Michael could smell the salt, Joshua explained that the city of Safdin sat on the easternmost coast of Prikea and worked mostly as a fishing port, so the smell of salt would grow stronger as they approached. Michael cringed at the thought of the smell getting stronger but consoled himself in the fact that he would only be here temporarily. He already missed Feldring. Along with the sea approaching, Michael noticed the trees thinned out entirely as they approached the city. An hour before getting even this close to Safdin, he could still see spinneys and woods popping up not far from the road. Now, he saw no trees which made everything feel far more open than he appreciated.

"If you look almost directly east of us," Joshua said, "you can see the spires of Harmpton Palace, where the royal family lives."

"I think I can see it," Michael said. "It just looks like a lot of spires from here."

Joshua nodded confirmation of Michael's observation. "Indeed. There are more than twenty of them, all of various heights."

As Michael and Joshua rode their horses further into the town, they eventually passed groups of guards who patrolled the outlying

31

areas in trios, venturing up and down the roads. Soon after passing their first cluster of guards, Michael and Joshua dismounted, leading their horses by the reins. Too many people crowded the roads for them to safely ride the horses as they grew closer to Safdin. Michael felt the walking necessary after such a long day of sitting in the saddle. His legs felt like they may never straighten out again.

Clusters of small houses and other buildings lined the roadside as Michael and Joshua rode further into the city. The population had exploded in this area since the construction of the original wall around the town that immediately surrounded the castle and caused many to move into the countryside. But as the city kept expanding, the countryside gradually grew further away. With an ocean on one side of the city, there was nowhere else for the city to grow except out to the north and west. It was a minor inconvenience for many, and the people Michael saw seemed happy enough. Streamers and pennants that bore the king's colors and crest flew on many of the buildings, the fabric waving in the sea-borne wind.

As guards saw Joshua, they lowered their heads reverently at him. Clearly, respect toward the priesthood existed, even if it appeared a little forced. Every guard wore polished metal cuirasses with mail underneath. The tan tabards they wore over their armor bore the same black striping as Joshua's robe, though a black eagle covered their chests instead of the raven that showed on the priest's. The only thing Michael noticed as unique among the many guards was their choices in weapons. Most carried long swords, some axes, even fewer maces, and only a handful carried polearms of one kind or another. Michael thought it was interesting that the soldiers here were given an apparent choice in their weaponry. In Feldring, all the guards carried the same weapons. A polearm and a long sword. Feldring's guards were lethal with either weapon in the rare instances they needed to use them.

A few dozen meters down the road, right before a portcullis that would take them further into the city, stood a boulder of a man with his thumbs tucked behind the polished gold buckle on his belt and his fingers laced in front. He wore ornate plate armor, lacquered tan and black with an eagle embellished on his cuirass. He wore no tabard and atop his helmet rose a black crest which rose rigidly nearly a hand's length above the helmet. In place of a visor, he wore a metal mask formed in an exaggerated, angered frown that covered his face from the nose down, allowing only his eyes to be visible with his great helmet on. The mask was lacquered black with tan accents in the same motif as the rest of his armor. The handle of a great sword rose from his left hip, and the blade fell beyond his knee. On his right hip hung a club, covered in large steel spikes. This man was clearly important, Michael noted even from this distance.

"You're late, priest," his voice boomed behind his mask as they approached. The tone of his voice matched the expression of his mask.

"I'm actually a day early, Bruce," Joshua replied flatly.

"I presume you had a safe journey, brother," Bruce replied, grabbing the priest in an embrace Michael hadn't expected. Spikes stood on the knuckles of his gauntlet; everything about the man seemed like a weapon. Michael did not doubt that even without his weapons the man could still maintain the same level of lethality as any of the other guards. Joshua clapped his hand against Bruce's heavy shoulder plates before breaking away.

"I've forgotten my manners," Joshua said as he stepped away from Bruce, "this is Michael, a carpenter's apprentice from Feldring. We have an appointment to see the king later today if that's still standing."

"Welcome, Michael!" Bruce said as he thrust his hand out. Michael clasped Bruce's forearm and then flew forward as the other man pulled him close and clapped a mighty paw on Michael's back.

"Bruce is the Commander of the King's Guard," Joshua stated.

With the introductions finished, Bruce turned, leading Joshua and Michael toward the portcullis behind him. He raised a hand, motioned to the horses, and two nearby guards grabbed the horses' reins, taking them down a side street. Bruce towered over Michael, who was neither short nor tall, and Michael felt the man was more intimidating while he walked than he was simply standing still.

"What have I missed, Bruce?" Joshua asked, his tone jovial once again.

"Another lunatic tried breaking into the castle again. If I didn't value my own time so much, I would pity someone so foolish, but here we are," Bruce stated. His honeyed words barely covered the obvious disdain in his voice.

"Where is he now?" Joshua asked.

"We are being very accommodating. We gave him a comfortable cell where he receives two adequate meals a day. More than some of the poorest in the city can say, that's certain. Sometimes I wonder if that's why we have so many people trying to break into the castle.

They may not actually be trying to kill the king but are seeking shelter and food even in the lowliest of places in the city. The dungeon isn't nice, but it's possibly better than living on the street," Bruce admitted with a shrug of his heavily armored shoulders.

"I'm surprised he's able to breathe without assistance from a priest."

"Your words wound me, Joshua. Had I found the bastard he would be sleeping with the crabs at the bottom of the harbor. Needless to say, someone else found him. His leg and a few ribs are broken and now he has all the time in the world to reconsider his life choices. I doubt he will breathe free air for at least a decade."

"Is this a common occurrence?" Michael asked, unsure if his question would be well-received by Bruce.

"Common? Not remotely. I think the last one we had was late last year, and I found that bastard myself. I wouldn't have caught that one if the king had requested wine instead of whiskey. This fool simply tried to walk into the king's study. How he managed to get that far into the castle undetected is something I'll never understand," Bruce replied. His hand remained on the handle of his club as he walked.

Michael took a closer look at Bruce and noticed rows of small knives sheathed along his wide leather belt, which widened around the back. Bruce was clearly a living weapon, not that there had been any doubts about that before seeing a dozen knives on his belt. *Not a single person should be able to stand before the king with ill intent and live a moment longer*, Michael thought to himself.

"We will take you to a tailor so you can have some more formal clothes made up before you meet with the king, if you would like, Michael," Joshua offered.

"I doubt we will have time for that, Joshua. His Highness is quite busy. I may be able to squeeze you in for your scheduled meeting now, but I make no promises. Otherwise, you will have to wait until tomorrow at the earliest," Bruce replied.

"Then we'll not keep his Highness waiting any longer," Joshua said.

With that, they walked faster, nearly jogging down the road; people stepped clear of Bruce and his large, lethal stature. Guards saluted Bruce as he passed, his armor faintly reflecting sunlight through the dark lacquer. His weapons, except the club, shone brilliantly in the sunlight. The man had to spend hours polishing his weapons to manage that shine. Not a blemish showed on his sword or his armor. *Perhaps his armor is more ceremonial than anything,* Michael thought to himself. Doubtful he had seen combat in any recent times. Prikea hadn't gone to war with anyone in nearly a century.

As Michael considered the condition of Bruce's armor and weapons, they reached the castle. Two weathered stone statues guarded the castle's gate, their monstrously tall stone lances pointed to the sky with the hafts planted firmly on the ground by their feet. These soldiers withstood eons of weather, their faces growing less featured each year. The heroic statues showed men with strong jaws and muscles that showed through their armor. *Perhaps the armor was shaped to show muscles,* Michael thought.

The castle's gatehouse was of an interesting design, Michael noted. There was one gate, a bridge that spanned a gap, then another gate. Two guards stood inside each of the gates, and they clapped their fists to their chests as Bruce led Michael and Joshua through the inner gate. Michael tried to look but couldn't see quite how far down the hole went under the bridge, nor could he see how far north and south it ran. Inside the second gate, in the courtyard outside the castle, stood a few dozen guards formed in a column three men wide. A man in armor similar to Bruce's, though not as weaponized, walked slowly from one end of the formation to the other. Michael could tell, even from this distance, that the man was inspecting the guards, and for the most part, his face showed only displeasure.

Inside the courtyard, tall stone buildings spread nearly wall to wall in a neat and organized manner. Streets and alleys formed a grid-like pattern between the buildings. As the road approached the keep, however, the buildings stopped, allowing for a clear view of anyone approaching the keep. Michael gazed up and saw several ballistae on the ramparts above, as well as on the outside bailey. Soldiers patrolled both along the ramparts and around the palace itself. Many guards carried swords or halberds with bows on their backs.

The further into the castle the trio went, the more the guards looked like Bruce, even down to the spikes in their armor. These men did not bear feathered crests atop their helmets like Bruce, but they looked just as lethal. These guards carried only swords and cudgels rather than the plethora of knives that Bruce carried around his belt. The guards slowly walked here and there as they made their rounds within the palace's outer walls.

The large, thick, wooden doors leading into Harmpton Palace stood closed until Bruce and Joshua started walking up the stairs. A guard with a much smaller crest approached Bruce, clapping his fist to his chest, motioning them through the door. Bruce and Joshua walked through the arched doorway, but Michael stopped as the crested guard placed his hand firmly on Michael's chest.

"The king is seeing no visitors today, citizen. Come back another day," the guard said through the visor of his helmet. Michael could barely see the man's eyes, but he knew annoyance flooded them.

"I'm with them," Michael said, motioning at Joshua and Bruce.

"No visitors, citizen. Come again another day," the guard said again slightly louder.

"Let him pass," Bruce's voice echoed from inside the palace. He had turned around and walked back to the top of the stairway.

"Sir?" the guard asked, confused by the order.

"Let him pass. Why must I repeat myself for you to follow orders, Captain?" Bruce left no chance for the guard to argue. He turned away with Michael in tow shortly behind.

When they were inside the palace, the doors closed behind them with a heavy thud. The hall was open with large, stone pillars on both sides of the walkway, and heroes depicted in stained-glass windows cast colored shadows on the floor. The light from the windows added extra warmth the myriad of candelabras and chandeliers simply could never provide. Three steps at the end of the hall led to another set of wooden, double doors. Two guards

38

stood outside, and they opened the doors, which swung quietly on their hinges, into the next room. The doorway spanned three meters in height and two meters wide, enough space for a merchant wagon and its horses to travel through were the doorway's arch less severe.

Within the room on the other side of the door, more stone pillars rose to a vaulted ceiling, stained-glass windows on the south side spread colored light onto the floor. A plush, green carpet covered the floor from the dais at the far end of the room to the doors. Gold tassels lined the edges of the carpet, and the sunlight playfully danced with the tassels. A small chair sat upon the dais at the far end. While simple in design and build, some ornate decorations made the chair seem of better quality.

King Daniel the Proud, Ruler of Prikea, lounged upon the throne, his head cradled on one hand, his elbow against the arm of the chair. As Michael, Bruce, and Joshua walked up the aisle toward the dais the king leaned to a man wearing polished steel mail armor with a white linen cloak around his shoulders. His hood rested upon his shoulders, and he held his hands on the clasp of his wide leather belt, thumbs tucked between his body and the belt. The man beside the king had a beard, full but trimmed, which had clearly been white for some time, but the man did not appear old beyond that. The king whispered something to the man, who gazed quickly at Michael, and nodded, then whispered his response. With his answer, the king stood and stepped down from the dais and waved his hand at the white-haired man. With that wave, the man left, his cloak catching a pocket of air as he spun on the balls of his feet and left the room. As the king approached, Bruce, Joshua, and Michael stopped and bowed at the waist. Michael followed the others' lead, unsure what else he should do.

"You must be the man from Feldring that Joshua went to fetch for us. I trust that both Bruce and Joshua have been most hospitable toward you," the king said, with a quick glance at both men with his statement.

"The whole journey has been nothing short of welcoming, Highness," Michael replied, rising from a bow.

"Joshua has explained everything to you, correct?" the king asked.

The king stood straight, half a head taller than Bruce, who already towered over Michael. His face showed few signs of age. Streaks of grey hair lined his temples, and a few wrinkles showed the merciless touches of age around his eyes. Beyond those signs, he looked hardly older than thirty. His eyes, the same bright blue one could see in the sky right after a thunderstorm's clouds empty themselves onto the ground, held a warmth Michael never saw before. His gaze was powerful, yet welcoming. Michael found it obvious why this man, more than any other, wore the crown and led Prikea. He couldn't recall any displeasure toward the king, and he had worn the crown for as long as Michael could remember.

"Highness, he knows enough right now but not everything. When we speak with the rest of the Order, he will learn everything else," Joshua replied. "They also wish to meet him. With your leave, sire, we will go to the Order now."

"Take your leave, Joshua," the king said as he broke his gaze from Michael and looked to his bodyguard, "Bruce, stay behind when they leave. I need to speak with you about the wretch taking up space within our dungeon."

"As you wish, Highness," Bruce replied.

"Joshua, please bring Michael to my study after dinner. I wish to speak with him privately this evening," the king said, glancing back to Michael briefly before holding Joshua in his gaze.

"As you wish, sire," Joshua replied.

With that, Joshua led Michael out of the throne room. As they opened the large wooden doors, the king began talking with Bruce about the prisoner the Commander of the Guard had mentioned on their way toward the palace. Michael followed Joshua down two hallways, up a spiral staircase, and turned left down another hallway before Joshua stopped and opened a simple wooden door. The door was plain, except for the raven carved and painted into the center of the door. When Joshua opened the door, seven priests looked up from a large oval table. When they saw Joshua and Michael walk in, they stood and approached slowly.

The closest priest seemed the eldest of the group. His head bore no hair, just as Joshua's, yet his bushy eyebrows were solid silver, matching his long beard which hid his neck. His eyes were a brilliant grey in the bright candlelight. Michael saw that he also had a raven on his right hand, like Joshua, but on his left hand was a golden rampant lion. Michael wanted to ask what the lion meant, but before he could ask, the priest reached and shook his hand.

"I am Gregory, and it's such a pleasure to meet you, Michael. We truly cannot say how much we appreciate that you chose to accompany Joshua when he asked you to leave the life you knew in

Feldring. If there is anything you need please let us know," he said, his face lighting up with a warm and friendly smile. Perhaps a bit *too* friendly of a smile.

Joshua stepped in and introduced the other priests from the left to the right: Peter, William, Oliver, Gerald, Francis, and Simon. Joshua introduced Francis, wearing four black stripes on the cuffs of his tan robes, as the High Priest of the Order of Ravens. Were he not wearing a priest's robes, Michael would have assumed he was a sailor. His face showed numerous scars, his eyes looked hard, and his face showed no signs of ever smiling. Francis also wore the most tattoo-like markings, some upon his neck as well as the backs of his hands. In addition to the same raven as Joshua and the others, he also sported a lion on his left hand, but the ones on his neck were the most surprising. Michael saw, among them, a cobra, an eagle, and a tree. Each of them shimmered, distinguishing them from ordinary tattoos. He remembered what Joshua said about these markings existing between this realm and another and wondered if there was symbolism behind how the markings looked or why there were different ones.

"Brother Joshua, we believe that we learned more about Michael's dreams last night while you were traveling here. We have yet to gain a specific location for Týr, but we have it locked down to a general area," Francis said. His voice was smooth like fresh honey and did not match what Michael expected, given the state of his face.

"Where is Týr?" Joshua asked, pulling a wicker chair away from the oak table and taking a seat. On the table sat a plain, stout teapot with matching porcelain cups. Joshua poured himself a cup and offered one to Michael, who accepted graciously.

"In that respect, we have encountered an…issue. We sensed his presence across the sea, but you likely already know what that means," Oliver said, opening a large, leather-bound volume and beginning to read feverously.

"Do we have a proposed solution, Francis?" Joshua asked, sipping his tea.

"I'm sorry for my failure to understand the problem. Where is Týr?" Michael asked, feeling the steam from his cup of tea wave across his face.

Joshua swallowed forcefully and looked deeply into his cup of tea before answering Michael's question. "Týr is in Drendil, a broken and dangerous land our ancestors left long ago. The King of Prikea at the time decreed that anyone who goes there cannot come back."

"What happened there that the king would make that kind of decision?" Michael asked.

"Dark Magic tainted the land beyond recognition. Rogue Mages performed rituals so dark they started wars and caused the deaths of thousands at a time. People still live there, but our entire world teeters on the brink of collapse the longer the continent goes unchecked," Joshua said before turning his attention to the other priests. "What is your solution to this issue?"

"The only solution we have is that we send someone to Týr. According to the dreams, these three are the ones to fight the Shadow Knight, something we all know may be the only thing that stands between this world and safety," Simon replied, his gaze growing intense as his eyes fell on Michael once more. "Randall the Ruthless is willing to prepare *Queller* for our purposes and will sail you to Drendil. Or rather, the king said that he will be *made* to prepare *Queller* for the voyage."

"Who is Randall the Ruthless?" Michael asked. The slightly bitter sting of the tea lingered on his tongue longer than he expected yet stayed satisfying somehow.

"He is the king's youngest brother and the fiercest Captain of the Prikean Navy, though he rarely acts in a way fitting of his rank," Joshua answered. This brought a quick glance from Francis.

"*Queller* is the first ship under his command. It is a perfectly middling ship of the king's fleet, but the man has a…reputation. You will understand when you meet him," Simon added before the High Priest could respond.

"This journey will be quite an endeavor. Has he not asked for anything in return?" Joshua asked, pouring another cup of the dark tea.

"When we spoke to the king, he made it clear that there would be a reward that Randall would be unable to refuse under any circumstances. I don't know what the reward will be, but it also doesn't affect me. As we speak, Captain Randall should be mooring *Queller* in the harbor and coming to the castle to speak with His Highness about the assignment," Francis said, pausing for a moment.

Joshua leaned forward in his chair, resting his elbows on the table, and intertwining his fingers around his cup. He held Francis's gaze for a long moment before peering into his cup, looking for the words he wanted to say within his tea. As he looked into his tea, his whole body grew eerily still. After a few moments, he inhaled deeply and sighed before he returned Francis's unmoved gaze. Joshua looked defeated, as if he had a bit of morbid knowledge, he could share with no one.

"You all have danced gracefully around what I'm about to ask throughout this entire conversation. I appreciate your concern for me, but I wish you would all take a more direct approach to deliver bad news just once," Joshua stated finally. "Do you wish for me to accompany Michael to Drendil?"

Joshua's voice broke as he asked, and beads of sweat began forming on his head despite the room not being overly warm. Blood drained from his face as he awaited Francis's answer. Michael saw Joshua's grip on his teacup tighten and feared the cup might break if he continued squeezing any harder.

"Yes." Francis's voice remained strong but smooth.

Joshua sat back in his chair as if the singular word possessed force enough to move him, his body reacting as if someone had buried a dagger in his chest and twisted the blade. The way Joshua looked, as he processed this information, is how Michael felt after waking up from the nightmares. He was limp, unmoving, and hardly breathing. Michael felt himself starting to sweat, the same cold sweat he had been drenched in for the past few weeks.

"Michael, you seem distraught by all this," Simon stated, looking up from the book he scrutinized.

Simon turned his gaze upon his guest, whom he seemed to have forgotten sat at the table with them. Michael tried to answer and felt his mouth move as it tried to form words, but he felt parched and could not find the words to speak. He brought his tea to his mouth and invited the bitterness of the tea and hoped it would help his words finally escape. As the last of the tea dripped into his mouth, Michael felt he could speak again. He set the cup down and cleared what felt like a beavers' dam from his throat.

"What am I to do about my life in Feldring? I thought I was only coming here for a week so you could learn about the dreams," Michael said, knowing he would have other questions when he heard the answer to this one.

"We initially did only want you to come here to study your dreams and your connection to prophecy, but as you entered the city we sensed your presence and touched it with our own gifts. Others have come here for us to study, but their prophetic natures pale in comparison to yours, Michael. We have little doubt that what you see in your dreams are actual events rather than mere fleeting images of events to come," Gregory explained. "We sincerely apologize for the inconvenience this brings to you both."

"Inconvenience?" Michael tried his best to keep his voice flat but knew the sound of fear and frustration babbled like a spring in the mountains. "I own a house and have a job in Feldring. Everything about my life is there including the graves of my parents. I have nothing outside that city. Yesterday morning I thought I was simply going to be gone for a short time, and now I am leaving for a land torn to pieces by Dark Magic and I can't come back here?" Michael asked.

"That is an oversimplification, Micha—" Simon started when Joshua cut him off.

"You're sending us away, to Drendil of all places, to find someone who you *believe* is there but without absolute certainty. Do we know when this Shadow Knight is going to attack? Do we even know where yet? When this mission is over is there any chance for returning to our lives here?" Joshua fumed.

"These are all questions which bring only worry, Brother Joshua," Francis said. "We must cast aside worry and live in the light of the Allfather, may he guide us toward His plan."

"What worries me is more than simply the exile I have walked into by going to Feldring," Joshua explained.

"Brother Joshua, please don't see this as a sentence of exile. We need you to accompany Michael through this journey. You are the best suited for this—" Francis began.

"Of course, you're going to say I'm the best suited for this 'calling.' You all have families that would be devastated for you to leave and never return. Why would you not send the *one* priest you found in the middle of a massacre without parents, a wife, children, and no connections outside of this room. Is this really why you are sending me?" Joshua questioned. There was a long silence before anyone said anything. Priests with cups of tea looked deeply into their cups as they searched for any kind of explanation that wasn't exactly what Joshua had spelled out.

"I'm sorry for this pain, Brother. Please don't see this as us sending you away simply because you have no family. That is not why we chose you." Francis finally replied. "Not entirely, at least. You are a far stronger priest than many of us in this room, and you are honestly more capable of the task than any of the rest of us are, and that is the truth. Beyond that, we believe *you* are in the dreams as well."

Michael sat in his chair for several moments, staring into his empty cup while thoughts flew through his head like leaves pushed through the air by a fierce wind. He tried to grasp these thoughts, but they escaped him too swiftly. He closed his eyes, allowing these thoughts to smolder in a warm blaze in the back of his mind. As he sat there, he felt a foreign embrace within himself. Visions of his life flashed through his mind. Feldring, the only home he knew, a city standing like a sentry in the mountains flashed inside his closed eyes. Never again would he see the star-filled nights of the mountains or the bright, mysterious colors that danced through the sky in the twilight hours.

Seasons passed like a breath exhaled in the cold as Feldring began to change. The city began growing, buildings rising higher into the mountains, spreading the city wider than he had ever known. As these buildings grew, countless people filled the roadways into the city. He saw merchants, as well as people looking for a new home in a city that showed promise of shelter and growth. The city continued to expand both upward and outward into the plains.

Then without warning, there was fire. Flames blazed through the mountains. People fled from the city in terror. Something was

48

happening, but he could help no one. Fire that should not spread across stone did just that. Fire that blazed in colors he had never seen until then. *Dark* fire. It consumed light around it; pillars of smoke flooded the skies as the city emptied. People ran down the road from the city, but they kept falling, flames rushing toward them. Escape was impossible. Screams of terror rang out from Feldring as women, children, and people he had spent his life with burned in a terrible fire that he knew even the waters of the seas could not stifle. Smoke rushed toward the sky in enormous pillars

Michael opened his eyes and gasped for air as the flames spread through the woods below the city. Joshua sat on the floor beside him. When had he gotten out of his seat? Why was he laying on the floor? He felt cold, and warm at the same time. His shirt was once again drenched in sweat and the cold fabric clung to his chest and back. He felt numb, but even that numbness could not stop the screams he still heard in his mind as Feldring burned in a dark fire that consumed everything.

"What did you see?" Francis asked.

All the priests had gathered around him on the floor. Before he answered, Joshua helped him sit up, handing him another cup of tea. The tea was welcoming, but the sounds of agony continued to torment his mind for a few moments as reality blurred back to his eyes. Finished with the tea, Michael grasped at words, wanting to share what he had seen. Would they believe him? Was this another nightmare?

"Feldring. The city grew and covered the mountains. Then there was fire, black fire that consumed stones. It came down from the mountains and surrounded the city. No one could escape. What does it mean?" Michael tried to stand, but Joshua pushed gently on his shoulder so he would remain on the ground.

"It sounds like the spread of Madness. Even our land is not safe until this threat is handled. I feel this Shadow Knight is only the first sign of what is to come. The void will push forth into our world if this Shadow Knight continues with his agenda. Michael, Joshua, we need your help. Find Týr and defeat this Shadow Knight for us. The world will burn unless we stop this," Simon said. His forehead bore smudges of ink. *He must spend every waking moment reading and studying texts,* Michael thought.

Before anyone else could say anything, a heavy knock resounded through the room. Francis opened the door, and on the other side stood Bruce and the king. Bruce still wore his mask, hiding his face; concern warped the king's face. Francis stepped away from the doorway, welcoming them in. Bruce stayed by the door while the king came fully into the room and looked questioningly at Michael on the floor surrounded by the priests

"Thunder rang out from a cloudless sky over the castle, torches and candles flickered, and a gust of wind blew through the windows. What happened?" Bruce asked, glancing at Michael, still sitting on the floor with Joshua beside him.

"Your Majesty, Michael had a vision of Darkness consuming Feldring," Joshua said, helping Michael to his feet.

"When did this happen?" the king asked, concern remaining on his face.

"It started half an hour ago. The thunder and wind started when he fell from his chair," Francis replied.

"Was this a vision or nightmare? Does it matter which it is?" the king asked. Michael was taken aback at how much time Francis said passed. To him, it felt like less than five minutes.

"That we do not know, Highness. Without testing his dreams to determine their level of Magic, it's hard to tell whether a nightmare or a vision could be more predictive. Would you like to speak with Michael now, sire?" Joshua asked.

"My dreams are Magic?" Michael asked. "Sorry to interrupt, Your Highness."

"No need to apologize. There is a lot to process here," the king replied.

"They are an incredibly weak form of Magic. We can discuss that more later, though," Joshua suggested, returning his attention to the king. "Is now a good time to speak with Michael? I know it's not after dinner as previously discussed, sire."

"I would like that, Joshua. Follow me to my study. We'll have privacy there. Make sure of that, Bruce." The king waited for Michael and Joshua to nod that they were ready before he and Bruce stepped out of the priests' study and turned left outside the door.

Bruce walked in front of the king, with Michael and Joshua following close behind him. Using the same spiral staircase as before, the kind and Joshua led Michael back up, passing the floor with the throne room, up another level and into a long hallway. Guards walked up and down this floor or stood along the walls in strategic places. Each guard bowed their head as the king walked by.

At the end of the hall stood a sturdy door with two guards on each side. The door was plain except for the king's eagle lacquered in the center of the wood. Bruce opened the door, and the rest of the party walked inside. As he closed the door, he gave a quick order to the sentries who were clad in the same armor, including the masks and spiked gauntlets, and Michael saw the sentries walk away, leaving just Bruce outside the king's study.

The king walked around his desk and sat in the tall, cushioned chair. On the desk, Michael saw a variety of maps, letters, and other papers he couldn't identify. After looking as closely at the largest map as he wished to look without being rude or intrusive, Michael saw nothing useful. He could see a land unknown to him, with little of the land actually drawn on the map. A wave of curiosity suddenly rushed over him, and he wanted to know what land that map portrayed. He felt himself staring rudely and reluctantly tore his gaze from the king's desk.

"This map shows the only portions of Drendil that we had records for. More complete maps do exist, but they were burned long ago to discourage our ancestors from venturing there. We remember only what we need: that the land overflows with Madness. We have allowed only one person that has set foot on this strange land to return, and he grew Mad immediately afterward. Intent on revenge for his Madness, he became the first man to attempt to assassinate the king at the time. He failed, though he killed one of the king's brothers," the king said, responding to Michael's obvious interest in the map. "It is because of that man, and others like him, that we cannot allow anyone to return from Drendil. While I am going to

52

enforce the same exile for you both, the reason for your journey to Drendil is different. You are not being sent there as a punishment, unlike some we have sent there."

"Sire, Francis has asked me to accompany Michael to Drendil," Joshua said. His voice held a thread of hope that the king would overrule this decision immediately.

"I know. This was a decision he approached me with during your absence. With your understanding of Michael, his dreams, and the situation, it was a hard, but necessary decision to second. I am sorry you are having this fate thrust upon you, Joshua. What are your thoughts about this?" The king sat back in his chair, rubbing his chin as he awaited the answer.

Joshua was quiet for a few moments before answering. "Sire, I have no reason to turn down this request. I don't wish to leave, though I understand that duty is a burden we all must take up when it calls us."

The king opened a drawer in his desk and removed a pipe and a small canvas sack about half-filled with tobacco. He packed the loose leaves into the bowl of his pipe, topping off the bowl with more leaves as he got toward the end of his packing, then retrieved a match from a box in the drawer. He looked up at Michael and Joshua and motioned that they could also smoke if they wished. The ever-familiar *fhisk* of the match sang out as the only sound in the study, the small flame consuming the wood as the king lit his pipe. He puffed vigorously at the mouthpiece and the flames danced across the surface of the tobacco leaves. Wisps of blue-grey smoke rose from all three of their pipes for a few minutes before anyone spoke again.

"Randall should have *Queller* moored by now. I'm expecting him shortly to discuss the details of his assignment with him. He knows he's setting sail soon, but I haven't told him exactly what he will be doing or who he will be transporting. Midday tomorrow his preparations will be finished, and the next morning, during high tide, you'll depart. *Queller* has a deep keel for a ship her size," the king said before he turned to Michael. "I understand you are a carpenter's apprentice, so forgive me, but I feel I must ask this question. Are you trained in any way to use a weapon? Regardless of your answer, I will provide you with a sword from Harmpton's armory."

"My father only taught me how to draw and sheath the sword without hurting myself. I've had no reason to learn to use it as my life has been peaceful up to this point," Michael replied sheepishly.

"I will make arrangements for Randall and his crew to teach you basic swordsmanship during your voyage. As a passenger on a warship, there's very little else to do, so this will help to pass the time. Few in our military can teach you better. He's a tough teacher though. You may not be immediately ready to fight this Shadow Knight, but he will at least get you started down that path. Do you have any questions for me?" the king inquired, striking another match to relight his pipe. Frustration twisted his face as he buried the tip of the match into the well-packed tobacco. Michael thought perhaps the king had packed too much of the tobacco into the bowl and he wasn't getting enough air flowing through the fiery leaves.

"I have no questions, sire," Michael said, keeping his eyes on the map still, slowly drawing on the stem of his pipe.

"Highness, I have one question: is there no way that either of us will ever be able to return from Drendil?" Joshua asked, puffing at his pipe for a few seconds before he realized it had also gone out.

"It pains me to say this, but right now I cannot allow anyone to return after setting foot in Drendil," he replied, knowing that would bring great pain to Joshua.

A bell outside the castle chimed six times, pealing through the quiet of the evening, marking the time. In about an hour, the sun would fall beyond the horizon and night would fall upon the world. Through the window, the sky began growing dark with streaks of colors, red, purple, and deep gold, splashed into the dusk sky. The colors reminded Michael of a painting he saw once in Master Gamel's shop. A customer brought the painting in for framing, and it only sat in their shop for a few hours before going back. Clouds at the horizon showed deep purple stripes with pink on the western edges. Michael sat puffing at his pipe with Joshua and the king, mesmerized by the colors that announced the coming of night. For a few minutes, the room remained silent, save the sound of the small, almost unnoticeable popping of the wicks of the candles around the room. As the king tapped the burned tobacco from his pipe, three quick knocks sounded at the door.

Bruce opened the door slowly. Through the crack in the door, Michael saw a tall, lean man with small scars on his face and a bigger one on the side of his neck. The scar on his neck was a deep purple, a ghastly reminder of something that would likely never

55

fully fade. His eyes were the clear blue, like the king's, and his nose hooked to the right, possibly from a close and personal fight. His face bore a close-trimmed, auburn beard, and he had his sun-faded brown hair slicked back into a ponytail. The man, whoever he was, nodded at Bruce, who stared at the man before closing the door again.

"What news do you have, Randall?" the king asked, placing his sack of tobacco and his pipe back in their drawer.

"*Queller* will be ready to sail the morning after tomorrow. You said this mission is urgent, after all, and I'd rather not disappoint you with delays. I still don't know why you want us to head back out to sea so quickly, though," he replied.

"Wonderful news," the king replied eagerly.

Randall leaned against the wood trim that ran all the way around the door and assumed an incredibly relaxed stance. He stood with his feet wide, appearing every bit as a sailor should. He wore simple clothes, which looked like they were made of canvas; a simple sword and a knife hung at his waist. The sword hung on his left side and the knife on his right. Michael felt quite concerned about the man's lack of footwear and wondered if he was actually a sea captain or someone who lived on the streets of Safdin. If not for the weapons he wore, it would be hard to differentiate the two.

"You will sail to Drendil. You will be taking these men there for a quest they need to complete," the king said, gesturing at Michael and Joshua. This brought a brief, sidelong glance from Randall. "Michael will have a sword but needs to learn to use one. Please teach him during the voyage."

"I won't step foot on that evil continent. Also, you know my feeling about the priests. I won't have one of them aboard my ship," Randall replied, looking at Joshua.

"As the king, it is *my* ship, and you will take whomever *I* tell you to wherever I tell you. Joshua is accompanying Michael to Drendil. You will take them both, and that is the last word of the matter," the king replied, his voice growing stern.

"Your wish is my command, *Brother*," Randall said, adding a bit of a sting to the end.

"Can you set off at dawn tomorrow?" Joshua asked, wishing to relieve some of the tension in the room.

"High tide isn't until the morning after and *Queller* can't leave until then," Randall said, nodding his head at Michael.

"Do you require anything else of us, Highness?" Joshua asked, turning to the king.

"I require some privacy with Captain Randall. Please find the others from your dreams and vanquish the Shadow Knight. You carry the fate of the world with you, Michael. May the Allfather bless you greatly," the king said.

"As you wish, Highness," Joshua and Michael said together.

Joshua opened the door and they found Bruce standing nearby. He closed the door softly behind them and motioned in the air for the sentries down the hall to return to their posts. They nodded their heads and took their places, tucking their thumbs behind their belts. As Michael and Joshua walked down the hallway, Bruce shook his head and muttered to himself.

"That man is a disgrace to his bloodline. Never have I questioned why he sails ships instead of serving any political role. He hasn't one tactful bone in his body. The man is more of a pirate than royalty. And the way he speaks to the king is disrespectful," Bruce said.

"Those are strong feelings, Bruce," Joshua said.

"They're justified, Joshua. He shows no respect to the king, neither as the *king* nor his own brother," Bruce said, his fists clenching. "The worst part is: the king allows this behavior, except in public."

"Bruce, we're going to eat and get ready for our voyage the day after tomorrow. Would you care to join us?" Joshua asked, looking at the larger man.

"Gladly," Bruce replied, his gaze directed elsewhere.

He stopped beside a guard leaning against a pillar and stared at the man for a few moments. Joshua and Michael stopped as well, and Joshua took a couple of steps away, standing at the far end of the hallway. Michael watched as Bruce came within inches of the man's face before shouting, his face nearly inside the man's ear. After flinching so much that he almost left his skin and armor behind, the guard fell to the ground after having lost his balance against the pillar. Bruce stood over the man, his hands at his waist.

"Are we allowed to sleep while we're guarding the king?" Bruce inquired loudly, his voice booming in the hallway.

"I wasn't asleep sir, honest!" the man replied, his voice quavered.

"The next person I catch sleeping loses their eyelids! Who is your relief?"

"Mathieu, sir. He should be here in an hour," the guard replied.

"Not anymore. He will be here in *four* hours. Test my patience again," Bruce yelled.

Before the man could protest the punishment, knowing he could have instead spent a night or two in the dungeon, Bruce turned and walked away quickly with Michael and Joshua behind him. As they entered the staircase, Bruce stopped and turned around, shouting at the sentry that his relief would instead arrive in the morning.

*   *   *

After eating dinner with Bruce and Joshua, Michael sat in his room at the palace where he would sleep for the two nights they had in Safdin before setting sail for Drendil aboard the *Queller*. Within the room, there was a desk, a bed, a wardrobe, and a small chest which opened to reveal many drawers and trays for storing things. Michael found only an extra blanket in the chest and nothing in the wardrobe. The desk contained things he would need such as a small stack of parchment, sealing wax, a quill, an inkwell, ink, and a clear liquid he assumed would clean the quill's nib. Michael sat at the desk and grabbed a piece of parchment off the stack and started writing a letter to Master Gamel explaining the situation so the carpenter wouldn't worry about Michael's extended absence.

Master Gamel,

First, I cannot explain everything going on in this letter, but I want you to know I am safe and writing this of my own free will, though I truly wish I were not writing this letter to you at all. I find myself in a predicament that seems to have no other solution. It turns out my dreams are premonitions of the future, and the world could be in grave danger. I think it's a good thing that I went to Safdin with the priest who visited my home the other day.

I want to let you know that I arrived safely in Safdin but will be setting sail for Drendil the morning after tomorrow. The priests I talked with said destiny ties me to that place. Please understand that I wish nothing more than to continue my apprenticeship under you, but for the sake of the world, I cannot.

If I have any unpaid wages, please donate them to the orphanage in Feldring either in my name or anonymously. Those children need the funds more than I do. I'm sure those overseeing everything there can make good use of it.

These past few years have been wonderful, and I appreciate your guidance and teachings. I will remember you and the rest of the wood shop fondly.

As always,

Michael

Michael set the letter aside and drafted another to the homeowner's registrar of Feldring. This office oversaw all matters on behalf of the homeowner should they not be present or able to accomplish something. Typically, as Michael knew, their duties involved the sale of homes for those who recently passed away without family to see to the homes. This would be a standard matter for them, though unusual given the circumstances. With his letter though, they would follow his instructions and ensure everything was taken care of according to his wishes. His letter to the registrar's office was similar to the one he wrote to Master Gamel, but less emotional and more down to business.

He once again asked that his possessions be sold at fair prices, and any proceeds be donated to the orphanage. Michael set this letter aside to allow the ink to dry and grabbed the sealing wax. He folded his letter to Master Gamel and heated the wax and pressed a glob onto the fold of the page. Without his own signet, Michael used the plain one provided on the desk to press a blank circle into the warm wax. He did the same with the other letter and set them both aside so he could see to their delivery the next morning. For now, he needed rest. His eyes felt heavy, especially after eating dinner with Bruce and Joshua.

Michael stood from the desk, stretched, and got ready to sleep. He folded his shirt and trousers and placed them atop the chest at the foot of the bed, then laid down and worked his way under the blankets. He put out the oil lamp that sat beside the bed and stared at a single spot in the darkness until he fell asleep, and dreams took him again.

Chapter Four

The morning to set sail finally arrived and Joshua and Michael walked along the wharf toward a galleon named *Queller*. Everywhere along the wharf, seamen scurried along as they completed various tasks among the fleet of moored ships in the harbor. Some worked among the riggings, sewing patches onto the sails; others swabbed fresh tar onto the wooden planks which formed the ships' decks. None of the sailors in the whole wharf paid mind to either Michael or Joshua. The wharf housed nearly two dozen ships, all of which floated beside their respective docks based on their size. The northern piers housed the brig ships, dwarfed by the frigates and man-of-war ships at the southern end of the dock.

Randall stood at the bottom of the gangplank leading to his warship with his arms crossed in front of his chest. His bare feet were spread slightly wider than his shoulders. His appearance was the epitome of a sea-faring man, much the same as a couple nights before when Michael and Joshua first met him. When his passengers walked up to the ship, he straightened his posture, revealing that he stood as tall as the king.

"I was told you would be here before dawn. You're late." Randall said, his voice flat and firm.

"We are here now. Let's set off," Joshua replied.

"I have one rule for you, priest. As a passenger aboard my ship, you will lower your hood. No man's face is to be hidden while his feet touch my deck," Randall said as he strolled up the gangplank. "It's bad luck."

Joshua lowered his hood reluctantly and walked up the gangplank onto the ship. Michael followed, unsure of what he should do once aboard *Queller*. The wood planks under his feet creaked as his weight shifted from one spot to another. Once aboard the ship, Michael noticed that the tar covered every portion of the exposed wooded floors. Here, the tar was less slippery than the smooth gangplank had been, and Michael watched as barefooted sailors ran here and there across the mighty warship.

"Quartermaster, are all supplies aboard that will be needed for the voyage?" Randall called to a man standing on the quarterdeck beside the helm.

"Yes, Captain, the supplies are all aboard," the quartermaster replied.

"Prepare to launch the ship at my command," Randall shouted.

Several sailors responded before scurrying off. Randall led Joshua and Michael into his quarters and closed the doors behind him. He also pulled the curtains over the windows. In the middle of his cabin stood a small wooden table, on which sat a variety of maps, a sextant, and other navigational tools, all of which looked brand new. Randall walked to the other side of the table and leaned over the map on the table, then picked up a match to light his candle. With the candle lit, he pointed to the largest map on the table and locked eyes with Michael.

"This is the portion of Drendil that I've personally charted through my various voyages. Our trip, without any adverse weather, conflicts, or other issues, will take about two weeks. Were my orders not coming from the king, I'd gladly sail around the ocean for that amount of time without seeing any land," Randall stated firmly, hoping he made his point.

"We have a mission to save the world," Michael said.

"You also fail to understand this my contention with that place." Randall drooped his head and sighed. "I suppose if you're both ready to leave, we can set sail."

"There is no reason to stay longer than we must," Michael replied.

"Very well. You are welcome to stay here in my cabin or come to the helm if you would like to watch the ship set sail. I only ask that you stay out of the way. I will leave that choice to you," Randall said, standing up and walking toward his door. As he got to the door there was a knock. When he opened the door, the quartermaster stood outside.

"Report, Quartermaster," Randall said.

"All crew members are aboard and ready to set off, Captain. We stand ready, awaiting your command," he reported.

"Very well," Randall said before he walked up to the helm. Michael followed closely behind, having decided to watch the ship being set to sea.

"Bosun, ready the ship to sail," Captain Randall called, looking at a barrel-chested man.

"Aye, Captain," the bosun said before he brought a peculiar-shaped, brass whistle to his mouth.

The bosun blew several blasts on his whistle. The sound carried well above the sounds of the harbor. Some of the sailors aboard *Queller* bustled about the ship, others took up their positions beside thick lines that held the ship to the pier. Others scurried up the masts and prepared to untie the sails for when that order came. The bosun looked about when all the movement settled as if he were counting every man aboard the ship. When he saw everyone where they should be, he turned back to Randall, quickly clapping his fist to his chest.

"Ready to sail at your word, Captain," bosun reported, letting the silver whistle hang at his chest on its thin, well-worn leather strap.

"Release the moorings and get us out into the harbor, bosun. You man the wheel until we are ready to leave the harbor," Randall said.

Bosun lifted the whistle to his mouth again, blowing three short blasts followed by a trilling long blast. The men aboard *Queller* loosened the ropes that tied the ship to the pier and hauled the lines in quickly. A repeated clanging sound came from the dock behind the ship, and Michael walked to the stern and looked over the rail to see what made the sound. Shirtless, barefoot men walked in circles around a contraption with large handles that let slack into a massive rope attached to the ship. As they walked around the machine, the waves brought into the harbor from the tide gently pushed *Queller* away from the pier and out into the harbor.

Michael returned to the rail beside Joshua and watched as the men pulled the mooring lines onto the ship's deck; the line would get drawn in, then doubled over as it formed a flat, neat pile of rope roughly two meters long and half a meter wide, one layer deep on the deck of the ship. Once they finished coiling the line, some of the sailors moved to other parts of the ship. Some stayed outside and a few others went below the main deck. Within fifteen minutes, *Queller* drifted far enough from the pier and bosun reported the ship's status to Randall.

"Very well," Randall said. "Don't unfurl the main sails until we are beyond the edge of the harbor. No need to get fined for moving too quickly even for this bloody awful mission."

The bosun nodded and acknowledged the captain's orders before blowing a few more blasts on his whistle; men on the masts released the smaller sails, the thick canvas falling naturally and snapping when the stiff, ocean breeze filled them. From the deck below, oars appeared in the side of the ship where cannons would show during a battle. The smooth wood dipped into and out of the water as they helped push *Queller* into a stronger wind and toward open waters.

"When we leave the harbor, open all sails, and set a course due west. Retrieve me an hour afterward," Randall ordered, clasping his hands together in the small of his back as he walked off the quarterdeck. His footing seemed very sure, even without shoes on.

Michael leaned against the rail, his back to the castle they left behind them. Joshua, a few feet to his right, gazed upon the city as they slowly drifted further away; the pennants that flew over the castle grew too small to count before he broke his gaze away from the city. As they continued sailing away, and the sailors let the remaining sails open with the wind, Michael watched as a lone tear dripped from Joshua's left eye, slowly traveling down his cheek unhindered. He neither attempted to stop the tear nor did he acknowledge its presence.

Queller cut through the water in the bay south of Safdin, small waves running from the edge of the ship as they moved further from land. As the warship sailed into the open ocean, Michael felt the ship rocking up and down as it cut across what would become waves crashing on the distant shoreline. His stomach lurched briefly, and he questioned how these sailors could do this so often without feeling sick. Michael watched as Prikea grew smaller, fading quickly into the distance.

*   *   *

Michael took a brief moment to catch his breath and gaze up at the sky. Light wispy clouds floated by as peacefully as any time he could remember watching the clouds as a child. Sweat collecting on his forehead now dripped down the sides of his face, some of it running into his ears. Breaths came and went quickly, and his chest felt tight. He never fought with a sword before. Even though he was only training, the sailors showed little mercy despite their claims of fighting at half power. The ship rocked back and forth and that only made the whole situation worse. Michael once again lost his footing and caught the training sword squarely against the left side of his ribs. The wounds, while minor and not at all life-threatening, still hurt like hell. His right side took a beating during the previous bout of sparring, which he knew would result in some bruises sometime within the next few hours. His muscles ached and he grew more exhausted as they continued to train. Just as the king warned, Randall was relentless with the training. Several hours per day and even into the evening or later.

Michael lazily rolled onto his side and forced himself to stand up. Jasper, the sailor he was currently sparring with, stood a few paces away with the tip of his practice sword resting gently on the tar-covered deck of the ship. He stood with his feet apart just as when Michael first met the man. Everything about the man loudly pointed to him being a sailor including the plain, black patch he wore over his left eye. From the way he fought, it was apparent that he saw his fair share of battles on the open ocean. Michael thought the eye patch was curious, but it seemed that all the men aboard *Queller* wore a patch over one eye or the other, so there had to be a reason for it. Perhaps Michael would ask one of them if he found himself not sparring any of the crew as Randall ordered. Michael felt odd taking orders while not being a sailor, but Randall explained that anyone who set foot on the ship in an official manner listened to his word. There were few laws on the ocean, but what Randall said accounted for enough of them, it seemed.

"You're improving, but your footing's still weak. Stand just how you were right before you fell, lad," Jasper said, a slightly disinterested look upon his face.

Randall stood off to the side as he watched over the training. Michael got back into the stance Randall had shown him, his left foot in front of his body, the sword in both hands, held close to his right side, and his right foot behind his body. His weight shifted with the ship, but he kept most of it on his back foot. The worn leather wrapped around the wood rod they called a practice sword had grown slippery from his sweating hands.

"There's your problem lad. Your feet are too far apart. You won't ever be able to stand like that when you get hit. Try putting this foot here," Jasper said, pushing Michael's front foot back with one of his bare feet. "Bend your knees a little too, like this." Jasper bent his knees slightly as if he were trying to sit in a chair that was not behind him. Michael mimicked the man, which brought a brief glimpse of approval to the man's face. "Now you're getting it, lad! We'll make a swordsman out of you yet," he said.

This round of practice went on for nearly two hours, with the only breaks coming when Michael fell. Michael hardly considered those breaks, but Randall did. If Michael took too long to get up, the captain started barking at him to move faster. Jasper still breathed normally, showing no signs of exhaustion. Randall stood on the quarterdeck watching the entire evolution from above, his appearance unchanged from the first time Michael met him, except for the eye patch he wore. Joshua also watched from the quarterdeck, standing next to Randall.

"How dead is he, Jasper?" Randall called from above. His voice carried across the ship well.

"Well, Captain, the lad is pretty dead. He's getting a hang of it though. Maybe in a couple of days, he'll only die four times instead of six," Jasper said, laughing when he said that.

"Give him rest, Jasper. You can spar again later if you think it will help," Randall called once more.

"Aye, Captain." Jasper collected the practice swords and took them below deck.

Joshua walked down the steps from the quarterdeck and joined Michael, who stood by the bulwark, his elbows leaning against the rail. Michael's breaths were rapid and shallow after hours of training. Sweat beaded on his brow and rolled down his cheeks and nose. His shirt was wet and clung to him like a second skin. A light breeze blew across the ship from the south, and it carried a cool, salt-filled air with it.

"Your swordsmanship has improved since you first started if that makes you feel better. I know it is difficult fighting on a sailing ship, but it should help you later when you're fighting on land," Joshua said as he leaned on the rail of the ship beside Michael.

They stood at the rail for a few more minutes, letting the breeze dance across them, simply taking in the sight of the ocean. Far away to the south, a few small islands rose from the unbroken sheet of still water, the only sign of land they had seen since leaving Safdin. A few fish and dolphins swam in the water beside the ship, and he could see more off in the distance. Michael enjoyed the voyage, even if there wasn't really anything to look at; simply being on the ship going somewhere new was exciting enough. Every once in a while, he remembered he would never see Feldring again, and that realization sat like a stone in his stomach.

The men aboard *Queller* followed orders periodically whistled by the bosun. They pulled lines and adjusted the riggings as needed, scurrying from here to there as they worked. With the ship out to sea, the crew followed a pattern of shifts for each position, including the bosun's. The bosun was a large, tan-skinned man with piercings in his face and tattoos on his chest, arms, and hands. Thin gold chains connected several piercings between his ears and his nose while other chains simply dangled. Michael wanted to ask the bosun what the chains meant, but the look on the bosun's face was not an inviting look, and the man was intimidating. It was unlikely he would welcome questions from the ship's new 'land-dog' as the sailors had taken to calling Michael.

Far to the west, behind the warship, the sun drew closer to the horizon, throwing splashes of color into the sky. Red and orange streaked across the sky, painting clouds in brilliant shades. Never had Michael thought that he would enjoy a sunset more than he had while he lived in Feldring, watching the sun descend beyond the mountain city, changing the colors of the mountains themselves. His time aboard *Queller* showed how much more there was to life than living in the mountains. After they finished the voyage, Michael doubted he would ever see such a brilliant display of colors again.

Joshua pushed away from the railing. "Get some sleep, Michael. Randall wants to spar with you tomorrow, and that won't be an easy fight. He likes the progress you've made so far. 'He has potential,' Randall said to me up on the quarterdeck before he put an end to your training today. That's something to take pride in at the very least."

After a few moments standing alone at the rail, Michael turned and walked below to the hammock Randall had assigned to him. The cotton supported him but was still soft, and the motion of the ship rocking against the sea put him to sleep quickly. As he drifted off, the same dream came to him as it had for many weeks now. Týr and Joshua fought by his side; in a city he knew but only through these dreams. Creatures that seemed familiar, yet still terrifying. And the darkness that loomed like a blanket being thrown over the world, smothering every speck of light easier than snuffing a candle that reached the end of its wax.

*   *   *

The next morning, Michael woke to the bustle of sailors getting ready for the day's work. The men moved with purpose, hurriedly throwing on their trousers but leaving off their shirts and shoes, as was their practice while out to sea. Michael still found that walking barefoot felt foreign, but the tar on the wooden decks of the ship felt strangely comforting against the soles of his feet. A few meters away, Joshua knelt under his hammock, the cowl of his robe still draped over his shoulders. He complied with Randall's wish on that aspect, as reluctant as he may have been to do so. The priest spent much of his time in the mornings and evenings in prayer, as he always had since leaving Safdin. Michael thought it could be his way of coping with the reality of exile, a sentence he received for following his orders. Guilt simmered within Michael like stew in a pot, even with reassurances from Joshua that his priestly calling meant many life changes, even those he disliked or even disagreed with. His eyes still bore a deep pain regarding that reality, which only added to the guilt Michael felt.

Michael sat up in his hammock and let his feet dangle above the deck for a few more moments before he stood. He threw on one of the soft, plain shirts Randall provided after they set sail. Michael had the option, as the rest of the crew did, to go about the ship shirtless, but he was still uncomfortable with that idea. The first day out to sea he had tried it but caught far too much of the unadulterated sunlight. He now had a reddish-pink hue to his chest and back. His skin stung under the weight of even the linen shirt. Strikes from the practice swords only hurt that much more. Perhaps the next morning when he woke up the pain would be gone. He already noticed skin peeling from the reddest areas. The biggest difficulty he found was not scratching himself to relieve the itching sensations.

A few sailors remained in the cabin area, one sewing a patch over a hole in a pair of trousers. Another sailor was eating some dried meat, fruit, and some bread. They ate simple foods, but that food kept the men alive and healthy, so none of them complained or found reason to, at the very least. Michael had certainly not heard any complaints during their time aboard *Queller*. Michael had grown to enjoy the food but thought it would grow old if this were his daily rations for longer than a couple of weeks. The sailors preserved as much of their food as they could to prevent such crucial food from spoiling. And as it turned out, dried fruit kept its flavor and made less of a mess to eat. In the evenings they ate cooked food prepared in the galley. The cooked food, while not great, was at least better than dried foods.

"Let's head topside and see if Randall is ready to start sparring with you if you're ready. Perhaps there will be something more in store for us today," Joshua suggested though he still knelt under his hammock.

"Sounds good to me," Michael acknowledged. He climbed out of his hammock and made his way through the area of the ship where the cannons were stored, then up a wooden ladder leading to the outside decks.

Reds, purples, and yellows splattered through the sky, much like the night before. However, the mood of the sailors seemed vastly different than it had when Michael went below deck to get some rest. Worry stained their faces, and several looked about, trying to find whatever scrap of hope they would need later. *Such an odd thing to be concerned about*, Michael thought to himself. The colors of the sky normally changed as the sun moved through it.

"To see red in the sky during a sunrise is an ill omen in a sailor's life," Randall called from his cabin door. He leaned against the open door, watching his passengers as they emerged from below. "The sky should only be red when the sun sets. There'll be a storm later. Hopefully, we get away from it—"

"Captain, a storm's brewing to the west. A big one, too," a man called from the top of the mast. "Appears to be heading toward us around twenty knots, still quite a few leagues off."

"Bosun, set a course for due south," Randall called, still leaning in his doorway.

"Captain, we'd be heading into the wind," the bosun questioned, shouting above the wind that had picked up from nowhere. The gusts filled the sails and the ship lurched through the water, which grew choppy as the storm approached.

"Set your course for due south. No further questions, bosun," Randall said.

"Aye, Captain," bosun replied, spinning the wheel to his right.

"Michael, Joshua, come into my cabin," Randall said, heading to the map table before speaking again. "The wind blew steadily in our favor until this morning. We'll be as close as I want to get to Drendil tomorrow evening. Unfortunately, for you to carry out your mission, I have to get much closer than I would like."

"How is that even possible? You said it would be a two-week voyage, but this is the start of our ninth day," Joshua said.

"You're misunderstanding what I said just now. I do not like being any closer to Drendil than a couple of days of sailing. But as I said, the wind blew in *Queller's* favor. Maybe not in your favor or mine, but the ship moves quickest with the wind at her back. The land is mad," Randall replied.

"You've already told us that," Joshua said, looking at the map of the west coast of Drendil to better understand their new home.

"I only mention it again because I really wouldn't have come out here if it wasn't my brother that gave me the order. I'd have told the admiral off if he said I had to sail here," Randall said. "The morning after we arrive, you can take a rowboat to the shore, but I'm turning *Queller* around the second I lose sight of you."

"You're giving us no support of any kind?" Michael asked. Suddenly he felt as if a stone had formed in his stomach and weighed him down. "What happens if we run into trouble?"

"My concern is that you arrive on that damned continent. After you reach land, I no longer have to worry about either of you," Randall said.

He slid his chair out from under the table and sat heavily on the worn black leather cushion. After he sat down, he propped his feet on the table. The heel of his bare foot crumpled the edge of a few maps. He picked his pipe up from his desk and packed quite a lot of tobacco into his pipe, lit the leaves, and blew out the harsh smelling smoke. The acrid smell of the smoke told Michael that the tobacco leaves had long since gone stale, but the look on Randall's face said the man didn't care. Michael and Joshua stood in the cabin watching Randall, hoping he would say something else to make up for his complete apathy toward their situation. Without acknowledging their presence in his cabin, he continued smoking his pipe, staring at the bare rafters, blowing the thin clouds of light grey smoke toward the ceiling, watching it dissipate before it even reached the wood beams overhead. For a few minutes, he sat without puffing at his pipe, the stem resting just far enough from his lips that they never met.

Without warning, he shot to his feet, pushed his passengers aside, and burst through his cabin doors. Standing in the doorway, his arms thrust straight to each side to hold his doors open, Michael peered around his frame and saw a large wall of water approaching the left side of the ship. It was moving fast too, and *Queller* began listing to the right as the water disappeared from under her to join the massive wave.

"Rogue wave! Bosun, steer the ship into the wave! All hands brace for impact," Randall shouted as loudly as he could. Sailors outside scrambled to the rails and lines, as they grabbed on to anything they could that would stay on the ship.

"Captain it's too late for that," bosun called back.

"How the *hell* did a rogue wave sneak up on you, bosun?" Randall shouted back.

Before the bosun could answer, the wave crashed over *Queller*. Water rushed across the deck, throwing anything not tied or nailed down off the ship, which included the coiled-up mooring lines that had remained beside the bulwarks since their voyage started. Randall continued bracing himself in his doorway, but Michael and Joshua flew against the bulkhead. Joshua crashed into a standing mirror, Michael into a sturdy nightstand. Lying on the deck, Michael saw his vision closing in, and the room started to spin around him; his breath came in shallow, pained gasps, and his back felt warm and wet. The darkness grew closer, and he found himself giving in to the irresistible call of the encroaching darkness.

*   *   *

Joshua sat against the wall amid the mirror splinters where the force of the wave threw him. He tried to realize what had happened, and how he ended up on the floor. Randall left the doorway shortly after the two of them hit the wall. The room spun, and he tried to stand but wavered too much and fell back to the floor again. Searing pain shot through Joshua's head and shoulder, and his vision blurred more with every blink. He leaned forward to stand up and his stomach lurched as it forced its contents to splash onto the floor. The *splat* sound was barely masked by the ringing in his ears. *Queller* rocked back and forth as she recovered from the wave.

When the ringing in his ears and blurry vision finally subsided, Joshua slowly got to his feet and looked around. He saw Michael on the floor with only a small table holding him on his side which kept him from rolling any further and ending up in the scattered pile of glass shards. The back of his shirt was torn slightly and showed a growing spot of deep red where blood already started to soak through the thin fabric. He appeared to be alive at least, just unconscious. His landing must have been significantly harder than Joshua's. *At least*, the priest thought to himself, *he hit the furniture and not that window behind the table.* While Joshua knelt and inspected Michael, *Queller* rocked again, and Joshua lost his balance, falling against the central table. Thankfully, he caught himself on the edge but knocked paperweights off the table. As he stood again, Randall rushed in, drenched in seawater. He had the appearance of a rat that just left a river and the room smelled heavily of salt the moment he walked in.

"What happened?" Randall asked, tossing his unlit pipe on the table, and pulling off his shirt while he rushed to Michael's side.

"We got thrown around in here like a girl's dolls," Joshua answered.

"I'm only making this voyage because of you. Neither of you is dying until I get you to Drendil. After that, you're free to do all the dying you want," Randall said, putting his shirt on Michael's wound. He had not thought of the salt in the seawater and Michael flinched through his unconsciousness. Joshua inhaled deeply and knew a quick spell would clear up Michael's wound, and any others they didn't know about. Randall would be furious, given his disposition toward priests. *What he doesn't know won't hurt him,* Joshua concluded as he reached for his source of Magic. He stopped and looked at Randall.

"You made it seem like you don't care about us. Why help him in that case?" Joshua asked, standing again.

"You're right about one thing: I don't care what fool's quest you're on. I only care that my mission is complete, and that means you stay alive until you get to Drendil. Take this as nothing more than that," Randall replied. "Besides, he should be fine in a couple of days. The wounds don't look deep, and the saltwater should help clean the wounds. He'll be in pain, though. Can you finish cleaning him up? I need to check with the bosun and see what the damages are."

"There's a way he could recover faster. You and I both know you're aware of my abilities," Joshua said.

"Not on my ship, priest. I will die before Magic is used on my ship. That's what got us into this whole mess with Drendil," Randall growled.

Joshua said nothing and instead applied pressure to Michael's wound with the shirt as he waited for Randall to leave the cabin. Once he heard the faint whisper of the doors closing behind the brash captain, Joshua started the healing spell. His hands faintly glowed white, and Joshua felt a chill run through his hands as he started the process of healing the wound. Michael's eyes opened wide as the spell started to work, and Joshua stopped the spell instantly. Now was not the time or place to explain the reality of the priesthood to Michael. This wasn't the first spell he had cast since he met the carpenter's apprentice, but it would be the hardest to explain. Starting fires was easy enough to do without raising questions. Healing wounds would be quite difficult. And there was still Randall's reaction to deal with. *Healing this time was a foolish move,* Joshua chided himself. The wound hadn't fully healed yet, but at least he wouldn't lose any more blood this way. Michael coughed harshly and tried to sit up on his own. Joshua held Michael against the floor until he finished coughing, then helped him to slowly sit. Once Michael was seated, Joshua leaned him against the table.

The door to the cabin opened and Randall walked back in, slamming his fists on the table, and clearing the maps that remained off the table. The papers scattered across the room, gently floating to the floor. His knuckles glowed white as he leaned against the table, breathing heavily through his clenched teeth.

"The main topsail yard and the foresail yards broke when the wave hit us. We have half the sails we had this morning. We either sit here until we can make what repairs we can, or we sail on much slower than we have been," Randall said, punching the table again.

"Which of those choices is easier?" Joshua asked, his eyes staying on Michael and his mostly healed wound.

"Neither choice is easy," Randall answered, speaking through clenched teeth.

"A choice must be made, Captain! That is your lot in this."

A few moments of enraged silence followed as Randall stared at where the maps previously sat before he tossed them aside in anger. He leaned against the table and breathed heavily, his face still red. A couple of veins showed in his forehead and neck. Finally, he slowly stood up straight and looked at Joshua.

"I will take him below to his hammock. Feel free to walk around the ship as you wish," Randall said, walking over to Michael and kneeling beside him.

"You've made a choice about the repairs?" Joshua asked; he was curious but wanted not to upset the man. Blood lightly stained his

82

knuckles from when he punched the heavy table. No doubt existed that Randall fought that table repeatedly and lost often.

"We will drop anchor here and see what repairs we can manage without being able to get any supplies. We may be able to set sail again in a few days."

Joshua continued to kneel beside Michael as Randall knelt. Surprisingly, he showed great care and concern toward Michael, lifting him as a small child who had fallen asleep somewhere besides their bed. Joshua stood and moved toward the cabin door. Before Joshua could reached the table in the center of the room, Randall had a door opened and stepped outside. Joshua stayed in the cabin a few minutes after Randall left and picked up the maps and other items from the floor. Once he put the maps and their paperweights back on the table, he made his way to the ladder going down to the crew's hold. He wanted to stay close to Michael during the remainder of his recovery.

Chapter Five

Fat raindrops crashed into broad oak leaves overhead and slowly trickled down to the damp, grimy forest floor. Sprouting trees, still green and without any signs of bark forming, stretched hopefully toward the distant sky from the moist dirt. Their leaves longed for the sunshine that was so scarce for any of the trees but the oldest and tallest of behemoths that made up the thick forest. Massive ferns and other shrubbery littered the forest floor between the trees. Shelf mushrooms could be seen on many of the larger trees, their slimy-looking surfaces reflecting what little light there was in the forest. Rain that made its way that far through the canopy high above pooled atop the shelf mushrooms. This added to their slick, slimy appearance.

The jungle was alive with a cacophony of animal chatter, the splashing of raindrops, the rustling of the broad leaves in the warm, humid jungle wind. Nearly every inch of the forest bustled with life. Ants crawled on tree limbs, across leaves, up and down tree trunks. Monkeys chattered high in the branches. Birds flew overhead, flapping their wings violently as they landed on branches far in the forest canopy. Crawling through the dirt and leaves that decayed on the forest floor were insects and worms, their bodies wriggling through the loose surface as they hunted for anything that could be eaten. Spiders formed ornate webs that spanned the gaps between trees. The webs had to be placed strategically to capture any insects, or small birds, which were foolish enough to fly into them.

One such web housed a rather large, yellow-striped spider, about the size of a man's hand, which was currently working its way down the web it built to a butterfly that had fluttered into the web and was now struggling to free itself from the horrid trap it found. The spider wasted no time biting the black and blue butterfly then converting it into a cocoon of web which engulfed the body and wings of the poor insect. With its food collected, the spider retreated to the top of its web where it sat and waited for the butterfly to fall victim to the injected poison. The process would take a couple of hours, but the spider was patient.

The violent roar of a monstrous beast elsewhere broke the sounds of the forest as it echoed through the trees and silenced many of the creatures within earshot. Birds took to flight, climbing for the open sky over the tops of the trees. The sound came from neither a man nor anything natural to the forest. This monster was something wholly unnatural, something which did not belong in this world. A beast created from Magic, spawned with evil in its heart and malice flowing in its very veins. The monster and a man in a dark robe stood in a small clearing where a boulder protruded from the ground and prevented any trees from growing in the soil it occupied. The dark man, his robes still as a windless night, stood before the beast with a large axe in his hands. He held the haft with the head of the axe resting against the ground, almost leaning against the weapon for support.

The beast was tall, over two meters at the shoulders. Thick, matted fur covered most of its body, with only its chest and stomach devoid of any of the fur. The creature stood on its hind legs, powerful hooves supporting it, rather than feet. A thick ridge of fur covered the creature's back, and the thick hairs that made up its fur stood straight out, like a stray dog that raised its hackles to show it felt threatened. And to the man, that's all this beast was. A cur he found that would serve him. A beast of burden. But the monster knew none of that. Not yet anyway. From the beast's head sprouted two horns; they jutted out then forward like a bull. The resemblance to a bull went so far as a ring piercing the septum of the creature's nose. The face of the monster was still too human, and human teeth showed under the bullish snout that jutted out.

"I name you Audro, King of the Forest. You shall serve me as my guardian of the trees. Let none come through unless they also serve me," a deep, resonating voice called out from inside the unmoving black robes.

Audro grunted his acknowledgment, bending from the waist as his shoulders, neck, and back were too stiff to bow only his head. The dark man, once the minotaur rose from his bow, handed over the behemoth of an axe that he held. On each side of the axe was a face, trapped in the steel, and each face showed great anguish. The faces on the axe seemed to be alive, trapped in time within the head of the axe.

Audro's axe was built almost like a bardiche, though the head of the axe was too large for the weapon to be used like a polearm. The axe's sole bit jutted out with a flared heel and toe. The heel nearly touched the belly of the handle, ending in a sharp point. The unsharpened toe curved less aggressively toward the point. The space between the beard and haft was large enough for Audro's mammoth hand. To provide balance for the axe, the butt contained a large, square piece of metal with rounded points which covered the flat surface. It resembled the hammer a butcher might use on a tough cut of meat, though with a more wicked intention.

"Use this axe to bring despair to anyone who crosses your path in these woods. All who see you shall tremble," the shadowy man said. Even his hands were cloaked in darkness.

"Yes, master," Audro grunted.

The shadowy man opened a doorway in the air and a man fell out, landing roughly on the ground, air gasping from his lungs as he landed. Seeing Audro, axe in hand, the man shrieked and started crawling away as best he could. Bindings on his wrists and ankles made it difficult for the man to crawl, and the dampness of the soil did not assist the man. Audro snorted, his hackles standing even straighter.

"This is your first test. This man has displeased me greatly, a grave mistake that I cannot allow him or others to make again. He is to suffer greatly for this choice he has made. You may be as painful as you deem sufficient while dolling out this punishment. Only after you have finished this task, and brought me his head, shall the forest be yours," the shadowy man ordered as he opened another doorway in the air and left the woods behind him.

Audro lumbered toward the man on the ground, who was slowly crawling away. The minotaur's hoofs compacted the dirt beneath them with each step. His left hand tightened around the haft of his axe and his knuckles crackled as they flexed. As he approached the man, Audro turned the axe around, putting the spiked butt between himself and the man he would be disciplining. He approached the man slowly which increased the tension he could sense in his captive. With only a few feet left, Audro smelled the air and noticed a new, musty smell that didn't belong in the forest. *Pitiful humans,* the beast thought. The ground was wet under his powerful hooves. The axe lifted and the spiked end came down on the man's right knee, crushing bones when it landed. The man shrieked in agony as the axe was lifted once more. Audro snorted and brought the axe down again on the captive's other knee, bones once again crushing under the force and weight of the spikes.

"Please, you don't have to do this!" the man squealed between anguished sobbing, his face a blubbering mess.

"You understand nothing, worm. You displeased our master and as such your life is already over. Whether I kill you, or he does, you die today. But I will not displease my master the way you displeased him. And I will be less cruel to you than he will be," Audro uttered, his guttural voice booming in the forest.

The man spat at Audro but missed the large beast completely. Audro looked at where the glob of saliva landed on the ground, the bubbles floating in a puddle of rainwater. The minotaur fixed his gaze on the man once more and turned the axe in his hands. The man chose pain. The forest resonated with the man's screams as Audro made him regret ever displeasing their shadowy master.

Chapter Six

The knife's sharpened blade slipped through the stiff, leather armor and between the ribs of the inattentive guard. His breath escaped his lungs one last time in a quiet gasp. With a quick motion, Iona quietly guided the body to the ground then moved it out of sight. She looked to her left at Týr, doing the same with another guard a couple of meters away. The pair moved through the shadows toward another pair of guards, striking swiftly and quietly. They both needed to drag these guards' bodies away as they stood too close to the main pathway through the camp, and they could leave no chance for anyone to find a body. At least, not before they were ready for any bodies to be found. That wasn't supposed to happen before the pair was already well outside the camp.

The dead man easily weighed twenty stones without his armor. *What did they let him eat?* Iona thought to herself angrily. Behind a tent, she quietly lowered the man down and buried the blade of her knife in his neck out of anger. Before she moved on, Iona checked the area and quickly looked for anyone that might notice her. With no one around, she ran to the left and met Týr outside a larger tent that had been marked on their maps as a supply tent. *Hopefully, they have plenty of food,* Iona thought, trying to ignore the emptiness of her stomach. Týr used his knife to cut a makeshift door into the back panel of the tent, making a hole just big enough for them both to go through. The soft light of the oil lamps flooded through the cut into the darkness of night.

"What took you so long?" Týr whispered behind the dark linen wrapped around his face. Only his eyes and the bridge of his nose were visible, the same as Iona.

"That guard was too big for me!" Iona snapped quietly, lowering her mask.

Týr huffed at that, rolled his eyes, and then disappeared into the tent. Iona slipped inside moments after and blinked at the light inside the tent. Oil lamps cast light throughout the tent from every corner; something about this tent felt wrong. *Why would a supply tent be this lit at night?* With a brief scan of the tent, she noticed a man lying on a chaise in the tent, his head propped up on his wrist and some fancy-looking pillows. She looked down and saw the rug in the tent, covering the wooden pallets that made up the floor. A goblet lay on the ground in front of the man. A deep red stain marred the rather elegant carpet where wine had spilled, most likely from when the fat man fell asleep. He clearly passed out after drinking too much of the sweet-smelling, spiced wine. His chest rose and fell with his rhythmed breathing and soft, wheezing snores.

She crept over to the man, knife in her hand, ready to bury the blade if he stirred. His silky robes and extravagant jewelry showed he owned more than a bit of wealth. He was probably some fat, pompous under-lord. Elsewhere in the tent, she heard Týr rifling through some canisters. He never really could be silent, unlike Iona. The two of them ended up in more than one dungeon cell because of that. That was back before the king lifted the ban on killing thieves.

Týr tapped Iona on her shoulder twice; they were leaving. As Iona knelt beside the sleeping man, his eyes fluttered, then snapped open. He looked right at her, his mouth opening briefly. Before any sounds escaped, she swiftly plunged the blade into his thick throat. Air gurgled from the opening as blood spilled onto the chaise, rug, and the goblet beneath the man. Involuntarily, she felt her stomach heave and empty itself onto the rug. Her eyes watered as she retched twice more, failing to be as quiet as possible.

"Is everything alright, lord?" a voice outside the tent asked. The heavy canvas of the tent slightly muffled the sound of the guard's voice, making him sound further away.

Oh shit! Was this *Lord Dennison?* Iona scolded herself. She had only heard stories about the man who oppressed the band of thieves and never saw him in person. If this were Lord Dennison, she would catch an earful from Lars when they returned to camp. Or she might be praised. It was really hard to guess what might happen when dealing with Lars.

A firm hand gripped Iona's shoulder and quickly yanked her toward the hole in the back of the tent. Once outside the tent, she saw only darkness. Her eyes slowly adjusted themselves to the blackness of the night sky. The hand dragged her a few tents away and finally stopped in a darker area between two other tents. Týr stood over her, his breath erratic and uneven, his mask pulled from his face. Even in the faintest light from the hidden moon, she saw beads of sweat gathered on his brow; his eyes burned with unbridled anger.

"Have you lost your mind?! We were supposed to grab the map of their supply routes and get out. 'Only kill guards, and only if absolutely necessary,' were the orders," Týr fumed. His fists clenched and the leather of his light gauntlets creaked as the leather stretched over his fist.

Before Iona could get out any response other than weak gasping, Týr dove beside her and threw his hand over her mouth. Shouts came from the large tent with the dead lord, and footsteps approached quickly, accompanied by the sounds of leather armor creaking and swords drawing from scabbards. Several guards ran past. Thankfully, none of them carried a torch. Only the slightest sliver of the moon shone in the sky, yet these guards expected to find whoever killed their lord? Escaping the camp would be harder now that the guards knew someone was here.

Pah, foolishness! Iona scolded herself crossly.

93

"We have to get out of here quickly and quietly," Týr whispered, motioning south toward the woods where they had set up their camp.

Iona put her hand on Týr's chest before they moved. He stopped, and their eyes locked in a few moments. She motioned to the west, where they could slip out of the camp faster, then double around to their camp. Týr nodded, looked around a few moments, and checked for more guards before getting up and crossing the path to the next set of tents where they could hide.

Iona followed and Týr moved on to the next spot before she fully settled between the tents. They kept this pattern up until they reached the edge of the camp. Týr motioned for them to halt, and they scanned the area to watch for any guards patrolling outside the camp. Neither saw any movement outside the camp, or near the edges of the tents, but guards could be patrolling without torches, which would make them especially hard to see in the nearly moonless night. It would be difficult to sneak away from the camp, especially after Iona killed that fat man. This group chose a nice spot for the camp. Fields to the north and west with sparse trees and few hills offered a good view for anything coming toward the site. To the south spread a vast forest, trees too thick for any enemy forces to march through. At least that is what the soldiers assumed, but the thieves built their own camp in the forest for that same reason. To the east, a small river flowed from the north to the south. The water source and clear visibility of the surrounding area made this an ideal location for the camp.

"We have to stay low and move quickly," Iona whispered to Týr, who only responded with a curt nod. "Did we at least get what we needed?"

Týr gave Iona a quick glance that clearly said they had missed their mark; Iona felt an instant pit forming in her stomach. Lars would surely have her lashed for this. He always punished failure swiftly and mercilessly. She turned her gaze from Týr, unable to take the relentless judgment in his eyes. He touched her shoulder to try comforting her, but she now feared returning to their camp.

They set off into the field heading west until they crested a couple of hills, then turned south where they came to a path the soldiers trampled through the fields. *Such disgraceful oafs,* Iona thought to herself. They stopped for a moment as a trio of soldiers rode their horses down the path toward the town a few kilometers southwest of the camp. Once they could no longer hear the *clip-clop* of horse hooves on the packed dirt, Týr and Iona continued moving south again. Týr looked around constantly, checking their surroundings for guards. Iona felt lost within herself as she thought about what Lars might do to punish her for this mistake; she floated in a pool of emptiness, only really aware that her legs moved as they ran through the tall grass. She couldn't tell if she was making her legs move or if they did that on their own.

Nearly an hour later, they reached the tree line and could move more freely through the woods. The soldiers only patrolled the very edge of the woods, but there was no sign of any soldiers being there today. After a few of them came back from the town's inn spouting fresh tales about a mysterious curse that surely accompanied the woods, they stopped venturing in. The thieves found it so easy to fool the soldiers with a few stories of curses once they had some liquor. It was really a disgrace how sloppy an army could be, all the while still functioning enough to oppress people.

Massive oak, maple, and pine trees stretched meters into the sky, their mighty arms blocking out the small bit of moonlight that wasn't already blocked by incoming clouds. Bushes, twigs, and dried leaves from years before rustled, as the thieves ran through the trees. Iona and Týr had grown familiar with these woods over the past season, learning the trees and their gnarled roots, which stones between the trees offered the best footing, and those that only brought injuries. As they came closer to their camp, they had to slow down, avoiding traps placed to keep interlopers away. Some traps were simple holes in the ground with wooden spikes in the bottom covered with leaves and sticks to hide them. Others were intricate with truly nasty consequences. One such trap always made Iona shudder to think about. High in the trees, they rigged logs that would swing down and crush whoever tripped the cord hidden amid leaves and twigs. The thought of the only person ever caught by that trap still haunted her dreams. *That was not a fun mess to clean,* Iona thought, feeling her stomach want to lurch again.

They passed through the last series of traps and reached the edge of their camp. No one stirred in any of the tents, but that seemed normal for this early in the morning. The first few hints of sunlight started coming between the trees as the sun came over the horizon. Týr and Iona moved through the camp as they made their way to the center tent where Lars would surely be leaning over his table, planning their next move on the map. The man spent his entire thieving career planning and strategizing; few of his plans had failed. Halfway to Lars's tent, Týr stopped and grabbed Iona's arm firmly right above the elbow. They stopped in the middle of the foot-worn path that ran through the encampment. Iona glanced at Týr's hand, then up to his face. She never saw his eyes that wide before and knew immediately something was wrong. Every drop of blood had drained from his face as he looked around.

"Something is *very* wrong," Týr said, his voice faint and almost cracking.

"What is it?" Iona's mind raced thinking of what it could be.

Týr composed himself before answering. "No one has welcomed us back, I don't smell any food, and it's far too quiet even for early morning."

Then, as sunlight broke through the trees, they saw it. Blood. Lots of blood. Everywhere. Blood that stained the canvas walls and flaps of tents and trailed into the packed dirt paths. Týr's hand loosened on her arm, and she turned around, seeing the faint glistening of blood throughout the entire camp, reflecting the soft morning sunlight. Her knees buckled and she fell to the ground where her stomach once again emptied itself. Vomit poured over her hands, warming them slightly. She didn't even care.

She heard Týr walk away while she knelt there, unsure how long she stared at her own vomit on the ground. When he came back, he draped a blanket over her and stood there with her. Iona finally felt like she could move, and Týr helped her stand slowly, supporting her with his arm tight around her waist. His body felt warm, a wonderfully welcome comfort at that moment. They stood there attempting to comfort each other as best they could, given the circumstances. Finally, she looked at Týr. His face looked ashen; blood drained from his cheeks. He looked at her and handed her a note he found.

"What's this?" Iona asked, gazed at the note, then noticed splatters of blood on the thick parchment. The edges of the paper were rough, like it was torn from a larger piece of parchment, and a slit in the top seemed like it was roughly knife-shaped. This note had been *pinned* to someone. Whoever left it clearly wanted to leave a message the massacre hadn't already left. Iona scanned the note at least half a dozen times, not knowing fully what it said any of the times she read it. When she finally focused on the words before her, she felt a white-hot rage boiling inside, threatening to spill over at any moment.

> By decree of Lord Dennison, on behalf of the two kings, the occupants of this camp have been found guilty of, and executed for, crimes up to and including high treason against the Kingdom of Drendil, and her Lords. Anyone who occupied this camp who was not present at the time of this sentencing is also considered guilty of these crimes and shall be punished as such.

The note bore a wax seal that belonged to Lord Dennison, but he was likely not the one to place the note wherever Týr found it. Iona also knew that only four people, all officers of Lord Dennison, would carry out his orders according to the note. Iona and Týr, belonging to a band of thieves, always knew there was a chance they would be caught. She just never expected it to end quite this way. As she finished reading the note for the third time, she handed it back to Týr, who pushed her hand back to her. The look on his face showed that he didn't want to keep it.

"Maybe someone survived. We should check," Iona said as she cast off the blanket and threw the parchment to the ground. As she started moving toward the central tent where Lars's table and map always stayed, Týr stopped her with a firm hand on her shoulder.

"If anyone survived, they're not here. I've already checked," Týr said. Iona felt tears welling in her eyes, her vision slowly blurring and a trail of warmth streaking down her cheek.

"Th—there's got to be someone who survived!" Iona said as tears ran down her cheeks.

"We need to leave. Who knows if someone will come back? Especially after our raid," Týr suggested, after a long pause. He scanned the woods around the camp, looking for signs of anyone coming through the trees.

"Where will we go? We don't have the map we went after, and I doubt we can get it now," Iona replied.

"Forget the map! It would have only led us to another map, then another and another. I don't know what Lars was so desperate to find. We have been searching for months for whatever he had his heart set on, and we kept finding nothing."

Iona and Týr went to their tents, the only two without blood splattered everywhere, to gather their belongings before leaving the camp. As thieves, they never maintained many possessions, but an hour passed before they met once more in the middle of the camp. The sun was now moving west and the shadows from the trees began to grow longer. Dusk was a few hours away, but they had to go somewhere. Týr looked at a map he grabbed from Lars's tent, and the surviving thieves tried to figure out where to go next. Nothing made sense anymore.

"We need to find whoever did this. They have to pay for what they've done," Iona said, her voice weak.

"Don't you think that's exactly what they'll expect us to do?" Týr tried to keep his voice down while speaking firmly.

"You think they expect anyone to have survived *this*?"

"I don't know. Would they have attacked the camp if they thought anyone was away? They'll be able to connect the murder to our camp. We're too close for anyone not to connect the two. We've been stealing from them for too long for them not to know exactly where to find our camp if they wanted to, and I'd say they finally wanted to."

"At most, they would think one person survived or they wouldn't have left the note. Why inform no one that a band of thieves was killed by a lord's decree?" Iona argued.

"We have a bounty on our heads now, Iona. It may not say our names specifically, but whoever did this wants us dead as well. If we go anywhere near the camp or soldiers from it, we will end up just as dead as everyone here," Týr replied.

"We can't do nothing. This camp was our whole life. We grew up with these thieves."

"We will figure out something, but first we have to get out of here. These woods aren't safe. The villages aren't either. According to this map, there are four villages nearby, all of which are likely to have any number of soldiers from the camp we just raided. We have to go far away from here. The coast isn't far, I think we can make our way there, and start new lives in Erith. There has to be something there for us. Lord Dennison doesn't have any control there either, so this," Týr said, as he waved the map at the bloody camp, "can't happen to us."

"Erith? We can't survive in a city that big! We're thieves. We've never known any other life," Iona replied.

"Well, we won't live if we stay here. Lord Dennison's men will watch these woods for anyone coming here. We already spent too long here as it is, Iona. We have to leave now," Týr said. Iona's face rumpled with frustration. She knew he was right but refused to admit that. She never liked to admit she was wrong, especially not to her brother. "For now, we need to head anywhere Lord Dennison doesn't have his soldiers."

"That's a good idea. Is Erith the closest city where he doesn't have a presence?"

"For now, yes. We could try to make our way to Shemont, but we would cross the entirety of Dennison's territory, with untold numbers of his soldiers who would recognize us on sight. It is safer for us in Erith. The line where Dennison's authority ends is about a kilometer west of here."

"Then let's head there. It doesn't seem there's much choice right now," Iona admitted.

"We should leave camp and head west toward the river. It leads to another river south of here that should guide us to Erith," Týr said, looking at the map.

With a sigh from Iona, the thieves started their journey toward Erith. Staying in the woods meant they couldn't take a direct path to the river. Traveling this way took more time than Týr wanted, and when they finally reached the river, they both were too tired to travel any further. The sun was only touching the horizon when they stopped, but without its light traveling along the river would be perilous. They settled among the trees without a fire, to Iona's protests, for fear that any passing soldiers would see the light or smoke and come to investigate. They couldn't risk drawing any unnecessary attention to themselves. Lars had taught them that Dennison was a cruel monster under the guise of a man. Iona and Týr drifted off to sleep watching the sky grow dark as the sun descended beyond the horizon with a gentle breeze rustling the trees.

Chapter Seven

aptain, I see something to the north and east, a few knots off!" a sailor called from the crow's nest. The sailor at the top of the mast wore an eye patch like the rest of the sailors aboard *Queller* but also wore a hat with three corners and a striped shirt.

Captain Randall, the Ruthless, the Commanding Officer of *Queller* felt a stone forming in his stomach. Men did not sail this close to Drendil without good reason, and the ship was still undergoing repairs.

"What are you seeing, Hagley?" the captain replied, fearing what the barrelman said next.

"A beast, sir. Large and moving toward us quickly!"

"Damn this entire voyage," Randall said to himself not under his breath. The bosun, at the helm of the ship, chuckled to himself before catching a menacing look from his captain. "Get that priest topside. I want him to see what his being aboard has brought us. Now!"

A sailor ran down below from the main deck and came back shortly with Joshua, his hood still draped over his shoulders as Randall asked. As much as Randall disliked the priests, this one had adapted to the life of a sailing man. He wore no shoes and seemed to be measuring his steps as he ran to the quarterdeck. Randall gave him no time to ask questions before barking information at him.

"What kind of beast is it?" Joshua asked, a grave look on his face.

"It looked like a sea serpent, but it moved too fast to get a good look, lord," the barrelman said.

"I knew having you aboard was bad luck," Randall snarled.

"Damn." Joshua looked more worried now. "What defenses do you have aboard?"

"We have sixteen guns each side, but if it's a serpent we stand little chance against it unless the ship is mobile," Randall replied. *Damn this whole fucking voyage.*

The ship rocked, gently at first, as waves from the serpent finally reached the boat. Based on the size of the waves it created, the creature was still a few kilometers away.

"Captain, I know you will disapprove, but I can dispel the beast. I'll just need time to concentrate." Joshua offered.

"Absolutely not. I will not have Magic cast aboard my ship. It's bad enough just having a priest as a passenger."

"You called me up here for a reason. This is the only way we will survive, and you and I both know that's Michael and I surviving is the only way you are getting your promotion to Commodore," Joshua countered.

Randall went silent and his face went neutral at that. *How does he know about that?* "Fine! Do whatever you need to do but keep this ship safe."

Michael came topside as Joshua started climbing the rope ladder to the crow's nest. Once up in the nest, Joshua knelt and held his hands in front of his chest, fingertips touching. Gazing out, he saw waves forming as the serpent approached quickly. He took a deep breath and began a few spells. Dark, unnaturally thick clouds formed overhead, cutting out the sunset and the stars that already showed through the evening sky. The clouds circled above the ship as if they were a soup in a giant cauldron being stirred by an equally giant spoon. Lightning streaked through the clouds and provided the only source of light besides a couple of oil lamps down on the main decks of the *Queller*. Joshua stood, still casting spells; he reached his hands forward, palms toward the roiling sky. A bolt of lightning shot down from the cloud, filled his hands, and formed an orb of great power between his hands. As the orb grew, he separated his hands, now forming a second orb of lightning. One hand he brought back close to his ear and looked for the serpent, peering through the darkness. Lightning streaked from the roiling clouds above to the water, illuminating the deep ocean, and revealing the snake for the priest.

The sea serpent jumped from the water, and Joshua threw his right hand forward. He released the first orb of lightning, which shot from his hand in what seemed to be a stream of liquid before it split into several shards of pure energy. One of the many bolts caught the snake's stomach, tracing across its scales toward the water. Scales shot from the snake's skin, the heat from the lightning rupturing its hide. The beast shrieked and dove back into the water as the last of the first lightning orb left Joshua's hand. The second orb was now ready. Joshua waited to throw it at the snake if it came back above the surface. He again lost sight of the snake when it dove into the water and hoped it had retreated but stayed ready in case.

He raised his empty hand and summoned another orb of lightning, prepared for the snake to return. After a quick glance, he spotted it again, approaching the surface quickly and at an angle that would allow it to reach *Queller* faster. Both orbs of lightning jumped toward the surface of the water, approaching the snake quickly. The beast emerged from the water and caught the streams of electricity as it did. The snake wriggled and shrieked, smoke rising off its scaly form, before it fell still, splashing back into the water and eventually floating at the surface. With the beast slain, Joshua relaxed and nearly fell over, supported only by the rope railing on the crow's nest. After a few moments of rest, he started climbing down the ladder before landing once more on the main decks of the ship, leaning against the repaired mast to catch his breath.

Michael stood nearby as he stared, unsure of what just happened. Randall and several sailors were at the port side of the ship inspecting the serpent to ensure it was truly dead before stripping some scales from its thick hide. The trinkets alone would bring them fortune beyond imagination. Sea serpents were rare enough, surviving them even more so. After he caught his breath, Joshua walked to the side of the ship to also inspect his work. Michael still stood where he had been, his legs suddenly feeling fused to the deck of the ship.

"Michael, I know you will have many questions about what you just saw. I...owe you an explanation about all of this," Joshua said, approaching his ward.

"Yeah, I'll say you owe me an explanation!" Michael agreed, shaken by everything.

"Can we go below to our hammocks to talk? I want to explain everything that you witnessed along with some things I should have told you before."

"I don't really know how you can explain your way out of this, Joshua."

"Give me some time, and I'm sure you will understand," Joshua said.

Michael followed closely behind Joshua as they walked between the rows of cannons and down into the crew's quarters. A few sailors occupied their hammocks as they slept before their shifts. To preserve the darkness for sleeping, lanterns and other light weren't allowed, so the men would switch their eyepatches to the other side, allowing them to see clearly in the dark. Michael thought it was a smart system and wondered if all sailors did this. Reaching their hammocks, Joshua sat on the wooden floor, adjusted his robes to be more comfortable, and motioned for Michael to join him. Michael did, though he hesitated a moment, wondering if he really had any other option.

"Let me start with what may now seem obvious," Joshua said. "Randall dislikes Magic and anything to do with it. *That* is why he dislikes priests and especially hates having one aboard his precious ship. A long time ago, at the beginning of the era, seven stars fell from the sky and landed in various places across the planet. So far, we only know of a few that were found. The first of those stars, discovered by an Elf who later became a powerful wizard, revealed what we know as Magic to the world. Many years later, the Elves opened a school for those who wanted to study and use Magic. They called this school the Sorcerer's College, and for a long time it was only open to Elves. Then humanity discovered a star and found Magic through their own star. This meant they no longer needed to depend on Elves to provide Magic. Humans struggled to learn the ways of Magic on their own and several were injured or killed in the attempts to master the gift from the stars. To prevent further harm, and with a deep desire to control the practice of Magic, the Elves decided to allowed humans into their College. Then, some devious humans and Elves discovered Dark Magic, and they began to experiment, creating terrible creatures and abominations in the search for greater power than the College taught them. Goblins, minotaurs, the Phoenix, and several others were created or summoned as a result of these experiments. Not all of the creations were created with malice, but enough of them were that the Elves exiled humanity from the College and outlawed the practice of Dark Magic.

"The laws never stopped anyone from studying Dark Magic, contrary to what the College's Elves intended. Instead, wizards and sorcerers studied it on their own, creating even worse monsters. These Dark Mages opened portals to other dimensions in the hope of gaining more powers than they already possessed. This worked until monsters that came from one of the portals killed those who opened the gateways. The College, upon learning about the experiments, slew the monsters and anyone who knew about their existence. This sparked a war, largely fought between humanity and Elves, over the right to practice all Magic. Countless lives were lost during the ten years the war raged on. Goblins were nearly wiped from the face of the world. Imagine an entire race that had done nothing wrong, but was simply the result of experiments, nearly extinct because their origin connected to Dark Magic. Goblins have turned feral since then, and their numbers are now stronger than they were during the war, and there are many cases of them now attacking anything they see. This is the Elves' doing. By not killing all the Goblins, they have instead made a feral species of what once were Elves who volunteered for these experiments.

"At the end of the Mages' War, men and Elves decided unanimously to outlaw the practice, study, and use of Dark Magic to prevent any further genocide from being anywhere close to considered necessary. By agreeing to these terms, the Elves felt humanity earned another chance at formally learning Magic and allowed men to once more return to the College. The Dark Magic ban, again, was not enough. Underground sects of Mages formed their own college of sorts specifically for the study of Dark Magic. Knowledge of these groups' existence spread like wildfire through the College, though the groups themselves somehow avoided formal discovery by the College's Council, who sought to punish the groups. They met and practiced somewhere unreachable by those who ignored the entirety of the Magic spectrum. To find and eliminate these sects, the Elves lifted their ban on Dark Magic, understanding this was their only option for balancing themselves with the Dark Mages.

"Humanity did not agree with this decision and withdrew from the Sorcerer's College entirely, refusing to attend until Elves once again banned the practice of Dark Magic. Then the Madness, which initially afflicted the world through the dimensional portals, began to spread starting with the Sorcerer's College. Monsters once again roamed the world, this time tainted by that very Madness the Elves fought to eradicate through the First Mages' War. This sparked a second war between the Mages," Joshua said, pausing to let Michael absorb the information and ask any questions. Getting silence from his companion, Joshua continued.

"The Second Mages' War ended with Drendil collapsing into Madness. Many fled the continent and found other places to live, such as our homeland. Thanks to the Madness, each of the new continents where humanity finally ended up exiled anyone going to Drendil, not wanting the sickness to spread. Prikea and the other new lands established the priesthood as a last line of defense against

Dark Magic and the Madness it brings. This fact isn't entirely a secret, though we don't broadcast it, and I'm not sure how Randall knows. Regardless, each order of priests is filled with sorcerers or wizards who serve their kings and queens as defenders of their lands. There are differences between those kinds of Mages, but they are too complex to discuss here and now. That is how we knew about your dreams, a form of Magic on their own, and could sense what you were dreaming. We had to get you close to us to actually know for sure, that is why I was sent to find you. Prophecy, and specifically premonitions like your dreams, show either what events will happen or how they can unfold. They aren't always perfect, but that's because it is a low-level form of Magic. Choice also plays a big part in their flawed predictions," Joshua explained.

"So, there is a chance that I could learn to be a wizard?" Michael asked, after several moments.

"More likely a sorcerer, but it's hard to say right now. Ultimately, it would come to whether you can naturally use Magic or if you would need years of studying to use it. Everyone has a different experience with this gift. If you would like, after we arrive in Drendil, we can conduct the requisite testing. I won't pressure you to choose either way," Joshua replied. "I also can't promise you anything will come from the test."

One of the sailors came down to the quarters a few moments later, telling Joshua and Michael that Randall wanted to speak with them both. His message carried great urgency, so Joshua and Michael stood and went with him as quickly as they could. He moved deftly through the dark quarters and up the ladder, skipping rungs as he climbed. Joshua and Michael didn't climb as fast but caught up with the sailor soon enough. He led them the entire way to the captain's cabin, knocking thrice on the double doors and waiting for the call to enter before opening the door.

Randall, hunched over the central table, looked up and waved Joshua and Michael over while he examined a hand-drawn map. "I have personally only charted the western coast of Drendil through my unfortunately numerous voyages near the vile continent. Some maps existed long ago, but the king at the time ordered them destroyed. Technically, captains are not permitted to keep such maps, as a way to deter people from defecting there or venturing too close to the Madness. Also, those maps, as old as they were, would be difficult to trust, as it's hard to tell what changed on the continent since the exodus."

"Sounds to me like you have contraband aboard one of the king's warships?" Joshua asked, to which Randall rolled his eyes and shook his head.

"I planned to take you to the closest part of the continent, here," Randall said as he ignored Joshua's comment and pointed to an area of the map which depicted a tree-covered peninsula that jutted out into the water. "However, that area is known as the Goblin Coast. It's reported to be infested with the bastards, and I wouldn't want you to get to land only to die fighting the wretched monsters. The king wouldn't take kindly to that, as you could imagine."

"What options do we have? Is there somewhere else we could go ashore?" Joshua asked.

"There is only one coastal city on this side of the continent, and it's my understanding that they have held off the Madness successfully since the exodus from Drendil so long ago. Supposedly, one of the local 'lords' has claimed the land immediately outside the city but has no power within the city limits. He has taxes and tolls set against anyone entering or leaving 'his' land. Erith, that's the coastal city, is a good place to drop you off, but you'll have to get some money to get through the tolls, especially since he has authority from one of the kings, it would seem."

"What kind of city is Erith?" Michael asked, curiosity coating his voice like honey.

"How do you know so much about Drendil if you haven't been there?" Joshua asked.

"The city isn't an easy one. Think of it like a clam: hard around the edges out of necessity to protect the soft middle bits. To answer your question, Joshua, I have stopped in Erith Bay a few times to take on supplies for extended voyages. Stopping in the harbor is as close to stepping foot on Drendil soil as the king permits. I never leave the ship, but the harbormaster comes to see me while the supplies are brought aboard. He's a talkative man who shares far more than I have ever wished him to, though now it seems to have been to your benefit," Randall explained, seeming genuinely helpful for the first time since the voyage started.

"How long will it take to get to Erith in our current state?" Joshua inquired as he examined the map rolled out on the tabletop in front of Randall.

Looking through his open cabin doors, Randall groaned. "This time of year, the winds push north and west, so it shouldn't take more than a couple of days. We're already a day's voyage from the Goblin Coast as it is. Going up to Erith would add a day, maybe two depending on the wind and tides. Erith Bay is shallower at low tide than *Queller* can comfortably sail through. At high tide, the bay is a lot deeper than we need. We just have to time our arrival for high tide and leave before the tide goes out. There is a chance that while we have the anchor dropped, we could end up on a sand barge. We should be fit to sail tomorrow morning. Any thoughts?"

"According to the books I've read on the matter, sea serpents are rarely, if ever, alone. Should we expect to encounter another?" Joshua asked.

"There could be more of those things?" Michael asked in surprise.

Randall inhaled sharply before answering. "It's certainly a possibility. The water here is deep and warm which makes a perfect environment for them to spawn. That serpent could have been a scout and the others might avoid us since it never returned. Or they could attack the ship out of revenge if a snake feels that emotion. It's hard to say."

It took Randall several moments to clean up his table. He spoke again. His tone was calmer than most of the other meetings the three had together. "The only thing I'm worried about is making sure the two of you get to Erith without issue. We have a rowboat I will give you that will let you dock at the harbor. The market shouldn't be far from there, but I can't say for sure since I've never been there."

"Is there anything we can do to help get the ship sailing sooner? Then at least we won't be a target for more serpents," Joshua suggested.

"The only thing needed for us to sail is to repair the holes in the mainsails. The crew has been working on that and they should be done in the morning. I'll have to replace the broken yard arms when I get back to port unless…are you able to mend wood, priest?"

"You *want* me to use Magic to repair your ship, Captain?" Joshua asked, a wry smile curling the edges of his mouth.

"It would make my life easier, as much as I hate Magic for all the trouble it causes. Is it possible?"

"Well, anything dealing with wood is more within Michael's bailiwick, Captain. When it comes to my skills, there are a couple of different ways that I could propel the ship. I can either cast a spell that creates a gust of wind for the sails, or I can manipulate the water to create waves that will push *Queller* through the water. Before I decide, you will have to inspect the remaining yardarms to see if they are sturdy enough to support the gale I would create."

"I will have the men inspect the yardarms, but I doubt they could handle much more than a gentle breeze at this point," Randall said.

Chapter Eight

Erith. Freedom. A new life where anything could happen. An escape from the life of a wanted criminal. Freedom from having to constantly look over their shoulders. Freedom from Lord Dennison and his goons. All of that was within sight. The air seemed fresher to Týr, knowing they wouldn't have to worry about the possibility of the soldiers snatching them up and taking them to a dungeon they would never leave.

Týr and Iona both peered through gaps in the slats of the wagon where they hid. The ride was bumpy and uncomfortable, but it was at least middlingly faster and stealthier than walking the whole distance across the open plains that stretched between Erith and the woods they escaped from a few days before. And the merchant into whose wagon they climbed was fine with them hitching a ride, even if that was purely because he didn't know or suspect two criminals were riding among the shipment of fruits he hauled to the city. Their plan was coming together perfectly well, until all of a sudden, Týr noticed something that could cause the whole operation to sink faster than a fishing boat shot with a cannon. He swore loudly in his mind, trying his hardest not to speak and alert the merchant to their presence.

The road ahead was closed. Týr could see guards ahead, three on his side of the road. Iona motioned with her hands that she could also see three on her side. The guards' armor shimmered in the midday sunlight, and their lances glinted as the sunlight danced off their polished surfaces. The guards stood still and inspected every wagon along the road. There happened to be many more merchants coming into Erith than Týr anticipated. As the wagons rolled forward slowly, the guards removed the canvas covers and inspected the goods within the wagons. *Perhaps this is for Lord Dennison's merchant tax, and they're just verifying the goods being transported,* Týr thought to himself as his hands started to quiver.

Inside the wagon, Týr and Iona made a sort of compartment underneath a few crates of fruit. They had climbed into the wagon while the merchant was asleep, an easy feat in the darkness of night, and rearranged a few of the crates to make room for them to hide without any of the cargo seeming out of place. They took a chance on the wagon actually heading to Erith and not any other city in Drendil. However, no matter where the wagon went, they knew they would leave Dennison's territory eventually, and could start their life over. Erith was simply closest and offered the best chance for them to start fresh in a safe place, even if it meant living in a walled city for the rest of their lives. Besides, they had always heard that Erith, as the 'last bastion against Madness,' was a hard city. They banked on the rumors holding at least a pinch of truth.

If the guards looked inside the wagon, unless they were looking *closely*, they should glance right over Týr and Iona. Based on how quickly the guards moved from one wagon to the next, the inspections were less than cursory. They lifted the canvas cover up, took a few quick glances at the crates or sacks of food, metals, and other goods filling the wagons, and dropped the canvas back into place. Týr's hands trembled more as the guards grew closer. He clasped his hands together to keep them from touching anything within the cart. Only one wagon stood between the guards and the fugitives. At this distance, the unintended passengers could hear what the guards were asking the merchant driving the wagon in front of them.

"What cargo are you carrying?" one soldier asked.

"Mined materials, sir. Brought from Vilyar, they are. You can see for yourself, sir. And I have my tax stamps right here," the merchant said as he handed a sealed paper to the guard. Two guards folded the wagon cover back, then waved at the one inspecting the papers, pointing at the cargo. Clearly, something was wrong with what the merchant said.

The first guard, who wore a crested helmet, inspected the goods in the wagon, glancing at several sacks filled with roughly cut jewels. Peering through the slats, Týr saw rough-hewn jewels that

118

were larger than his hand. The unguarded wagon carried what had to be worth tens of thousands in gold coins. *Why is it unprotected?* Týr thought to himself. *There should at least be a half dozen guards riding with the wagon.* The guard with the tax stamp inspected the paper, but his face warped as he read it. Then without asking any other questions, he tore the paper repeatedly. The pieces grew smaller as he continued to tear the stamp before he threw the scraps of paper on the ground.

"Sir, you are in possession of goods for which Lord Dennison has not collected a tax. You must forfeit your wagon and all untaxed goods. You may take this up with my Lord in his estate on the third day of every other week. We cannot permit you to enter Erith with these goods," the guard explained.

"He already collected the tax! You just tore up the proof of that! This is an *outrage* that you would make me stop, send my horse-bound guards away to another line designated for foot traffic, a line which I don't see by the way, and then you seize my..." the merchant protested before the tip of a pike was planted firmly in his chest.

The guard removed his pike and blood spurted from the wound; the merchant, who stood on his driver's bench, fell from his wagon onto the ground below. One of the guards grabbed his body and dragged it away from the road, while another drove the wagon off the road in the other direction. Iona stifled a squeak inside the wagon, seeing the innocent merchant suddenly dead. Týr immediately snapped her a look that didn't need any words. She could have ruined their whole chance at getting through the line of

119

guards undetected. And they were so close to freedom. Blessedly, the man driving the wagon took no notice of Iona's sound. The guards motioned the wagon forward. Týr felt an intense burning in his stomach, sure that the guards would catch them and afraid of what might happen if they did, especially after watching them kill the merchant. *Likely for the gems, rather than a* false *tax stamp,* Týr thought to himself.

"What goods are you transporting?" one of the guards asked the merchant.

"Good morning, Captain Rufus. I'm just making my weekly trip bearing fruits and vegetables from Canalin. I have all my papers in order if you need to see them," the merchant said, rifling through the knapsack sitting on the bench beside him.

"That won't be necessary. Simply need to see your cargo to verify," the guard said. The other two guards on Týr's side walked to the back of the wagon, ready for the inspection.

The guards pulled back the curtains on the back of the arch-topped wagon, saw crates of apples and other fruits and simply shrugged. They made their return to the front of the wagon, reporting nothing unusual. The guards waved the wagon on, and the merchant snapped the reins. The horse walked forward, and the wagon started rambling down the road. The wagon shook as the wheels rolled over stones and rough holes in the packed dirt that served as a road. Týr felt his heart pounding in his ears and sweat dripped down his brow. Something so simple ended up being among the most stressful things he experienced. Now, it was all over, and they could relax again. They could almost taste the freedom. Erith was getting closer by the slow, agonizing minute as the wagon rolled down the road.

Chapter Nine

"ring the ship to larboard, six degrees, bosun. Reduce our speed to harbor's rules," Randall called. The bosun repeated the captain's calls to the crew through his whistle. Sailors about the ship scurried to fulfill the captain's wishes.

The crew was beyond relieved to set sail again, leaving the potential nest of sea snakes behind. The evening before, two more had come within sight of *Queller*, setting the nervous crew even more on edge. The men found it hard to concentrate on finishing the repairs, instead constantly eyeing the water, anticipating another attack. Now, with land in sight finally, the crew seemed both happy and anxious; happy to see land again; anxious because that land was Drendil. This was a place where people went but never came back.

To Michael, that felt like a great reason to be on edge, and one that he couldn't contest, no matter how hard he thought about the subject. He started to feel uneasy at the thought of leaving the ship.

As he leaned against the rough wooden rails of the quarterdeck, gazing onto the water, Michael realized he would actually miss sailing. He would long for the salty tinge of the wind and deep blue color of the water, which at times looked smoother than glass far away from the ship. The sunrises and sunsets, the pure, unaltered colors of the sun morphing the clouds into purples, pinks, and oranges were an undeniably euphoric experience. Even the water changed color to match the clouds. The life of a sailor pulled at Michael's heart so firmly, but he knew there was another life for him, and one that would likely end tragically, no matter how heroically he fought. That's what Joshua could make of the nightmares. The dreams always ended too soon to see for sure, which was something else Joshua said was a characteristic of premonitions. They showed only some of the future, sometimes not enough to know with much clarity what was actually going to happen.

Joshua also seemed to enjoy the time sailing across the ocean too, despite his apparent feelings toward being sent to Drendil. After convincing Randall to ignore, or at least put aside his hatred of Magic, Joshua ran Michael through the tests for Magic wielding capabilities. Together, they found that Michael was only sensitive to Magic and was unable to learn or cast spells. The priest still meditated at sunrise and sunset, but instead of staying below the main decks, Randall allowed him to meditate on the main deck if he chose. Still, Randall did not relax his rule about anyone hiding their face while aboard the ship, but the two at least made progress considering his abhorrent feelings toward Magic at the start of the voyage.

With the ship finally moving into the harbor, Randall called for the anchor to be dropped as a small boat made its way toward *Queller* with two men aboard. When they approached, Randall, now wearing some semblance of a uniform, stood beside the railings on the larboard—Michael had learned that meant 'left' in sailing terms—side of the ship awaiting their approach. Randall made it quite clear on several occasions that he would have to deal with the harbormaster coming to the ship trying to aide them in docking. Randall possessed no interest in docking *Queller* in Erith. He simply wanted to drop anchor, give Joshua and Michael one of the rowboats, and make sure they safely arrived on land. Then he could aweigh his anchor and return home to Prikea, where his anticipated promotion waited for him. "Commodore Randall" had a nice ring to it, and, while the title might not match his normal bare-footed, bare-chested sailing attire, Randall preferred to stay comfortable at sea, dressing up only when absolutely necessary.

Randall, in his uniform, certainly appeared more like a military sea captain than a rough brigand. He sported a dark blue jacket with gold brocading and epaulets, in addition to a tricorn hat which made him look…*professional*. His uniform also swapped his roughly-patched, baggy trousers for elegant ones that were quite puffy at the hips, white with a silver stripe down the outside seams. The silver looked like a velour fabric against fine cotton and nearly blended

124

with the white. A saber hung from his white leather belt. The scabbard extended slightly beyond his knee. The sword, Michael was sure, saw plenty of battles on the high seas. In addition to wearing a uniform, Randall had removed his eye patch, the same as most of the crew. Only a couple of members of the crew still wore eye patches, and as Michael understood, they actually needed to wear them. He shuddered at the thought of how they lost an eye.

Even Randall's boots, something he had not worn the entire voyage, showed that he had put in significant effort to shine them. Michael found it hard to believe Randall could care about anything so trivial as the condition of his footwear. The black leather came just shy of his knees, and a slight heel added to his already impressive height. The toes of his boots curled slightly, in the tradition of the Prikean Navy's uniforms. The leather itself gleamed in the sunlight, the surface polished enough to almost reflect like a pair of mirrors on Randall's feet

"Ahoy, Captain! Thrown down a ladder for me," the harbormaster called as the small ship finally reached *Queller*, pulling up to her larboard side.

"I am not mooring my ship today. I have two passengers who must reach the city. They will be taking one of my rowboats and can follow you unless you have space for them in your boat," Randall said, responding to the man's request.

"What do you plan to do with your ship while your passengers row into the city? Also, if you would like, or if they would like, we may provide them transport so you don't lose one of your dinghies," the harbormaster called from the water.

"I plan to drop anchor right here, where I am not blocking the harbor and can watch as my passengers make it safely to Erith. However they choose to get to land is up to them. I will not make that choice for them," Randall replied.

"Very well, Captain. Are your passengers coming to stay in Erith?" the harbormaster asked.

"We are simply passing through, sir," Joshua answered.

"You a priest?" the other man in the boat asked.

"Coxswain shut your yap," the harbormaster snapped. "Apologies about him, he just gets skittish around Magic. How long will you be here before passing through?"

"A week at most," Joshua said.

"You will have to register yourselves with a magistrate if you stay longer than three days, sir," the harbormaster responded. "And to register, you have to be seen by a Mage to prove you haven't the Madness. It's a standard procedure, it is. We mean no offense with the registration. There just have been a lot of strange happenings around here lately is all," the harbormaster explained patiently from the water

"What sort of happenings?" Joshua asked.

"Nothing terribly out of the normal here in Drendil. We had some merchants killed outside the gate. They apparently were transporting valuable goods and Lord Dennison's men, despite having taxed them, wanted those goods outright. If you ask me the whole situation with him is mighty dreadful," the harbormaster responded.

"Anything else?"

"I have heard tales of a man in dark robes being spotted in the area not far from here. I think that is more just a rumor going around, or some of the Madness making people see things that aren't really there if you ask me. But my job is only to manage the harbor, not to ponder the origin of rumors."

"Thank you for the information, harbormaster. We will be ashore shortly," Joshua said.

The harbormaster tipped his hat quickly and ordered the coxswain to paddle back toward the harbor. The surface of the water gently rippled as their oars dipped in and out of the water. As the small boat drew further away, Michael and Joshua gathered their belongings and prepared for their own boat ride to land. Randall accompanied them to the quarters and ensured they grabbed everything before setting off. He was being uncharacteristically friendly, but it could be because he was about to sail back home where a hefty promotion awaited him. Were Michael on his way back to Feldring, he would be happy too.

* * *

Shortly after the tax stop, Týr and Iona departed from their transportation. The wagon rocked sharply as the pair exited, but the merchant paid no mind, attributing the movement to the unevenness of the road. The tax stop was a few kilometers from the edge of Erith since Dennison's reach technically stopped just after the river east of the city. It was Týr's hope that Dennison's goons would be powerless out here. The guards didn't even appear to patrol anywhere beyond their tax station. Now the pair of thieves just needed to make it into the city, and while the Erith guards were likely checking everyone coming into the city, that's the only thing they would be doing. The only checks would be Madness examinations performed by a local Mage of some kind. Týr and Iona hardly had to worry about that sort of thing at all.

The Madness wasn't something tangible or visually evident. It was a disease that struck the mind, though more often it struck the soul. People who went their entire lives without committing crimes could one day wake up and become serial murderers. It changed who a person was at their very core. It was rumored that Lars had fallen to the Madness and that was why he so aggressively searched for some treasure. It was also possible that was the reason why Lars could never fully explain the motive for his search without getting an obsessive look in his eyes. Týr found himself thinking about Lars and the other thieves, and how the raid on the camp would have happened. *How many soldiers did Dennison send to wipe out our brethren?* Týr wondered to himself before Iona brought him back to reality with a gentle touch on his arm.

"Are you also thinking that it was too easy getting away from Dennison, Týr?" Iona asked as they walked. Their footsteps kicked up small, nearly invisible pockets of dust, a few stones bouncing ahead of their toes.

"It was as easy as it needed to be, Iona. Dennison doesn't even know we survived, let alone escaped. We are *free* and can start a new life here in Erith. That's what we said we would do, and that's what I plan to do."

"Why not start with new names? I know father liked the name Iona because it was mother's name, but I want a different name. What do you think?"

"A clean start might not be a bad idea. What name do you want?" Týr replied, curious about her choice. She was a creative person and would be able to get something good.

She thought for a moment, her brow furrowing as she came up with an answer. "Svenka."

"I like it. Father would approve, too," Týr replied, reassuringly.

"What about you, Týr? What name do you want?"

Týr thought for several moments and contemplated a new name. "Týr" had been his name for nearly thirty years. While it was just a label and didn't change anything about who he was, he rather liked his name. It was *his* name. Could he throw that away and simply pick another one? Would he respond to it, or would he still only listen for the same familiar sounds his mind had known for so long?

"I don't think I will change my name, Io—Svenka. Sorry. It will take me a bit to get used to your new name," Týr finally said.

Before Svenka could respond, horse hooves thundered nearby, approaching quickly. Someone was in a hurry. With such a monstrous roar, there were at least four horses, all galloping on the packed dirt road. Shouting accompanied the sounds of the horses, causing Týr and Svenka to turn and look at what was happening behind them. It was a rapidly approaching cacophony of thundering hooves, snorting breaths, shouting men, and the clanking of metal on metal.

Týr saw seven guards wearing Lord Dennison's colors, crimson with silver suns, quickly approaching them. The soldiers had their weapons drawn, rough looks on their faces. Two of the soldiers carried spears or pikes, but the rest carried the usual curved scimitars that Dennison preferred for his soldiers. More than likely, the witless lord had his men use the curved swords because they looked scarier than a straight sword. While mounted on their horses, the soldiers typically proved deadly, but out of the saddle, the soldiers fought like children. Admittedly, the swords weren't entirely to blame for that. Throughout his years thieving, Týr fought or killed dozens of the soldiers. His knives and short sword were always more efficient. *Perhaps it's an issue of training. These soldiers don't train as aggressively as they need to.* Lars made it a point that the thieves would train as often and as hard as they could, often having them fight each other with real weapons.

Týr wore a cloak, his weapons concealed underneath. He wanted to avoid attention by keeping his numerous knives hidden while walking into a city many sought as a bastion against violence and Madness. There was still a chance these soldiers weren't charging at Týr and Svenka, so he kept his weapons sheathed for the moment, though he drew his hands into his cloak, ready to draw his knives if he needed. The leather wrappings on his knives creaked under his firm grip. He could feel the bumps in the leather where the wraps overlapped, a familiar feeling that he would miss with this new life he and Svenka planned.

The horses passed the travelers on both sides and some of the soldiers looked closely at them as they passed. The entire group moved as fluidly as a rushing river. A few hundred feet away, the cluster of horses and men turned, moving into a circle around the travelers. The circle tightened as they grew closer, until the horses nearly touched each other nose to rump, forming an impenetrable ring around the two travelers. The soldiers drew their weapons, sunlight glinting off the polished metal, pointed toward the middle of the circle. The tips of the spears came within a few hands of Týr's chest, and the tips of the pikes came even closer. Týr and Svenka stood, their backs together, moving slowly in a clockwise circle, never taking their eyes off their adversaries. Týr kept his hands inside his cloak and slowly drew his knife from its sheath, the blade resting against his leather-clad wrist, the unsharpened side toward his skin. In his left hand, he grabbed a few throwing knives, ready for the guards to make a move they wouldn't live to regret.

"You are wanted criminals. We will take you before Lord Dennison willingly, or otherwise, so you may receive your punishment in his courts," one of the guards, the only one wearing a helmet, declared. His voice was smooth yet firm, a velvety gentility behind his authority. "Lay down all weapons on your person and come with us."

"Tell us what crimes we have committed that Lord Dennison would send men out of his lands to fetch criminals!" Svenka demanded, fiery strength in her voice.

"You are wanted for theft over five hundred marks, murder of legion soldiers, trespassing in military camps, treason against Lord

Dennison and his realm, and arson. Shall I continue the list, or are you going to surrender and come with us?"

As Týr and Svenka looked at each other, trying to decide what to do, a doorway opened outside the ring of horsemen. The edges of the door shimmered and wriggled like the air above a fire. On the other side of the doorway was a brightly lit study with shelves lining the walls. Hundreds, if not thousands, of books covered the shelves from the floor to the ceiling high above. A writing desk stood in one corner of the room, facing the doorway that had opened. Various quills were set upon the leather-covered wooden desktop. Everyone stopped to look at the doorway, confused about its existence.

A tall, frail, old man dressed in silver and crimson robes, matching the colors the soldiers wore, gingerly stepped through the doorway. He wore a cloak over his robes with the cowl down, draped over his shoulders. His gaunt face was covered by a grey and white, medium-length beard that was longer at the chin than at the sides. His wispy hair, also the same grey and white mix as his beard, was drawn back and tied near the nape of his neck. Deep-set blue eyes gazed at the group from under his steel-colored, bushy eyebrows. A bereft sorrow filled his gaze so much that Týr thought he could touch the man's sadness. Despite walking like he needed one, the man bore no cane or walking stick of any kind. Instead, his hands were tucked into his sleeves, only a sliver of his wrists showing between the flaps of fabric.

The old man stopped hobbling for a second, and in a flash, the doorway behind him, and the room beyond, vanished out of

132

existence. The only sign the doorway ever existed was a small strip of grass that was now shorter than the rest.

"Master Eidu, what are you doing here?" the leader of the horsemen asked, lowering his sword. Clearly, this was a man of great respect among the soldiers.

"Lieutenant, I am here with grave news," the old man replied, the despair in his eyes growing somehow deeper.

"What news have you, sir?" the soldier asked.

"Lord Dennison has been murdered," Master Eidu said, his voice breaking and becoming grave as he made his announcement.

So that really was *Dennison in the tent. We don't have to worry about any of his soldiers. Without Dennison they don't have authority. And that means...* Svenka wondered, her thoughts flashing through her head like lightning.

All weapons pointed at Týr and Svenka lowered as the soldiers donned bereft looks as they processed this news. Svenka, still standing with her back against Týr's, repeatedly tapped his arm excitedly. Maybe this news meant they wouldn't have to live in Erith! Perhaps they could simply settle in one of the villages, living out their lives in peace. Peace. Grief. So many lives were lost, but no more blood would be shed for this war they fought for so many years. The war that never bore a name.

"What does that mean for us?" Svenka asked, her voice bearing too much excitement.

"Excuse me? What do you mean 'what does this mean for us'?" the old man replied.

"These men were going to arrest us for charges against Lord Dennison, who is no longer alive. What does that mean for our situation?" Svenka responded.

"Svenka, allow them the time to mourn their lord," Týr whispered. They may have hated, fought, and stolen from Lord Dennison, but he was still a man, and still deserved that much.

"No, Týr! He made our life a living *hell*, and his men killed Lars and the rest of our family. I will not be arrested for defying a dead man!"

"Was Lars the leader of the thieves' camp that we dispatched nearly a few days ago? He and that band of forest-dwellers were little more than a pack of rabid dogs, a pest to be put down and done away with," the old man said, the hint of a smile showing on his face.

Svenka dashed forward, darting between two horses that stood between her and the old man who taunted her. Before Týr could register what was happening, she tackled the old man and planted a knife in his neck. As the man crumpled to the ground under Svenka, the portal he opened snapped shut. The soldiers, in shock at the news and sudden assault, responded a fraction of a second slower than Týr, who pulled one of the soldiers from his horse, burying a blade in the man's ribs, sliding it between plates of armor. A sword swung far too close to Týr's head, thankfully missing him as he was still crouched beside the dying soldier, gasping on the ground with a collapsed lung, a trick Týr learned from Lars.

Svenka turned her attention from the dead man, her bloodied knife pulled from his neck and ready for any of the soldiers to get too close. One of the soldiers charged at her on his horse, his spear angled too high to hit her and the distance between them too close to do anything about it. She stepped to the side, grabbed the soldier by his belt, and swung herself onto the horse's back, ending up on the back of the saddle in a matter of a second. Her knife rapidly punched through his skin, his neck pouring blood as she threw him from his horse. Týr blinked in surprise, unsure that what he witnessed actually happened. Týr watched Svenka as she shifted into a saddle that a soldier occupied only moments before.

Pain. He felt a sharp, burning sensation in his left shoulder. Agony. He looked briefly and saw something sliced across his arm, from the back around to the front, a little higher than halfway up the shoulder muscle. Seeing the wound made the pain instantly worse. He scolded himself for looking at a wound in the middle of a battle. Lars taught him to never take his eyes off the enemy in a battle, and he learned well enough on his own not to look at a wound. It always made the pain more real, harder to ignore. Týr dropped to his knees and grabbed his arm. Blood oozed between his fingers, now free from his knife which clattered to the ground. He couldn't remember dropping his knife. *When did that happen?* Týr wondered to himself.

Svenka, now in control of a horse, grabbed the reins and turned the horse around, kicking its sides so it would run back toward the old man, now lying still in his own blood. The grass under his body grew dark as his blood flowed onto the ground. *Serves him right,* Týr thought mercilessly. She looked into the cluster of horsemen still scrambling to react to what happened around them. She saw Týr kneeling on the ground, clutching his arm with a bloody hand.

Quickly, she yanked the reins and kicked her heels again. The horse beneath her responded instantly and turned to charge into the group of soldiers. Svenka bolted toward the group of soldiers, commanding the horse to vault. She knew what was about to happen but wanted to make sure Týr could get away.

Her horse obeyed her command, his front legs coming off the ground in time for his powerful hooves to connect with the lieutenant's chest. Svenka only knew he was the lieutenant because of his helmet, with its feathery crest of red and silver plumes. The man and his horse toppled beneath Svenka's. A terrible crunching sound, like a crusty loaf of bread being broken open, came from beneath the horse just before both toppled to the ground in a whinnying mess of broken bones and crumpled armor. Svenka found herself sliding a meter across the ground as she was thrown from the horse during the tussle.

Once she stopped rolling, Svenka stood, grabbed one of the knives from her belt, and tossed it at the nearest soldier, who caught the knife in the side of his thigh. The man wailed as he grabbed his leg. He leaned to grab the knife and, his balance thrown off, fell from his horse. The soldier landed roughly with a heavy *thud* sound and the *tung* of armor as it contacted the packed dirt beneath him.

As Svenka stood and pivoted to see Týr, still clutching his arm while he knelt, and pulled another soldier from his horse, a group of soldiers wearing blue and black coats with a boar emblazoned upon their chests, rushed down the road from Erith's gate, halberds drawn at the ready. The guards were tall and thin, much like the deceased old man, though none of them walked hunched over or as if they needed a cane. The group was mixed men and women, their rounded ears showing they were humans, instead of Elves. One of the women, in the middle of the group leveled her halberd at the group, her knuckles white around the haft.

"By order of the duchess, everyone stay where you are! Raise your hands where we can see them," the soldier called, her voice heavy with authority.

Svenka, after she verified the soldier she knelt beside was dead, raised her hands and turned to face the new soldiers. Týr, on the other side of the circle of death, raised his right hand, still dripping with blood that only now was starting to dry into his cloak. After an attempt to raise his left hand freely, he grabbed his wrist and yanked his arm above his head, trying his best to suppress the wince that followed. His arm oozed blood down his sleeve, the fabric now showed maroon instead of light grey. The leading soldier motioned one of the others toward Týr, saying to get him some assistance. One of the soldiers who ran toward Týr reached into a pouch on his belt and removed a small cylinder, which he held toward the sky. A bright streak of fire shot into the sky, leaving a trail of bright green smoke that stayed in the air behind it. The orb of fire, having reached its apex, erupted into the sky. The resulting burst was a magnificent, glittery, expanding ball of sparkles and shimmers. Svenka watched the fire, enrapt by the mysterious presentation.

Another doorway opened in the air, not far from where the soldier stood over Týr, and a woman stepped through. She was short and stout and wore tight blue and white robes that revealed more of her plump body than Svenka cared to see. The newly arrived woman took a quick look around, saw Týr and his wound, and rushed over to aid him. She held her hands out and her palms began to glow as she gingerly moved them across Týr's wound and inspected him. Once she found the problem, the color of her hands changed from the faint white to a more menacing crimson. Týr's face wrenched with agony, and he visibly stifled a cry, but in a few moments, he was left gasping for air and sweating profusely. The woman's hands once again changed, returning to their pasty color, as she continued inspecting him for further injuries. Finding none, she removed her hands from Týr and walked to one of the soldiers writing on the ground, Týr's knife stuck between his ribs.

"No, madam healer. Those are Lord Dennison's men, and they started this whole conflict. Leave them as they are," the leading soldier called, which stopped the woman, who only responded with a furrowed brow and a huff. She clearly had no qualms with letting men die, even as a healer.

"What do you mean we started this? She," one of the other remaining soldiers questioned as he pointed at Svenka, "assaulted our wizard unprovoked. We had nothing to do with this."

"Then why did your unit surround them with drawn weapons? As we saw it, you were the aggressors, and if you say another word to the contrary, it will be the last thing you have to say about anything," the soldier responded, her voice cool and as level as her halberd. Svenka shuddered hearing how calmly she was handling the whole situation. "How many of you that stayed behind are still alive?"

"I believe we are the last two alive, if my comrade even breathes," the soldier responded between labored breaths.

"Sir, please retrieve your blade from the man at your feet. The pig should already be dead," the soldier ordered, as she looked firmly at Týr, who obeyed quickly. "Good, now follow me. We will escort you the rest of the way to the gate. There may be more of Dennison's soldiers coming when the one survivor returns to his camp. We don't want you getting attacked again."

No further attention was paid to the man on the ground who gasped like a fish removed from the water while blood pooled around him. Týr and Svenka exchanged a quick look before dropping their hands and following the group of soldiers. The healer, her brow still furrowed, bowed at the soldiers as they departed, then set to work collecting the bodies. Sometimes healers had tough days. Svenka tried not to dwell on the healer having to collect the bodies and dispose of them. Curiosity gripped her and she wondered how she would dispose of the bodies. Perhaps a fire would be used? Maybe she would simply leave them for the carrion birds and other scavengers? That option seemed less likely, this close to the city and the road. A pile of rotting corpses would likely not sit well with any of the merchants coming into or out of Erith. Fire made the most sense.

"We didn't need you to rescue us," Svenka said, walking with the group of soldiers, making sure Týr was fine. He massaged his healed shoulder, wanting to avoid any stiffness after the healing.

"From what we saw, you more than needed the rescue. Dennison's men are more aggressive now that their Lord is dead," one of the other soldiers replied.

"How did you know about that? The old man just told the horsemen a few moments before and they all were taken aback by the news," Týr said, rotating his shoulder gently.

"That's simple: our duchess dispatched a group of soldiers to kill him a couple nights back," one of the other soldiers replied. "The team of covert soldiers from Erith were sent to put an end to his barbary. What's weird, though, is they said he was already dead when they got there. Regardless of how he died, without Dennison and his mercenaries, we won't lose so many merchants or their supplies coming into the city. That fat slob has been stealing far too many of the goods meant for our city. It's gotten worse in the last couple months."

"Yeah, we saw the guards kill a merchant whose wagon was laden with gems at the stop a few kilometers back. Their officer had the tax stamp in hand but tore it up and killed the man in cold blood," Týr mentioned.

"You saw what, exactly?" another soldier questioned. Týr recapped the events and without warning three of the soldiers in the group turned around and started galloping toward the taxation checkpoint. Clearly, there was unfinished business for them to deal with immediately.

"Those *bastards* have been doing that for months and they will die the death they have inflicted on so many of our merchants. Now, where are you coming from?" the leader of the group asked. Týr and

Svenka shared a glance and nodded to each other before telling the guard about their experience with Dennison as briefly as they could.

"Exactly how long were you scavenging off Dennison?" the leading soldier asked. "I'm going to choose to ignore the obvious law-breaking for the time being as I would like some answers about this whole matter. The duchess will have questions for sure."

"About...two years. Our leader, Lars, was dead set on Dennison having some map or treasure or something. He would send a pair of us into various camps that Dennison controlled to see what we could find. We happened to have bad intel and went into the wrong tent that night. I wouldn't have killed that fat asshole if he hadn't looked right at me," Svenka replied.

"You should have had your face covered in the camp," Týr sniped.

"Wait, you killed a fat man?" the soldiers stopped their horses, as their leader questioned this news. "What did he look like?"

"Wispy blonde hair, beak-like nose, slack jaw, one eye was green the other a dull brown, really oily skin," Svenka replied. "I stabbed him in the neck when he saw me. It was purely an instinctive reaction, and I shouldn't have been so foolish."

"So, *you* killed Dennison!" one of the other soldiers replied, his face rumpling at the thought.

"We saw a group of soldiers running through the camp on our way out, but it was too dark to see what colors they had been wearing. Was that your group? Or were Dennison's soldiers responding to your group?"

141

"Your guess on that is probably better than mine since you were there. You mean to tell me that in the two years you spent stealing from someone, you never learned what he looked like? " the leading soldier asked, a puzzled look on her face.

"Lars never told us what he looked like. He simply told us the targets and trinkets we were after, and whether we could kill anyone. Usually, we weren't allowed to kill unless necessary. Guards were the only casualties we could inflict without permission. Lars had a run-in with Dennison a few years ago and started recruiting thieves for his group. We were close to him, almost like a family, took care of each other, watched our backs." Týr replied.

"Well, I'm sorry your group was killed. I assume you come to Erith to start new lives?"

"That was our plan. We wanted to escape Dennison's reach, and this was the closest city we could get to that let us do just that," Svenka said.

"Erith can be a rough city for newcomers. Stay out of trouble and you will be fine. If you go back to thieving, I'll personally gut you like a fish," the leader said, her countenance changing drastically. "Register with the magistrate if you plan to be here longer than three days."

The soldiers departed and returned to their patrol route, leaving the thieves alone standing before one of the gates into the city. A large, black stone wall surrounded Erith, creating a barrier between the wilderness that Lord Dennison laid claim to and the city. The wall was a boundary between the Madness spreading through Drendil and the last bastion of sanity. It provided protection for the people who sought common, everyday lives. Every few hundred meters a tower jutted from the wall, a parapet atop, likely with archers inside, ready to launch arrows at perceived threats. The road leading to the eastern side of the city lacked trees, shacks, buildings, or any other kind of cover, ensuring the archers would have a clear line of sight for kilometers around the city, able to observe carefully and diligently.

A lone gate marred the beauty of the dark, stone wall. The gate, two wagons wide, stood open, three guards on both sides of the road that led through to the city. The guards wore plate and mail armor with thick cloth padding covers over their torsos which showed the same colors and patterns the earlier soldiers had worn: blue with a black boar. This was undoubtedly the signet of the duchess and her lineage. These guards, armed with glaives, stood still as stone, the pennants and tassels on their weapons only wavering from the breeze that had picked up since the fight with Dennison's soldiers. The glaives were held, shaft touching the ground near the right foot, angled slightly outward with small banners flying from the spear point at the end of the axe blades. Even without seeing their faces, due to the visors on their helmets, Týr could tell they scrutinized the former thieves through their entire walk across the small bridge leading to the opened gate. Their future, a life not spent running, not spent looking over their shoulders, worrying about where their food would come from was just beyond the gate.

Chapter Ten

The temple to which the harbormaster directed Michael and Joshua was quiet from the outside. Inside, stone pillars rose to the vaulted ceiling half a dozen meters overhead. Windows made of colored glass brought in sunlight and muted its intensity from the harsh light of midday. The altar at the front of the temple was set in a rounded wall. It was furthest from the double doors and a group of priests gathered around, preparing for some ritual or another.

As they stepped into the temple, Joshua lowered his hood, once more showing his shaved head, his scalp tanned from their time aboard *Queller*. After he lowered his hood, he made a motion with his hands and breathed a quick prayer. Michael wasn't sure of the meaning of either, but it was clearly something meant for the Allfather. The other priests looked up, a glint of recognition on their faces as they saw Joshua. They may not have known him personally, but his robes and the raven on the back of his hand appeared to be all they needed to determine he was one of their own. The temple's priests also wore hooded robes, though they wore blue robes with a white wading bird on their chests. Their hoods, just as Joshua's, rested on their shoulders. Michael noticed markings on their hands similar to the one that Joshua wore, although these resembled herons with long legs and beaks. Unlike the raven on Joshua's hand, which appeared in flight, the herons appeared to be walking, as if wading through a pond searching for their next meal.

"These priests are from the Order of Herons, Drendil's only surviving sect of priests. There are five orders of priests that are each marked by different birds. Drendil is the heron, Prikea the raven, Ofari the owl, Udin the hawk, and Istraes the swallow. Each governs the Magic within their continent. At least, that is the hope. Here in Drendil, there is also the Sorcerer's College that I mentioned aboard *Queller*, though they do much less governing over Magic than they used to," Joshua explained when he saw Michael eying the markings.

"Welcome Brother. We weren't expecting visitors from outside our own continent, let alone a priest. We get very few visitors from the other continents, for obvious reasons, but it is our pleasure to welcome you to our temple. How may we help you?" one of the Heron Priests said, walking over to Michael and Joshua.

Joshua briefly explained the purpose behind their visit, with the Heron Priests nodding their understanding. During the explanation, and hearing their need to find the Shadow Knight, the other priests motioned for the visitors to join the rest of the priests in their study downstairs. They would be more at liberty to speak behind closed doors. The Order of Herons' study looked quite similar to the Order of Ravens' that Michael saw before. In the middle of the room stood a large table. Shelves surrounded the room, and the shelves bent slightly under the weight of the many books they bore. On the center of the table was a small teapot with a matching set of seven mugs. Oil lamps, placed in strategic locations throughout the room, cast light evenly throughout the cozy room. The study appeared to be the perfect place for Michael and Joshua to learn the necessary information that would aid them in their quest.

Just as in Prikea, the priests prepared tea for their guests. Unlike the Order of Ravens, the Herons used spells to heat the water, speeding up the process significantly. There apparently were fewer trepidations concerning the priesthood openly using Magic in Drendil than there were in Prikea. While they prepared the water for the tea, Joshua explained their visit, going into greater detail about Michael's premonitions, the nightmares that plagued him for over a month now, the Shadow Knight and the army he led to destroy the unknown city, and the last person Michael needed to find for his mission. The Heron priests took a few moments to consider the information they received before providing their suggestions.

"Brother Joshua, I believe there are some things you are failing to consider," one of the priests with long silver hair drawn back in a ponytail said.

"What else should we consider?" Joshua asked.

"Being an outsider, you wouldn't know the liveries found across our continent, but we already know the city you seek based on that alone. You are looking for the city of Shemont, where the human King Orson II resides," the priest replied. "Something else to consider is this Týr fellow can be located fairly easily. Have you considered the possibility of a bond existing between you and Michael? The same thing could exist between you and this third person you seek."

"A bond?" Joshua pondered. He sipped at some of the tea for a brief moment before an idea struck him. "Do you think we could investigate it and search for anyone else that may be connected with a similar bond? If we did that, it could lead us to Týr!"

"Great thinking, Brother Joshua," one of the other Herons replied. "Michael, would you allow us to delve into you so we might examine this bond between you and Joshua?"

"What would be involved with that? It sounds like something that will hurt. Will it hurt?" Michael asked, suddenly rethinking his desire to stay in the room.

"It won't hurt, child. In fact, the only thing you should feel is a remarkable lightness, as if you are a cloud floating above the world. We simply need to find this bond within your soul that connects you and Joshua so that we might examine it," the priest replied.

"As long as this won't hurt, I don't see any issues with this spell you want to cast," Michael said, a fluttering sensation appearing in his stomach.

He turned to the other Heron Priests before continuing. "Brothers, join each other and when I find this bond, search the world for the remainder of it. We must find who else, if anyone, the bond is connected to before we let them go on their way."

The other priests started casting spells, creating a large cloud of light in the space above the table. Michael looked at the cloud and saw the continent he stood on as if viewed from a few kilometers above the ground. He only recognized that he was looking at Drendil from the maps he saw aboard Queller and here in the temple. There was something about the sight of the world seen from that height that confused and overwhelmed him, and he felt the room starting to spin under his feet. Then a Heron Priest came over and, using both hands, grasped Michael's head gently. His hands were clammy, but his skin was noticeably soft. Suddenly, the hands against his head grew warm, the temperature rising until it was just shy of uncomfortably hot, then stopped.

A gentle pulse jolted through Michael starting from the priest's hands. His entire body tensed then everything felt…different. Michael's body felt lighter, almost as if he could levitate from the chair he was sitting in. His arms felt like they were floating in the air, unsupported by anything. Despite this feeling, his arms were still firmly planted on the arms of the chair he sat in. Every muscle in his body relaxed from his neck to his feet. Michael decided he wouldn't care if this feeling stayed forever, though he knew that was unrealistic.

"I've found the bond. As we assumed, it doesn't look like a familiar form of Magic, but it is certainly there. There is another link that branches off elsewhere. Brothers," the priest turned to the others, "can you grab the bond and search across Drendil for it? Quickly, please. I wish not to risk harming Michael by keeping him under this spell for longer than is needed."

The image in the cloud changed. No longer was it the entire continent. The view of Drendil jolted and closed in on Erith. As the picture changed, it turned grainy but eventually became clearer. The view inside the cloud showed the road inside the main gate on the eastern side of the city, not far from the temple. Michael could see two travelers, a man and a woman, floating inside the cloud over the table. They wore simple clothes and cloaks showing the rough signs of travel. The man, tall and slender, walked on the woman's right. Despite the difference in their heights, their faces were similar; both had beak-shaped noses, green eyes, and brown hair with golden highlights throughout. The imagine in the cloud froze showing the two travelers and the priests removed their Magic from Michael who felt a cold wave crash over his body like a wave breaking against a sea cliff. With the priests now out of his head, he felt the room spin momentarily and he planted his hands firmly on the table while the vertigo sensation faded. After nearly a minute, the room steadied, and Michael was able to drink some of the tea in his cup.

"Are they both connected with this bond? Perhaps they came to Erith because of its strong pull? Coincidences happen, but providence is a marvelous and more likely cause, I think," one of the priests said.

"They certainly look aggressive but not hostile. I advise using caution when approaching to tell them about a quest such as yours," another priest stated. "They may be more than wary against strangers speaking to them, Brother Joshua."

"If they're bonded to us, we need them, right?" Michael asked, finally free from the priest's touch and the delving spell.

"That is my thought, though I have been wrong in the past. For all we know, they could be bonded because of the Shadow Knight. It's very hard to say," Joshua replied, refilling his cup of tea, thankful to have a hot beverage. Randall had not let them heat any water for tea during their voyage, one of Joshua's multiple irritations with the ship captain.

"We can use the bond and attempt to locate the Shadow Knight, though I don't know what could happen if we do that. With only ten priests, we might be too weak to touch something so dark. This is a difficult endeavor without currently knowing how powerful your foe is. What are your thoughts, Brother?" one of the priests asked, looking to Joshua for help.

"We must find out where the Shadow Knight is if he is in this plane at all. Can we look into another plane of reality, like he can?" The room grew silent at this question.

"You are asking for something that has been prohibited by every Order of priests on all five continents. We cannot use spells beyond this mortal plane, Brother Joshua. And even staying on this plane to search for the Shadow Knight is too risky. The weakest Shadow

150

Knight we have run across was still stronger than four priests," someone finally replied.

"We have to try something!" Joshua shouted as he slammed his fist on the table. He missed his cup of tea, but only just. "We cannot possibly expect to fight this Shadow Knight without any knowledge or expectation of what is to come. Yes, the Orders and the College have all banned the use and study of Dark Magic, and the Order has banned the practice of anything that reaches beyond this realm, but realistically this plane didn't have Magic of any kind until those stars fell from the sky and Master Fylson discovered a secret that had previously been hidden beyond this world. If the Order wishes to ban everything from beyond our own realm, all Magic would be cast aside."

"You're making a fair argument, Brother Joshua, but as priests, we took an oath—"

"The oath means nothing to me if we cannot do what needs to be done," Joshua growled as he cut off the other priest. "I know that goes against what the priesthood stands for, but what is the purpose of an oath if the lives of all people are at risk? Do you understand what we are dealing with here? Madness will return and hit the world harder than it had before if this Shadow Knight isn't stopped. That same Madness drove people from Drendil and left Erith as the only city standing freely on the entire blasted continent. That same Madness is keeping Michael and me from returning to the only lives we have ever known because Prikea has exiled us for fear we will spread this disease with us if we were to return. I am going to do what I must to stop that from happening because this is not the only continent at risk. The entire planet will fall if we do nothing. Stick to your oaths if you must."

The Heron Priests sat silently around the table, sharing looks amongst themselves but not bringing their eyes to Michael or Joshua. They stared into their cups of tea and pondered the statements that Joshua made and the treachery of his words. Saving the world *was* more important than maintaining an oath and list of prohibitions. By the same token, Dark Magic was prohibited for reasons many of the Mages alive today wished not to contemplate too strongly. The Mages involved with the Wars certainly had their reasons for the banning.

"This response will not please you, Joshua, but we cannot decide anything regarding this situation right now, at least not without discussing it amongst our entire Order first," one of the Herons replied finally.

"What more is there to discuss? We either save the world by finding this Shadow Knight or risk all life as we know it," Joshua replied.

"We need, and request, a day to decide what our choice will be. We cannot be hasty in making this choice, Joshua. We are talking about the foundation of our Orders, something which cannot be taken lightly," one of the Herons replied finally.

"Please, understand," another Heron pled.

"Fine. We will return this time tomorrow. Make the correct choice, that is all I can beg of you," Joshua said as he finished the last of his tea in a single gulp and stepped toward the door.

Joshua opened the door, walked out, and slammed it behind him. Michael sat at the table briefly, waiting to see how the Herons would react to Joshua's tirade. The Herons sat around their table, idly exchanging glances back and forth, unsure about what just happened. Michael took another sip from his cup of tea, not wanting to waste anything his hosts provided for him. Despite Joshua's frustrations, they were quite a hospitable group of men. He finally stood and looked each priest in the eyes before he made his way toward the door. With his hand on the knob, he stopped and turned to the priests once more.

"Some rules are meant to maintain the safety of civilization. Others simply hurt people. I hope you can make the right choice here, no matter how hard that is for you. I'm sorry about Joshua. He's still upset about not being able to return to Prikea. Our entire lives are on that other continent, and they were suddenly taken away from us. You must understand his frustration with our situation. Please, consider that while making your decision, no matter what that decision may be. Have a good rest of the day."

Michael met Joshua in the hallway outside the study, and together they walked up the stairs to leave the temple. Joshua remained silent for the whole walk to a nearby inn, obviously bothered by the Order of the Herons. The stress of their mission didn't help to alleviate any amount of worry over what would happen. There was plenty for anyone to be worried about at the moment. Finally, after enough silence, Michael stopped in the middle of the inn's courtyard. Joshua stopped as well, turning to Michael.

"You shouldn't have apologized for me. The Herons refuse to listen to reason and the day they need to make this decision is simply wasting our time. We need to find supplies, money, everything. And I don't know how to do all of that in the day they have given us, nor in the two days we have left in this city before we have to register with the magistrate," Joshua said, his face finally calm.

"Perhaps we can talk to the Herons about getting some assistance with supplies that we need for our mission. Even if they don't want to help us by looking for the Shadow Knight, I'm sure they will help us with that. For right now, we need to get a place to sleep, and this inn looks as good as any. Should we try to find the other two people the priests identified with the spell?" Michael asked, unsure what reaction his question would bring.

"That's not a bad idea, Michael. Let's get a room here, then we can try to find them. I can track the bond the Herons found. The spell they used, while effective, is not the best one. I need you to be able to walk with me, and for too long after their spell, you weren't able to do that. This is one of the problems with Magic. There are so many solutions to problems and none of them are wrong."

"Let's get a room then, and we should eat too. I'm sure the inn will have better food than *Queller* had," Michael said, longingly. "Dried fruits and meats only go so far."

The Snorting Pig was a quaint inn, with a small walkway that cut through a nice, well-kept lawn. Butting right up against the front of the inn was a small garden with various plants that sported blooms of various colors. Michael recognized a couple of herbs planted amid the flowers. At least they looked similar to some herbs he grew

154

in his own garden. He never claimed to have a green thumb, but herbs were infinitely harder to kill than flowers were. Delicate things, flowers. Above the garden, to the right of the door as they looked at it, was a colored glass window with an unrealistically corpulent pig that looked quite cheerful. The words 'The Snorting Pig' showed in white letters over the happy boar, and Michael felt the window was a nice touch, rather than a simple painted sign bearing the inn's name.

Inside the Snorting Pig, a few men sat around a table as they drank and played a card game while the innkeeper stood behind the bar cleaning glasses and wiping down the bar top. The tavern maids moved gracefully through the room, seeming to almost dance across the straw-covered floor. Oil lamps, sconces, and the light coming through the leaded glass windows cast ample light throughout. Unlike many of the taverns Michael visited in his life, the Snorting Pig seemed a step above in many respects. While there was loose straw littering the floor to absorb spilled drinks, Michael didn't notice any unpleasant smells. It was quite the opposite. Whatever food the innkeeper made, in the large cauldron which hung over the hearth, filled the tavern area with a savory, appetizing smell.

"Please take your hood down, master priest," the innkeeper called to Joshua, who lowered his hood compliantly. No reason to cause any trouble with the man before getting a room from him.

"We need a room for the night, possibly two," Joshua said as he removed a small, leather pouch from his robes and tossed it onto the bar. The bag clinked and the innkeeper's eyes grew excitedly large at the mere sound of coins.

Looking inside the bag, the innkeeper jolted, seeing foreign coins. He counted what was in the pouch, shrugged, and tucked the coins into his own pouch, jostling the coin purse after to hear the satisfying clinking of gold once again. His payment received, he removed a small lockbox from beneath the bar and handed a key to Joshua, then provided directions to the room. Upstairs, the last room on the left. That would be their home for the immediate future. He also offered the bathtub and one of the tavern maids to aid with the bathing process if they so wanted. The innkeeper claimed a single bath per customer was included with the price of the room per week they stayed. Michael would definitely be taking a bath later, as it had been a couple of weeks since his last, and he felt dirtier than the tavern floor.

"What have you for dinner tonight?" Michael asked, hoping to see a menu or at least have a few options.

"We have a peppered boar stew with potatoes and veggies. Comes with some good, hearty bread. I can have some sent up to your room if you would like," the innkeeper replied, wiping his hands on his once-white apron.

"That sounds perfect. Thank you," Joshua said, heading toward the stairs at the other end of the room.

"Would you like the stew sent up before or after your baths, master priest?"

"Before is perfectly fine," Joshua replied. The innkeeper nodded and whistled at one of the tavern maids, who fetched two bowls and a tray.

The staircase went up to a landing then curved to the right. Once upstairs, the hallway went to the left and right. A few torches lit the hallway enough to see the numbers on the doors. Small bronze plates with the numbers etched in and lacquered black was sufficient for anyone to identify their room properly. The last room on the left was room number one. The key in Joshua's hand slid into the door easily and the latches inside the lock clicked as the key turned. He opened the door and walked inside with Michael following closely.

The room was simple, with two beds and a small dresser between them. The beds, slightly larger than the hammocks Queller had for her sailors, looked plush and inviting. Michael sat on the edge of one of the beds and watched as Joshua removed a small trinket from another pouch hidden amongst his robes. It was a flat, smooth stone carved in the shape of a raven small enough to fit in the palm of his hand. Joshua closed his hands around the raven and breathed into his closed palms. A faint light shone through his fingers as the soft light seeped through his skin.

"If you're ready, I can connect the bond to the trinket, and we can have a way of tracking the others without having to delve into you each time we want to check it. Once I have the bond connected, the light will fade or shine as we get further from or closer to them. Once we have an idea of where these two are, we can find them easier," Joshua explained.

"Won't doing this attract the attention of the Shadow Knight?" Michael asked.

"Not that I'm aware. We aren't going to attach the trinket to his portion of the bond. That said, exposing ourselves to him is a risk *I* am willing to take if it means finding the rest of our party, even if the Herons refuse to assist us. We must find the others and get them to join us. Without their help, we cannot take on such a powerful foe. Are you ready to start?" Joshua asked which received a nod from Michael.

Joshua reached one of his hands toward Michael and cast a spell that immediately made Michael feel as if he had fallen into a frozen river. The chills ran up and down his spine, leaving goosebumps as they moved. Michael could feel the hairs on his neck standing up, his skin drawing tight as the tiny bumps popped up all over. As the icy sensation spread across his body, the raven token in Joshua's hand started to glow, gloriously illuminating the room. Cracks in the wall previously invisible under the light of the single oil lamp were now so obvious as to make Michael wonder how he could have missed such flaws. A moment later the raven stopped glowing entirely, leaving the room dim once again, lit only by the lone oil lamp on the dresser between the two beds.

"The link has been established, so now we can find them," Joshua said, putting the raven on a thin leather strap.

A knock on the door announced one of the tavern maids carrying a tray laden with two bowls of the boar stew and two hefty chunks of thick, crusty bread. The stew was light in color, contrasted with the bread being dark in color. Chunks of boar floated amid vegetables and potatoes in the thick broth of the stew. Michael and Joshua each grabbed a bowl, thanking the maid for bringing the food. She left the room with a spring in her step and a bouncy sway in her hips.

The stew was warm, not hot, and both Michael and Joshua ate quickly. Neither realized how hungry they were until they started eating their food. Both bowls and chunks of bread were devoured quickly, leaving only menial crumbs and strips of gristly fat in their bowls, which they set on the dresser by the oil lamp, stacked to conserve space. Michael thought about going back downstairs to ask for another bowl. Perhaps after his bath he would do just that.

"We can begin our search for the others in the morning. Now that I've eaten some real food, I'm tired. What do you think, Michael?" Joshua asked, stretching and yawning.

"That sounds like a good plan. Do you have an idea of where in the city the other two are?" Michael asked with a stretch and yawn of his own.

"I have an idea of where in the city they will likely be, but it's just an idea. I believe they're nearby since there are inns near the temple and in the market area, but they really could be anywhere. Given their cloaks and travel gear, I would think they would need to buy supplies, so we can check the market. We should both get some rest. Sleeping on land will be a welcome change from a ship out at sea," Joshua replied.

Before getting ready to sleep, Michael ventured downstairs and asked about the bath. The innkeeper snapped and called over one of the tavern maids. She was tall, nearly Michael's height, with straight blonde-brown hair, green eyes, and a smile that could warm any man's heart. The dress she wore boasted a low-cut square neckline that revealed a touch too much. She glanced at Michael, and at the direction of the innkeeper, turned and walked spiritedly down a hallway at the back of the tavern and into another room with a bathtub and a clean chamber pot.

The large copper-colored tub was empty, and a large cauldron of water sat above a hearth. Steam wafted from the top of the pot. The tavern maid, Michael hadn't thought to ask her name, started to fill the bathtub, and told Michael that he could start stripping down to prepare for his bath. Michael removed his shirt, boots, and belt, though he left his trousers on until he got assurance from the tavern maid that she wouldn't look at him after he undressed. He saw a woolen towel sat, folded, on a small table beside the bathtub and wrapped the towel around his waist before removing his trousers, which he folded neatly and placed atop his shirt.

"Would you like any oils added to the bath?" she asked with a breathy voice. Her smile was just as warm as the room.

"No, oils won't be necessary. Thank you very much," Michael replied.

"Enjoy the bath. There is a bell on the back of the door. Ring it if you need anything and I will come to help you," she added before she turned on her toes, walked out, and closed the door behind her. Michael wondered, after she left, if she was this welcoming to everyone.

The bathwater was just on the warm side of the perfect temperature. Hot, but not scalding, and he could feel much of the stress and grime from traveling, and sailing, melting away as he laid back in the bathtub. On the table where Michael had found the towel, he found a few different bars of soap, as well as a few bottles of fragranced oils he could add to the water. He relaxed in the warm bath a few minutes before he started to clean himself. When he was finished, Michael dried himself off, got dressed again, and made his way upstairs, after finding the tavern maid again and letting her know he was finished with his bath. She smiled warmly again and flounced off toward the back room as he made his way up the stairs back toward their rented room. Inside the room, he saw Joshua laying in his bed, atop the blankets. The soft sound of his snoring told Michael that his companion had drifted off to sleep already, and Michael felt jealous of his friend. He climbed into bed, under the blankets, and put out the oil lamp before getting truly comfortable.

Still warm from his bath, and under the cozy blankets, Michael felt himself quickly drifting to sleep. The bed, which was far more comfortable than the hammock he grew accustomed to during their voyage, soothed his travel-weary muscles and embraced him for what should have been the best night of sleep since setting off from Feldring. Were it not for the nightmares he expected, it would have been. As he drifted off, Michael wondered how much longer he would be tortured by these dark, repetitive dreams.

Chapter Eleven

aple, oak, and pine trees rose from the ground, their mighty roots gripping the soil as they towered high into the sky. Their branches, high above the ground, provided shade and protection from the weather. Rain was something that Vor'Kath came to loathe about the mortal realms and likely would never grow accustomed to. Water belonged in lakes, rivers, and ponds, not falling from the sky. But that point was moot today, as none of the accursed stuff seemed to be ready to drop. Somewhere high above the trees was a blue sky with some fluffy white clouds floating around. It was disgusting.

Vor'Kath walked through the forest aptly named 'The Goblin Forest' toward a cave that sunk deep into the ground. The opening was shallow and rocky. Inside was total darkness, just the way he preferred. The darkness was much more welcome than any amount of this unrelentingly bright sunlight. Vor'Kath made his way into the cave, ducking his head under a low-hanging rock formation just inside the entrance.

The smell was immediately overwhelming. Acrid. Caustic. Goblins always smelled so foul, even when they were gathered in small quantities. The confines of the cave only served to compound their smell. Hundreds of the little bastards were gathered in the cave. How could something so small smell so bad? But they were free combatants who required no additional training. That was an advantage that might outweigh their smell. Since their spawn, goblins were angry little runts. This had only worsened after they became feral. In-fighting was a serious threat to their existence, but Vor'Kath would get around that. Any goblin who killed another goblin would *wish* to be drawn and quartered. Audro would prove to be a very useful overlord for them. But first, they would need better weapons than their current armaments. Stupid, smelly goblins. They couldn't figure out how to forge metal if their lives depended on it. And in this case, they very much would.

The sea of goblins stretched further than Vor'Kath could see. He could see better in the dark than he could in the light of midday, especially in this mortal plane. The army was coming together nicely. He simply needed to pick his first target strategically. Very few of the goblins spoke the common language of the continent, having little exposure to the clunky common tongue spoken among the humans and Elves. Vor'Kath only found two goblins that could

163

speak the common tongue so far and immediately made them commanders for his army. They would lead the goblins into battle, willingly or otherwise. Their knowledge prevented his need for learning the vile goblin language. He was thankful for only having to clamber his way through the common tongue and not struggle with the coughing sounds of the goblins. They were crude beasts that served little purpose to the world. *It's a shame those excuses for Mages didn't wipe them out entirely during their pathetic wars*, he thought to himself.

Now that he had a chance to see the start of his army, it was time to consider a target for his army to attack. Erith was out of the question. He couldn't accept the miniscule risk of encountering a priest who could overpower him. Feeble though their powers may be compared to his own, strength certainly did exist in numbers. Shemont and Anselin were viable options, but it would take time to decide between the two. There were strained ties between the two cities that served as the heads of the Kingdom of Drendil. The humans had a displeasure toward the Elves, and no matter which city he attacked, one was unlikely to come to the other's aid. The goblins could help with this decision. Their size and their sheer presence across the continent made them great for scouting, something that Vor'Kath would use them for extensively. If anyone killed the goblins found scouting, it was a small loss. It certainly was a price he was willing to pay, and the goblins would have to accept their place in this plan. They were merely cogs within a greater machine. A machine they could never possibly understand, but a machine, nonetheless.

"Send scouting parties to Anselin and Shemont. I need information about the cities that I cannot get myself," Vor'Kath commanded. The goblins attempted a bow, something else they would have to learn.

"Yes, master," one of the goblins gurgled as it went to the group and passed on their new tasks. Goblins scattered, running toward the exit of the cave. They were curious creatures, making their homes underground, yet comfortable enough outside to venture into the woods for hunting and foraging.

*   *   *

"Brother Joshua, we have made our decision," the head of the Order of Herons said. This was a priest that Michael and Joshua had not met the day before. His long white beard touched the Heron embroidered on the front of his robes. His wispy hair had thinned with his many years of age, showing a scalp with dark spots scattered around.

"And what is your decision?" Joshua asked impatiently.

"We have decided that we cannot abandon our oaths, or the priesthood, even at the cost of the world's safety. Dark Magic is far too dangerous of a thing for anyone to wield, and we, as priests, are not an exception to that rule. If anything, Dark Magic is a far more dangerous thing for *us* to even think about. We will not help you to look beyond this mortal plane, Brother Joshua, and I advise you do not search for this Shadow Knight within our own realm."

"Then Drendil forever shall be lost to the shadows of Madness. I cannot believe that your order has decided to abandon the lives of countless innocents. The very oath we have all taken was to protect the world against dangers that others cannot defend themselves against," Joshua replied. The muscles in Joshua's jaw clenched as he spoke, his frustrations visible to Michael who sat beside him.

"There is simply too much at stake for us to go delving into things that are prohibited—"

"They are prohibited by *your* priesthood! Ever since the kingdom of Drendil fell after the Second Mages' War, it has been the priesthood that has governed Magic and its uses. Even the other continents based their prohibitions on the Herons' rulings."

"The Sorcerer's College banned the practice of Dark Magic—"

"And then started practicing it themselves after their Council was infiltrated and they banned humans from learning Magic. You are not making any arguments to support your decision, *brothers*," Joshua said, standing from his chair. "I will do what must be done to save the world, while you sit here in your temple with your rules and wait for salvation to come. History shall, for time immortal, tell of your unwillingness to step in and uphold the very oath you have sworn."

Furious, Joshua stormed out of the room before the Herons could protest his words. Michael stood, nodded at the Herons, and followed after Joshua. Outside the temple, Joshua fumed about the priests and their inability to adapt to the present and how they lived with their rules from the past.

"There comes a point in time where obsolete, outdated rules must be cast aside to meet the present world's demands and situations. They just sat there and decided not to help with something that will save the world! Can you believe that? The priesthood is supposed to protect humanity from the dangers in the world, not only from this realm, but from others. Ever since the first Dark Magic rituals opened up gates to other realms, our world was opened up to disasters and threats we were never before exposed to. Yet, they see no reason to cater our rules to the problems at hand," Joshua fumed.

Just as Joshua finished venting his frustrations, one of the Heron Priests walked out of the temple and quickly approached Joshua and Michael. He cautiously looked around, clearly not wanting to be seen. Once he was sure that no one watched him, he removed a book from inside his robes. The sinister-looking book was bound in scaly black leather with runes scrawled on the cover, and the other priest handed it to Joshua, whispered something, and ran back into the temple. No other words were passed between the two, and Joshua stood in the courtyard inspecting the book, running his fingers over the etched runes. Somehow, the runes seemed to glow as if something were giving them light. *How can that even happen?* Michael asked himself, curious but not enough to ask that question specifically.

"What was all that about?" Michael asked, slightly afraid of the answer he would get.

"Apparently some of the Herons disagree with the decision that was made. We saw at least one of them disagrees, or he wouldn't have provided us with this book with the etched runes. He said it contains spells that will help us track down the Shadow Knight. While not Dark Magic, it is darker than what the priesthood, even the Order of Ravens, allows anyone to practice. If I use these spells, I could be expelled from the Order. But for that to happen, someone with authority in the Ravens must bring up the accusations of Dark Magic practices or rituals. And only someone within my Order can do that. Other priesthoods cannot have someone removed from an order they do not belong to," Joshua explained as he concealed the book in his robes and removed the raven trinket which he had bound the previous evening.

Even in the daylight, the trinket was shining brightly enough to see. The light it produced was soft, like a candle compared to the sun. Something about the raven was comforting to Michael, a reminder of Prikea. It reminded him of the first time he spoke with Joshua. The light began flashing and moved to one side of the raven, highlighting its right wing. If the Magic was to be trusted, the other two were off to the east, though how far east couldn't be determined. They had to be within the city, at the very least. The day before they were walking just inside the gate, and it was hard to imagine they would leave the city after just getting there. Joshua motioned for Michael to follow, and they started walking east to search of the pair of travelers.

Týr and Svenka stopped by the market to get some food. The previous night they stayed in a shifty inn and ate a hot meal, which neither of them overly enjoyed. Still, they were thankful for some amount of food in their bellies, compared to the previous night where they went to bed with nothing to eat. The day before they visited a banker who assessed all the belongings they were willing to part with, then took the assessment to a merchant where they sold many of the remaining pieces of their previous lives. While Týr knew they could have bartered with their possessions, coins spoke volumes above the claimed value of things. While not necessary to keep, the pair refused to part with their weapons purely out of sentiment.

The food in the market varied, but it all looked hearty. Dried and fresh fish, fresh meats, fruits, vegetables, spices, herbs, and grains were all available in whatever quantity was desired. Týr longed for some fried beef. Even after selling what possessions they could, they didn't have as much money as they would have preferred and wanted to save as much as possible. Dried meats, while not as savory, were cheaper. Dried fruits and vegetables, too. Both Týr and Svenka long for the day they could get away from eating dried foods, though any food was welcome at this point. Týr bought some fish, some rice, and a few different vegetables. They could certainly try to make something with that. Maybe the vegetables would do well in a nice stew.

"We have forty coins left. I think we have enough money to buy food for another two days, if we buy the same things we have been eating," Týr said, putting his coin purse back after counting their money.

"We need to eat. Having even something is better than going without," Svenka replied. "It doesn't matter if it tastes good or not at this point."

The merchant wrapped up the food for the travelers, tying everything with a plain brown string. Two small parcels of food wrapped in a waxy paper were handed back, one to Svenka, one to Týr, who both tucked the pouches away in their cloaks. Turning away from the vendor's stall, Týr saw two men approaching, one wearing a cloak and robes, his hood covering most of his face. The front of the tan robes showed a black raven on the chest. In one hand the robed man held a small white disk that glowed brightly, like a torch. The men approached quickly, and Týr grabbed Svenka's arm and motioned toward the men with a slight nod. Neither of them appeared threatening, but the speed with which they approached alarmed Týr. Something was unusual about the two, that was certain. Before either could react, the men were upon them, speaking immediately.

"I'm sorry to bother you both, but we need you to come with us. There is a matter of great importance that you are both destined for," the robed man asserted as he tucked the disk under his robes.

"Who are you? What do you need us for? How do you know who we are?" Svenka asked.

*　　*　　*

Joshua quickly explained who he and Michael were and that more details would be provided out of the open. The group moved from the marketplace toward The Snorting Pig; they walked down the winding, stone streets of Erith. Once they reached the inn, Joshua asked the innkeeper if they would be permitted to use the cellar, and the innkeeper opened the door without batting an eye. Clearly, the amount of gold provided for the room was sufficient enough to grant them some privilege at the inn. As the group moved into the cellar, the innkeeper called out to his visitors.

"Master priest, if you would like I can have some of the boar stew and some tankards of ale sent down for you and your guests." The man wiped his hands vigorously against the once-white apron he wore just like the day before.

Týr and Svenka lit up at the idea of something other than dried food, and perhaps at the idea of having something stiff to drink, and Joshua asked for four bowls of the stew to be brought down promptly. The innkeeper nodded and once more wiped his hands on his apron as the door closed behind the group.

The cellar was cool, but not cold, and it smelled musty, but was dry. In the middle of the room stood a table and some chairs which were surrounded by barrels that undoubtedly contained ales, stouts, lagers, and other varieties of beers. Michael gazed at the half dozen barrels, each a little shy of a meter wide and not much taller. The night before the only drinks the innkeeper seemed to have been serving were ales and stouts, but Michael imagined there were other types of beer available. Perhaps not to typical guests, but Joshua seemed to have a way of working with the innkeeper to match his wants and needs. A few moments after everyone sat down, the innkeeper lumbered down the stairs with a wooden tray, laden with four bowls of the peppered boar stew and chunks of the same crusty bread. Also on the tray were four tankards, which the innkeeper filled with a brown ale from the only opened barrel in the cellar. He dipped a metal ladle in and poured the ale quite skillfully. Clearly, he had been doing this for some time. *Maybe he kept the table and chairs down here for a special purpose,* Michael wondered.

"Help yourselves to as much of this ale as you want, but please don't open another barrel. I have to have enough beer to serve my guests later today, and the Allfather knows that the soldiers in this town are thirsty bastards. Please let me know whatever you may need, master priest," the innkeeper said, bowing slightly and wiping his hands on his apron.

"Thank you," Joshua replied, dismissing the overweight man.

Týr and Svenka, smelling the stew, asked if they could each get another bowl. The innkeeper started up the creaky stairs and he bowed and nodded. When the upstairs door to the main tavern closed, the four ate their stew. While they ate, Joshua explained in greater detail what was happening, and why the two travelers were needed. As he went on, he removed the black leather book the Heron Priest gave him and explained his intentions. Týr and Svenka stared at Joshua with puzzled looks on their faces.

172

"Let me see if I understand this correctly. *You* want to use Dark Magic to find a Shadow Knight that *we* are supposed to fight?" Týr asked.

"It hardly constitutes Dark Magic. The only problem the Heron Priests have with it is the potential for looking at realities beyond our own."

"That seems pretty 'Dark Magic' to me," Týr said.

"Do you expect us to simply take everything you're telling us as fact and agree to do this for you?" Svenka questioned.

"I don't expect the two of you to fight the Shadow Knight alone. The four of us will fight him together. But basically, yes. Again, as I said before, this is hardly Dark Magic. It happens to be something that few enough priests understand and therefore labeled as bad. There is very little risk of us catching or even coming in contact with the Madness; however, I must let you know that casting this spell could alert the Shadow Knight to our presence if he is in our realm and put Erith at risk of being attacked. Shadow Knights like to work from the background, unseen and unknown. If he learns that he is known, he might retaliate or flee into another realm and become craftier with whatever plans he is executing right now. I know this sounds hard to believe. A priest wants to use a spell that will put a whole city at risk of being attacked by an immensely powerful Dark being. Please understand the urgency with which I have made this decision. I do not risk danger for anyone lightly."

Before the conversation could continue, the door at the top of the stairs opened and the innkeeper returned with another set of four bowls of the peppered boar stew. He cleared away the empty bowls

173

and placed the new ones in front of each of his guests. The man had sweat beading on his brow, likely from when he had filled the bowls from the cauldron hanging over the fire. With the bowls placed on the table he set down a basket with more bread for his guests, then walked back upstairs and closed the door behind him. Týr and Svenka both started eating their stew, attacking it as if they went days without a proper meal before resuming their conversation.

"Are you wanting our approval to cast this spell? You're the only Mage amongst the four of us in this group, and clearly know more about Magic than the rest of us," Svenka said before she finished off her thick slice of crusty bread.

"I still don't understand what the bond that you found is, how you found it, or why we are tied to the two of you," Týr said, eying Joshua as his hands settled on the black book.

"Svenka, you make a valid point in saying that I am the only Mage in the group. That really has nothing to do with the decision to cast this spell or not, though. Týr, the bond is a connection that exists between the four of us in this room. Beyond that, it would be arduous to explain a bond of this level and how the Heron Priests thought to check for it. It was only a matter of time before we would have found each other is the easiest way to explain the connection it creates. The bond pulled you to Erith, even if you didn't know that was why you came here," Joshua explained.

He gingerly opened the book in front of him. The leather creaked quietly as he opened the book. The pages, with their torn, uneven edges, were thicker parchment than most books that Michael had ever seen before. Joshua sat at the table, the bowl which formerly contained stew pushed away. The book lay on the table, Joshua skimmed the pages, quickly glancing from top to bottom and then flipping to the next page. This continued until he stopped and read the same page several times. His lips moved silently as he read the page once more, and his finger moved from one side of the page to the next, as if he was trying to further absorb the knowledge the book contained. He read the page once more, nodded, then closed the book. While Joshua scoured the book, looking for what he hoped was contained within the pages, Svenka glanced up at Michael from her food, a puzzled look on her face as she gestured toward Joshua with her eyes. Michael, unsure what else to do, shrugged quickly and continued eating his stew.

After he finished reading the page, Joshua stood and moved back from the table, clearing some space in the cellar, and started casting a spell. Part way through the spell, he chanted something and the light of the oil lamps in the cellar flickered. A dark orb appeared over the table, displaying the image of a thick forest of maple and oak trees. Some pine trees were scattered through the forest, their pointed tops standing out from the sea of rounded trees. A mass of goblins ran from the forest, moving north and east, away from Erith by a considerable distance. A second orb appeared and focused on the dark entrance of a rock cave. The Shadow Knight, clothed in robes that never moved with him, emerged from a cave deep inside the forest. The cowl on his robes was raised and completely hid his face, even though it should have only covered him from the elements. The only portions of his skin which the group could see where his hands, pale as snow in the sunlight. Despite wearing no scabbard or belt, in his left hand, he held a sword with a slightly curved, midnight-black blade. The blade showed only one sharpened edge. The Shadow Knight stopped and focused his attention on the orb. Without any hesitation, his sword flashed, and the edge struck the orb, though nothing happened in the cellar.

"I know not who you are, but clearly you are strong enough to resist that. You meddle in things you do not, and cannot, understand," his voice echoed through the orb.

The Shadow Knight raised his right hand, started a spell, and both orbs wavered, flashed dimly, and then closed before anything further could be seen. Joshua rippled, recovering from casting the spells, then dropped into the empty chair behind him. His breath came in shallow gasps as he recovered from something unknown to the others. Sweat that collected on his forehead now ran down his face. His whole head, face, and neck shone in the dim lamp light of the cellar. Michael handed Joshua his tankard of ale, though he raised his hand, declining the offer of a drink. That was odd since Michael surely thought the cool ale would help him right now.

"The goblins," Joshua gasped between ragged breaths, "are doing his bidding. What that is right now, I can't tell. I need to find out though. I believe it has something to do with where we have to go."

"They were running northeast, right? What if we looked at a map to see if there is anything worth his attention in that direction? That could help us narrow down his potential target," Michael suggested.

"Northeast of the Goblin Coast are the capital cities for the kingdom. Anselin, the Elven capital is far to the north, and Shemont

176

is almost directly east of here. There are also the Dwarven mines in the mountains, but the Dwarves want little to do with Drendil beyond selling us whatever gems and metals they can mine. I can't imagine he would find anything of interest in Vilyar or Nalum. That means it has to be Anselin or Shemont, right?" Svenka wondered.

"Don't forget about the College between the two capitals. They supposedly have many Magic artifacts that could be valuable to a Shadow Knight. Maybe he is interested in something they have there?" Týr asked.

"I doubt that any of the artifacts that the College maintains are even worth his time to consider. Unless the one he serves is interested in obtaining more power through those artifacts, his seeking them would be a waste of time," Joshua replied. "I agree with you, Svenka, that he likely won't go after the Dwarven mines. I haven't heard of any Dwarf coming above ground for anything, short of when Madira collapsed and the few who were fortunate enough to do so escaped before the mountain imploded."

"So, that brings us back to Anselin or Shemont," Svenka said again.

"This would be easier if we had an army that could scout the continent for us like he appears to have. I doubt I can cast the same spell again without giving our location away to the Shadow Knight," Joshua sighed.

"Is there a way we could watch the goblins without him knowing that we are watching him?" Týr asked before he took another long drink from his tankard.

"I very much doubt that I can cast any spells from this book without alerting the Shadow Knight right now. He is incredibly strong and likely knows these spells better than I do. When his sword hit the orb, I *felt* its strike. I believe his sword is made from Magic. I have no idea how that is possible, or how such a thing can be done. I also don't know how he can strike a spell with a Magic-made weapon and make me feel its strike. That said, I *do* know, now that we have seen him, that he is a Vor," Joshua replied.

"What does that mean?" Michael asked, taking a sip from his second tankard of ale.

"From what little I have learned in an exceptionally small handful of texts, the Vor are beings from another world who are born of pure Magic. They aren't wholly good or evil, but individuals are certainly split between those camps. There are extremely few records of them that even exist, and the sight of a Vor usually means trouble. Using this knowledge, can we potentially narrow down his intentions? Also, since he can travel between realms, he is likely to have picked up different spells and weapons that we will have difficulty fighting without support from, at the very least, the priesthood, if not other Mages," Joshua answered.

"If he is meant to disrupt order, and you said Michael's dream involves a mine being dug under a city with a moat? Well, that leaves us with Shemont as Anselin has no moat. In that regard I agree with the priests' assessment," Týr said as he finished his second ale and poured a third. "I imagine any kind of attack against Shemont that is Magic-based would only bring further tension between the Elves and humans. This could be something the

178

Shadow Knight uses to get another war started between the two. Another all-out civil war could bring Drendil crumbling down, Erith would likely get involved in the war, as the 'last bastion of sanity' they claim to be. If Erith did join the war, they would lose too many soldiers and they wouldn't be able to hold against whatever else the Shadow Knight plans next."

"That certainly aligns with what the Herons said yesterday," Joshua confirmed.

"Would there be anything to gain from attacking both Shemont *and* Anselin?" Michael asked, drawing attention from the rest of the table.

"He would need a massive army to assault two heavily fortified cities," Týr reminded. "Both halves of the kingdom employ a legion of Battlemages augmented by the College."

"Don't you know a lot about politics," Svenka muttered.

"Lars always said to know your enemy better than yourself."

"Let's remember that we *are* talking about an extremely powerful entity from beyond our planet. I'm sure he could amass such an army if he really wanted to. But why attack two cities if you would want them to fight each other?" Joshua wondered aloud. He had finally stopped sweating from the encounter with the Vor.

"It's possible that both sides of the kingdom would be angered toward the other side if he attacked both capitals. Would that cause enough of a disruption of order for his purposes? Would another war in Drendil get the other continents involved? Joshua, you said the priesthood is full of Mages who serve to defend the kingdom against

Magic like this, right? Can't we ask them for help?" Svenka asked after emptying her third ale.

"After my last interaction with the Heron Priests, I doubt they will offer much help to us if any. I can speak with them about this matter, and any other questions we can come up with. I think, in this effort, they might be willing to answer questions to help us. I will simply not tell them what I did and hope that they don't already know about the orb spell. Are there any other questions you want me to bring before the priests?" Joshua asked as he quickly drank the last of the ale that sat in his tankard. The bubbles that had formed at the top when the innkeeper poured the beers disappeared, but Joshua seemed unconcerned about that.

The group fell silent as they drank more ale, thinking of more questions to bring before the priests. After another ale, and no further questions to ask, Joshua stood, wavered slightly on his feet, and walked to the stairs. As he left, he assured the others he would return shortly.

*   *   *

Joshua walked into the temple, doffed his hood, and dipped his fingers in the basin of holy water the priests used for cleansing rituals. The entirety of the priesthood was already waiting in their study downstairs, grim looks upon their faces. When Joshua walked in, the head of the Order, a wizened man named Harold stood, his face betwixt by annoyance. His long grey eyebrows turned down in a furious rumple splitting his green eyes from his brow, wrinkled with the force of his eyebrows.

"Brother Joshua, we cannot help you with your quest. We told you that to do so would go against our oaths that everyone in this room took to enter the priesthood. You have forsaken your oath by casting these dark spells. Brother Timothy told us of the book he gave you and the nature of what is found within its pages. Surely you have found more questions through these spells, or you would not have returned for the second time this day," Harold scolded.

"I still think it's wrong for us not to help them," Timothy argued, clearly speaking when none of the other Herons wanted him to.

"I will deal with your insubordination later. For now, sit there and know your place," Harold snarled. Normally, priests were far more restrained than this.

"You were correct. I do have further questions after what I saw," Joshua said.

Joshua briefly described what he saw through the spells he had cast. Once the priesthood came to understand his findings, Joshua began asking the questions he had come up with, making sure to ask in ways that would elicit specific answers from the priests, rather than roundabout ways for them to tell him off.

"This certainly sounds like a Vor, as you stated. What purpose is there in causing a rift between the Elves and the humans? What could be gained by the kingdom collapsing?" Harold asked, somehow not giving Joshua an answer while also answering his question.

"That's what I came here to find out. The Vor have, in the very little documentation that we have concerning them, typically been the masters of chaos. Could attacking Anselin and Shemont cause another war between the races? What of the Dwarves?"

"The Dwarves have not left their mines since Madira collapsed, and even before then very seldom were they seen above the surface. Even the merchants that come and go from the mines aren't Dwarves," Timothy said, not meeting Joshua's gaze. "We honestly only know that the Dwarves still exist because ores and jewels keep pouring out of the mines, and even that evidence is speculative."

Why help me then tell the priests about the tome you gave me? Joshua wondered.

"Brother Timothy I already told you to sit there quietly," Harold snapped once more as he waved his finger at the stubborn priest.

"Dammit, Harold. That's enough! I will not just 'sit here and know my place,' while the whole world could be destroyed. If I know an answer to one of Joshua's questions, I'm going to provide it rather than beating around the bush and wasting precious time we don't have. You can remove me from the priesthood right now if you want. I will still stay here and help him through this issue. And that's not because I'm being 'insubordinate' to your backward authority. It's because I value the countless lives on this planet that count on us to fulfill the oath we took and protect them from harm." The priests in the room all looked taken aback by the words. Some clearly thought and wanted to say the same thing, but none dared to say what needed saying.

"I will not make this decision before I—"

182

"Have time to think about it? That's what you say about everything, and I will endure it no longer! You don't deserve the title of head priest and should be removed from *your* post! You are running our order into the ground with your indecision, and I will not have it anymore," Timothy cut off the old man.

"Enough! You are expelled from the Order immediately!" Harold shouted back. This took all the priests by surprise. There was a process for removing a priest, and this certainly didn't fall into that process.

"There has to be a vote for that to happen!" one of the other Herons objected as he stood to defend Timothy.

"Thank you for standing up for me, Brother."

"I could care less about whether you stay in the order, honestly. Giving that book to Joshua is just as damning as if you had cast the spells yourself. And how are we to know you weren't casting the spells, feeding information to this Vor all along? But I agree with you that Harold has sat back and let the world fall to ruin. We not only let that happen, but we did nothing to prevent it. When was the last time a new priest joined us? When was the last time a temple has opened? Since when have we—"

"Stop! If you want to change your Order, do so without me present. We have more pressing matters at the moment and your insolence is not going to get anyone closer to saving the world," Joshua interrupted, getting the attention of all the priests in the room. "What I'm getting from you is that the Dwarves care not one iota about the surface races, their mines are not the target for the Vor's attention, and indecision runs rampant through this room."

183

A deep silence struck the room before anyone replied. Not one priest so much as coughed. They stared at each other, still taking in what went down before Joshua interrupted the argument. Clearly, tensions among them were high, and no one could simply put aside that hostility. The harsh words. The spoken truths. Several minutes passed before one of the priests finally leaned forward in his chair to answer Joshua's statement.

"Correct. And the Dwarves haven't cared since they first discovered metal and gems were buried deep underground."

"Let's get back to the main questions I asked," Joshua said, corralling the priests. "Are we certain the dreams point to Shemont being the Vor's target?"

"The dreams certainly point to *an* attack happening in Shemont. Whether he also attacks Anselin or not, we cannot be certain," a priest said.

"What is the benefit to attacking both cities?" Joshua retorted.

"Tensions already exist between the halves of the kingdom. If he attacked both cities, another war could break out. If another war involving Magic starts, the priesthood would have to get involved, and as you see, there are twelve priests to fight against untold legions of rogue Mages. We would *lose* the priesthood, and Madness could spread to the other continents. Perhaps that is the reality this Vor wishes to bring about," Harold said.

"Should we concentrate on saving Shemont or fighting the knight there, or should we split our focus between the two cities? If we prepare for an attack against the humans, and he attacks the

Elves, we have done nothing to stop his mission of bringing chaos to Drendil's doorstep, correct?" Joshua asked.

"Were it me that was on this quest, I would start in Shemont until you get some evidence that says you must head to Anselin. None of us want any city in Drendil to fall, especially if, in so falling, a war is started. Should you split your efforts between two cities? I don't believe that would be beneficial," Timothy replied, sipping from his cup of tea. Tendrils of steam wafted toward his face as he drank.

"I agree. Splitting your focus would simply leave part of your group too vulnerable against the Shadow Knight, a risk that must not be afforded to him. Have you conducted any of the tests for Michael to see if he can wield Magic?" Harold added. As he spoke, he glared at Timothy, though said nothing further toward their hostilities.

"He is only able to sense Magic at best. His real gift is the premonitions, which are helpful enough on their own—" Joshua said, cutting off as he heard a distant sound like thunder as the ground started shaking.

The priests all left the study quickly and ran up the stairs to find the source of the noise and vibrations. Outside the temple, people ran in all directions, screaming, as hordes of goblins poured through the city streets, attacking anyone within their reach. Thick, unnaturally dark clouds covered the sky to the horizon. Joshua and the other priests, formed into a ring in front of the temple, began casting spells, eliminating goblins as deftly as they could. Fire, lightning, gusts of air, and blasts of water shot in all directions, cutting down goblins by the dozens. Týr and Svenka, with Michael

185

following closely behind, emerged from the inn, the two in front drawing their weapons as soon as they saw the goblins in the streets. Týr held a knife in his right hand and a short sword in his left. Svenka twirled two wickedly curved knives, the blades flashing in the remnants of sunlight that shone through the suddenly, Magically darkened sky.

Michael awkwardly drew his sword, assuming one of the stances he learned aboard *Queller*, his feet slightly wide as they were in training to accommodate for the movement of the ship. That was something he would adjust for fighting on land, Joshua knew. Michael moved, more fluidly through stances than Joshua expected, but it was still obvious he only had a month of training with his sword. Some of the goblins he attacked sported deep cuts from his sword, others had shallower markings. He needed to learn consistency in striking, but Joshua knew he could focus on that later. Blades flashed, spells shot through the air, and goblins fell in all directions. Bodies piled up in the street and most belonged to what used to be goblins. Sadly, some of the others were the fallen citizens of Erith. Screams echoed through the city.

Three of the priests cast a spell toward the sky which parted some of the clouds. A circle broke through the solid curtain of darkness overhead, allowing some sunlight to shine in the city momentarily. A few moments after the spell shot into the deep darkness overhead, the clouds closed in once more, shutting out the sunlight again. With the midday sun now blocked out, the world plunged into near midnight darkness. Still, the group fought the goblins, dropping their sickly colored bodies throughout the small courtyard around the temple and the surrounding streets. Down the street, Joshua heard more weapons clashing and, with a quick look, saw the city guards also fought the wretched creatures. *It's hard to imagine that goblins were once tame beasts capable of thought,* Joshua thought to himself as he struck down half a dozen of the monsters with lightning that arced between their bodies in a gruesome display.

A bolt of lightning darker than the sky on a moonless night shot through the air, struck the temple, and brought the steeple tumbling toward the ground. Carved stones fell to the street and smashed anything in its path. One of the priests, as he pushed a goblin with a blast of air, crumpled beneath the weight of a large stone, which looked as if it easily weighed over a hundred kilograms. His body produced a stomach-churning *crunch* sound as the stone impacted the ground.

Within moments of the lightning strike, the Vor appeared within the circle formed by the remaining priests. The Vor's sword flashed through the air, which brought down two priests. Joshua turned and released a bolt of lightning from his left hand. The sparks jumped through the air, connected with the dark robes that remained motionless, jumped through the Vor and into one of the priests beyond him, and sent the limp, felled priest's body into the air.

The dark being turned to Joshua, an orb of darkness forming in his hand. Dark lightning shot forth from his hand and danced through the air toward Joshua. Harold and one of the other Heron Priests quickly stepped between the Vor and Joshua and opened a portal in the air. The lightning shot into the portal and raced through

187

the air over the priests' heads. The portal closed after the end of the lightning reached it. A stream of fire shot from the Vor's hand, and another portal appeared with the same results. Harold and Joshua squared up against the Vor, spells at the ready. Flashes of lightning and fire shot toward both, portals opening to divert each of the wicked spells.

The black blade of the Vor's sword flashed through the air, heading toward Harold. As the blade approached, Svenka jumped forward, her knives, their blades crossed, caught the dark blade in a fury of sparks. The sword bounced back, and Svenka yelped as one of her knives melted out of her hand, the blade severed less than a hand's width from the hilt. Her left shoulder oozed red with fresh blood, and another spot appeared on her right calf, the end of an arrow sticking through the leg of her trousers. As the Vor struggled to regain control, Svenka lunged at him, her good blade moving quickly. Týr stopped, his sword stuck through a goblin's head, shouted, and ran toward the group.

Svenka planted her remaining knife firmly into the right shoulder of the Vor; as her blade sank into his flesh, the dark steel blade flashed through her right arm, cutting through the muscles in her arm but bouncing after contacting the bone. A resounding snap followed the cut as her muscle bounced away from the cut and toward her joints. Svenka screamed and clutched the wound as bright red blood gushed through her sleeve and fingers. The Vor clutched his shoulder, clutching at the knife planted there, a high-pitched shriek echoed through the plaza as he removed the blade and dropped it on the ground. The blood on the knife's blade was a dark

188

maroon, nearly black. Drops of blood fell from the knife as it raced toward the cobblestone floor of the plaza. The knife landed on the ground and clattered as all sounds from the battle seemed to stop within an instant.

Týr lunged at the Vor, his blades readied and a wave of fierce anger in his eyes. The short sword swung as he approached, and the fine blade closed in on the Vor's back. As the blade touched the edge of the dark robes, a portal opened under their collective foe's feet and he disappeared, leaving only the sound of goblins racing through the city. Týr's blade struck nothing but air as the portal closed within an instant. Goblins who fought furiously now stopped as fear washed over them, their master gone without a trace.

The clouds departed in a matter of seconds, and the goblins scattered like cockroaches under the uninhibited light of the sun. As they ran, Joshua threw spells, killing a dozen of the creatures in a fury of lightning. The bolt of electricity arced from one goblin to the next as the lightning made their muscles tense and they fell over. Wispy tendrils of blue smoke rose from their bodies, now limply crumpled onto the cobblestone street.

Týr straddled Svenka, who now lay on the ground, no longer writhing in agony, her energy long-since spent. His hands firmly covered the wound in her arm causing her to wriggle under Týr's weight. Her agonized scream filling the courtyard and downing out the cries of fallen citizens, guards, and goblins alike. Joshua rushed over and held his hands over her arm and cast a spell. His hands glowed white, a slightly green hue in the glow. Soon the blood stopped pouring from between Týr's fingers, and Svenka groaned fiercely as she fainted. Her head lolled onto the ground as the muscles in her neck relaxed. Sweat that pooled on her face now rolled toward the ground and left tracks through the thin layer of dirt that covered her face. All the color in her face vanished instantly and left her deathly pale, like an opaque spirit. Týr shot a glance up at Joshua, a bewildered look on his face, his eyes holding a thousand questions and accusations he left unspoken.

"This wound looked nasty. Do you think she will survive?" he asked, finally calmed down enough to speak, wiping sweat from his face and neck.

"The healing spell I just used should stabilize her long enough that we can get some proper healing done in the temple. With proper attention to the wound, she should recover just fine. Harold," Joshua said, turning to the last standing Heron Priest, "we should gather the wounded in the temple."

Harold stood in the plaza, only a couple feet from where he cast portals to stop the Vor's attacks. His eyes, filled with emotions earlier in the study, now showed an emptiness. He gazed at the remnants of the chaos. Bodies, and pieces of bodies, lay strewn throughout the street, blood pooled on the stones. Men, women, children, and goblins; those few who lived through the attack shrieked in agony. Michael stood in front of the inn, staring at the blood on the blade of his sword, a few shallow cuts running up and down the outsides of his arms and legs. Svenka lay on the cobblestone street, her clothes soaked with her own blood. Týr stood over his sister, his hands dripping with blood from holding the wound in her arm. Priests lay scattered throughout the courtyard, their bodies mangled by the Vor and his spells.

"So much death. It came because of *you*, Joshua. *Your* spells and curiosity brought this destruction and torment to our peaceful city. This is a city that will never be the same again. Is this what you wished? You could have simply said you wanted my help under threat of attack. Do you think that offering to take care of the wounded will return you to my graces?" Harold was nearly yelling, his voice low and resolute. "You ventured far from the oath you took."

"My oath was to stand between innocent people and the forces of evil that haunt the world from *this* continent, a land *you* oversaw and allowed to slip into Madness. This Vor went unchecked and amassed an army of goblins to this scale while you and the Heron Order sat back and got fat, living *comfortably* within a city and its walls. If anything, *that* betrays the oath. If you ask my opinion, Harold—" Joshua started.

"Keep your opinions. I still believe that you have betrayed the priesthood and should be removed from your order. You are beyond lucky that I am not a Raven and cannot remove you myself," Harold interjected.

"The weight of today is as much on your shoulders as it is on mine, Harold. We both know that. You cannot sit back and let evil grow, then become angry when it knocks down your door," Joshua growled, his knuckles popping as he spoke.

"Leave this city and never return. You are not welcome here," Harold ordered.

"There are wounded to deal with. You can banish me once they are tended to."

Harold inhaled deeply before he responded, "Fine. Let's bring the wounded inside the temple and get them triaged. I will prepare the temple; you gather the wounded. Start with the young lady, as she needs immediate attention. Get the others into the temple based on the severity of their wounds."

Týr and Joshua lifted Svenka and gingerly carried her limp body into the temple. Michael stood, his feet unmoved since the battle ended, watching them. The color drained from his face, seeing the amount of death in the plaza. Once the priests and Týr vanished inside the temple, Michael doubled over and emptied the stew and ale from his stomach. Týr returned shortly, a grim look on his face. Something was wrong. Joshua left the temple shortly after Týr and started directing the other two to the wounded. Michael's feet finally moved, reluctantly, though his face regained no color. Týr reassured Michael. He offered some wisdom that killing, and battles, were always like that at first, but that it would grow easier as they happened.

"Why is there so much hostility between you and that other priest?" Týr asked Joshua, his voice strained.

"I am willing to cast spells they dislike. Unfortunately, the Vor located and attacked us. Harold is the only surviving priest of his order, now. I can't imagine that's an easy reality to face," Joshua replied. "I can only imagine the struggles he will face on his own."

"Svenka and I know that feeling well. We were part of a group that was killed by a local lord who is now dead, by her hands it turns out. While we were out of the camp, everyone else was killed. Slaughtered."

"Life will get a lot rougher for us all, Týr. I cannot guarantee that any of us will survive this endeavor before us," Joshua said.

Until the sun journeyed beyond the wall and no longer shone its light on the world, the group assessed wounded from the battle, getting those with serious injuries to the temple, where Harold treated and cared for the wounded. Svenka remained unconscious even after Joshua, Michael, and Týr finished gathering the wounded. Though her wound was cared for, her pulse remained rapid and shallow, and her breathing was sporadic. Joshua and Michael went back to the inn for some food, bringing some stew to Harold, who scoffed and refused to accept anything from Joshua. Michael left a bowl and some of the crusty bread for him in case he changed his mind later. Týr remained at the temple by Svenka's side well into the night after Michael and Joshua returned to the inn. Before retiring for the night, Joshua made sure that Harold needed nothing else in the way of assistance. Again, the man scoffed but said nothing.

Chapter Twelve

The next morning, sunlight flooded the plaza by the temple, showing once more the horrors that took place the day before as Joshua and Michael went to the temple. Týr remained by Svenka's side through the night, despite her not regaining consciousness. Early in the morning, around the fourth bell, Harold had pronounced her dead, a proclamation that struck Týr harder than a hammer swung at a plaster wall. A likely cause, Harold had said, was the combination of infection from either the Vor's sword or the goblin arrow, and the loss of blood she suffered before Joshua healed her. Goblins, disgusting creatures, were not well known for their cleanliness. Týr sat beside her and stared at nothing, his gaze locked on some distant, unseen object. He clutched

194

her hand firmly in his, not ready to leave the last connection to the only remaining member of his family. Even now, Joshua was unsure if they were blood relatives, but he knew that regardless of how they were related, a strong connection existed between them.

Finally, at the sounding of the seventh bell elsewhere in the city, Týr released Svenka's hand, stood, then leaned down and pressed his lips firmly against her forehead, a singular tear falling from the crest of his cheek. Before he turned to face the others, he retrieved her knife from beside the mat she lay on and tucked it into his own belt in the small of his back. With a token to remember Svenka, Týr turned to Joshua and Michael, his voice faint.

"That goat-fucker will pay for what he did to my sister. How do we find him again?"

"Master Týr, please watch your choice of words in this temple," Harold called from the other side of the room. "I understand your frust—"

"Sod off, old man. Sit back and let others fight battles that you are better equipped for as much as you'd like. That's fine by me. But don't sit there and tell us what we are supposed to do inside four walls," Týr snapped.

"I have been far more than hospitable for you three given what you have done to Erith. Leave now, before I call the guards," Harold said.

Before any further confrontations arose between Harold and the trio, Joshua, Michael, and Týr left the temple so Harold could tend to the wounded in peace. Outside, guards gathered to clear out the bodies of the goblins and place them on various fires constructed throughout the city. Thick, black smoke and a grim aura clung to the city like a wet shirt and accompanied the heavy, harsh smell of burning bodies. A handful of nearby guards stopped to glare, angrily, at the three companions as they moved to the end of the plaza outside the temple. Word had gotten around, likely from Harold as the guards brought him wounded, about who was responsible for the attack. The guards judged without knowing the full story, but then again, the whole story would have only muddled the waters and caused further confusion. There was little that could be done to explain this situation clearly in a short time.

Joshua told Týr and Michael to stay behind and went to speak with the guards. After a brief exchange, one of the guards pointed toward the gate beyond the market, where a half-day before Michael and Joshua met Týr and his late sister. Týr, Michael thought to himself, must still be processing Svenka's death, as the man was quieter than the dead scattered across the city. Joshua returned to the group, and they started moving toward the market, snaking their way through the body-littered streets. Despite the fact the battle ended about ten hours before, there was a lot of work to be done to clean up Erith. There were only so many guards to call upon for such an endeavor. In the market area, another fire burned close to the city wall. Goblins were piled nearly two meters high, their flesh charred by the flames. The acrid smoke stung the eyes as it floated on the lazy wind that wafted across the city. A pair of guards ahead dragged a goblin by his ankles toward the fire, despite protesting sounds the creature made. It was still alive, yet they dragged the goblin toward the fire all the same. Joshua walked over and ordered the guards to kill the goblin before throwing it onto the fire. Michael heard one of the guards ask why they should care if an abomination should suffer a little extra compared to the others.

"You may only see the goblins as monsters, but they are still living beings. It deserves mercy," Joshua replied.

"Fuck giving this monster any mercy. Do you know how many people died yesterday because of these things? I wouldn't care if you're the King of Drendil, I'm tossing this thing on the pyre and letting it die that way," the guard replied.

Joshua, his hands behind his back, wiggled his fingers, which briefly flashed white. The guards shook their heads gently, a confused look showing on their faces. Joshua once again reminded them to show mercy to the goblins, and one of the guards drew his knife, slitting the goblin's throat and watching it go limp before tossing it into the fire. Fire flashed around the goblin as it was consumed by the flames. Once again, Joshua rejoined his group and they turned down a side street.

"Why are you so concerned with them showing some monster any mercy? Goblins are just the results of some experiments gone wrong. They're scavengers with little quality of life that provide no utility for anything alive," Týr wondered. "Don't tell me your priesthood believes that all living things are valuable and should be given fair lives."

"We are taught to be kind to all life, no matter how small that life may seem. Throwing a living creature on a fire is not right, Týr, regardless of its origins. There was a time when goblins were not the feral creatures we know them as today. They became what they are now after the wars when they were almost made extinct by their cruel masters forcing them to fight for a cause they couldn't possibly understand," Joshua replied.

"That goblin would have shown you no mercy. You even admitted they are feral beasts. Besides, they are aggressive, violent monsters. No different than a cur that bites a village child," Týr countered.

"That may be true, but that changes nothing of my principles," Joshua answered.

"Your principles are going to have to change if we are to kill this Vor, friend. Will you go soft and let him live because he is a creature that should be shown mercy?" Týr argued.

"That is a wholly different situation, and you know it. He is not feral and only exists to cause evil in our world. If there is a way to end his threat against us without killing him, I don't think we should excuse that option simply because you seek revenge. I know death is a hard part of reality to deal with, but that is not always the answer we should seek," Joshua countered.

"You're going to go soft and let him live. Mark my words, priest," Týr huffed.

Joshua let the argument die before it grew any more heated. He saw no reason for two people to fight in such a way over something that *might* happen. As they walked in silence, the group turned down a few more side streets until they arrived at a stable. The smell of horses floated heavily in the air, even over the smell of the fires and burning flesh, a block away from the stable. The horses inside danced back and forth in their stalls, on edge from the attack the day

198

before and the smell of nearby fires. Several stable hands were inside attempting to calm the horses, some with better results than others. One of the hands, seeing the three in the doorway, walked over, wiping his hands on his trousers, leaving behind streaks of dirt.

"Welcome master priest. What can I do for you today?" the lead hand asked.

"We're looking to buy some horses from you. Have you got three for sale?" Joshua asked in turn.

"I'm sorry, master, but the horses we have aren't for sale at the moment. You could check back in a few days, and we might have something available then. There is another stable inside the western gate that you could check with as well," the hand suggested.

Joshua removed a pouch from his belt and tossed it to the stable hand who looked inside; his eyes widened at the sight of coins. Putting away the pouch, the stable hand whistled at the other hands, made a whirling motion with his hands, then motioned for the men to follow him. He pointed out three geldings, one grey with a white smudge on its face, another tan from head to tail, and the third as dark as a moonless night sky. The black horse bore a white patch on its chest and one white hoof, the only color marring its pristinely dark coat. Each horse whinnied, stamped their hooves, and shook their manes in various order as the three travelers approached.

"We can part with these three if they suit you," the hand said, patting the black horse on his neck. He pulled a few carrots from a pouch on his belt and fed them to each of the horses, which made them each visibly more settled.

"I thought you said there were no horses for sale?" Týr asked, his brow furrowing as he questioned the sudden change of heart.

"I said that yes. But the master priest jogged my memory."

"I won't allow you to sell us horses that belong to someone else," Joshua said.

"That won't be a problem, sir. The stable's owner, Master Gerald if you know him, has a policy that any horse stabled here can be sold if the owner is behind by two months of payments. These three horses are all well over that time, but very few people buy horses anymore these days. And since you are a priest, I will throw in the saddles and any other accoutrements that you may need for your journey, sir. Let me know what you need, and we will retrieve it for you," the stable hand explained.

"That would be incredibly helpful. Thank you," Joshua replied.

As Joshua, Michael, and Týr picked out their equipment, the stable hands readied the horses quickly, though the creatures were still jittery and excited. Once the horses were ready, the travelers mounted their steeds and worked their way to the nearest gate. Because they were still in the city, they were only allowed to walk the horses by the reins rather than riding in the saddles, especially with the streets more crowded and cluttered with bodies. This made getting out of the city difficult, even though there was only a short distance to travel to the gate and the open road.

Outside the city, open fields stretched to the north and east as far as could be seen; hills rolled in the distance. Northeast of the city, barely visible from this distance, spinneys attempted to form some woods before the trees collected and formed a small, thick forest.

This was the same forest from which Týr and Svenka just traveled in their escape from Lord Dennison and his goonish soldiers. To the south, more plains stretched to the edge of the Erith Bay, a river cutting through the plains toward a quaint village. The river cut south, then aggressively north. The village rested in the crook of the river as it gently broke off toward the east into the woods.

Beyond a few hundred meters, no real roads left Erith, though paths were carved into the grassy plains after years of people wandering to the city, years where horseshoes trampled the grass and the dirt to form packed down trails that marked the paths of long-forgotten travelers. Several of these paths cut through the fields, one heading south to the village. Two bridges spanned the river to the north and south of the village. A few men gathered along the river; they cast their nets into the rushing water as they hoped to catch fish that swam downstream. As the travelers rode through the countryside, Michael wondered what fish were found in the rivers and lakes of Drendil and how much different they were from the fish found in Prikea. Feldring always had lots of pike with the mountains keeping the water frigid throughout the year. Maybe there were pike in Drendil too. What if the fish were different than his home? Could the Madness be spread through the food? That was a question he neither wanted to ask nor to receive an answer to. Especially after that exceptional peppered boar stew.

Groups of deer ran through the grassy plains all around the travelers. They chewed on various plants that couldn't be seen from horseback and looked up at the men thundering by on their horses before they darted off, hopping through the thick grass. They bounded through the grass with ease, venturing toward safety from the humans, though there was little reason for them to fear. Well, maybe they should fear Týr. The man still scared Michael to a point. Týr very openly was a thief until no more than a few days ago. Michael found it hard to trust him, but if Joshua could, Michael figured he should as well.

Since they were out in the open, the group let the horses run. They galloped, then cantered to ensure the horses didn't tire too quickly. This process repeated for a few hours. The travelers chewed through leagues of open ground that day before they finally stopped when they reached the larger portion of the river they saw earlier after it made another bend northward and met with the forest. Týr, as the group settled down and set up their campfire, looked northward into the tree line with sorrow in his eyes. Joshua cast a spell, which sparked the kindling they gathered. As the fire blazed, and they prepared some food, Týr sat beside the fire and explained the last mission he and Svenka went on together. He told in detail of the guards and the large man that Svenka killed. While he told this tale, Týr removed Svenka's knife from his belt, which was the very knife she used to slit Lord Dennison's throat and checked the blade's sharpness. He removed a whetstone from a small oilskin pouch and sharpened the curved blade of the knife, checking its edge periodically. Michael, inspired by this, drew his sword, and checked its edge, but found his sword was sharp enough.

The food cooked quickly on the roaring fire. Joshua divvied out the food to the group; he took less food for himself than he gave to the others, which Michael found odd. He let it slide though, thinking perhaps Joshua just wasn't as hungry at the moment. They sat in silence and ate their food, dried fish that Týr and Svenka purchased the day before, and roasted vegetables. Michael found the food filling, though a little bland. The fish was rather salty, perhaps from the drying process, Michael figured. After eating their dinner, the group settled in for the night they would spend under the stars. Nocturnal birds called from the nearby forest, their hoots and screeches dominating the stillness of the night. Týr perked up at one point and threw a few logs on the fire as it began dying down. By this point, Michael slept soundly with his head propped against his saddle.

"You seem uneasy, Týr," Joshua noted.

"I didn't tell Svenka for fear it might startle her, but I heard something in the woods the night after we left our empty camp. It sounded like a dog, but I've never heard anything natural make those sounds. There is something evil in these woods. I don't know what it is, but it is certainly out there," Týr replied.

"Madness is already starting to spread through the land again," Joshua replied as he looked toward the tree line, silent for a few moments. "Get some rest. I will cast a spell to ward off any predators. It will also alert us if anything gets too close to the camp."

Joshua cast a quick spell, and a dome appeared in the air. The dome shone a bright white that slowly turned clear as it came down to the ground. Once the dome touched the ground, the sounds of the creatures in the woods faded slightly and the camp grew quiet once more. Joshua and Týr fell asleep as the fire picked back up, growing bright as the new logs were consumed by the flames.

The fire burned through the night, and the wood grew into embers then into ashes; the fire popped, sending sparks toward the top of the dome. Columns of smoke rose from the fire, gathering near the top of the dome before dissipating. Outside the dome, creatures stirred in the woods. One such beast, a mixture of a wolf and a man, with more wolf than man, sat perched in a tree and watched the travelers far below. The beast snarled through its wolfish snout and let loose a brief howl, to which two others responded. Their master would want to learn of the travelers. If only the beasts knew how to contact the dark man from another world.

*　　*　　*

Joshua was the first to wake with the first hints of sunlight in the sky. The sky looked grey as the night sky started its exchange with the morning light. Watching the lights change in the sky felt like watching an infinitely great battle between good and evil. In times like this, good always won and evil seceded, regathering for the next battle in the dusk, where the forces of light lost to the overwhelming darkness. Joshua sighed, knowing that such things came in waves and never ended, then opened the small book Timothy gave him. He found himself longing to study every spell the book contained. None of these spells were Dark enough to have been banned by any of the orders, though the Herons reacted so angrily at the existence of the spell book. That remained a perfect reason to Joshua that the priesthood was outdated and needed to adjust to the times. As he studied, he learned spells that would cast a new type of *liquid* fire that could consume stones, another spell that would turn a person to stone like a statue, the dark bolts of lightning that the Vor cast during their battle in Erith, and many others. *These tools might prove useful in our final confrontation with the Vor,* Joshua thought. Several of these would come into great use, he felt, studying the spells further.

Michael and Týr woke up shortly after the sun peeked over the horizon and threw mighty streaks of red, orange, purple, and yellow through the sky far to the east, driving out the darkness that was the night sky. Wisps of clouds captured the colors of the rising sun and reflected them beautifully, adding to the brilliance of the world's fresh start. Each morning brought a reminder that every day was a new day with a new beginning and that, no matter how dark the times just were, there was always room for hope. Though clouds were gathering overhead, none of them appeared large enough to bring any rain that day. Rain would slow their traveling greatly, something they couldn't afford right now.

Týr removed a map from one of the saddlebags on his horse and examined it closely. Once Joshua finished his studies of the spell book, the three travelers consulted the map as they considered the best route for them to take to Shemont. It would be a few days of riding before they arrived, and then they would need at least a few weeks to build trust with the city's guards and the King of Drendil. Without that trust, their mission would fair no better than the goblin attack on Erith.

"What do you know of Shemont?" Michael asked, his voice hopeful.

"Nothing. I was born to a thief and have lived as a thief in and around these woods. I have heard that Shemont used to be a brilliant, dazzling city before the Wars, though now it is supposedly a shell of what it once resembled. Joshua, is there a way to cast a spell and preview the city as we did with the goblins and the Vor?"

"I believe there is a way to see the city without attracting any unwanted attention as we did before, but I cannot promise as clear of a view as we had with the previous spell. It's another one I learned from this book, but I've never cast it before. I don't know what might happen if I get the spell wrong. That happens from time to time. Sometimes the results are fine, other times it's catastrophic. We should prepare to leave before I cast this spell in case we give away our location again. I would hate to end up having to ride away from goblins, let alone the Vor himself. Especially since he travels through portals."

The group cleaned up their camp site, buried the ashes from their fire from the previous night, and readied the horses, all three of which had calmed down since leaving Erith. Michael saddled his horse and Týr helped synch the straps around its belly. Once done, Michael loaded up his saddlebags with the few things he took out of them, then helped Týr get his saddle situated. The saddles were heavy to lift, but they were moved such a short distance it was not much of a burden. The horses stood still as they waited for the saddles to be placed and tightened, showing they were used to being equipped.

Michael removed a small brush from his left saddlebag and brushed his horse while Joshua finished his preparations. The horse whinnied and stamped its hooves as Michael brushed and it leaned into the gentle caress of the fine-haired brush. Once finished, Michael replaced the brush and removed an apple from the right saddlebag, which the horse devoured promptly in only a few bites. With everything else ready, Michael mounted his horse and adjusted his scabbard to his back, where it was most comfortable while riding. Týr also mounted his horse, but his knives stayed right where they were before: scattered across his person on leather straps. The knife he recovered from Svenka remained in the small of his back, the blade facing to his right.

Joshua remained on the ground, as he read the page from the spell book once more. He moved his finger across the words and his lips moved silently as he read. He flipped a few pages, read the new page, flipped back to the previous page, and stopped and looked up at the sky, a confounded look on his face.

"What's wrong, Joshua?" Michael asked.

"I don't know which spell to use. There are two viewing orb spells that I can use, and both mask our location. There seems to be very little difference between the two spells. But there surely has to be something different between them," Joshua replied.

Joshua pondered on this a few minutes longer, gazing at both pages independently and together. Finally, he decided which spell to case and after a small motion of his hands, a small white orb appeared, similar to the one used in the inn's basement. Unlike that orb, no sound came from this orb, and the view was clearer, proving Joshua's theory wrong.

Through the orb, a great city, surrounded by a channel of murky water, spread out north of twin lakes which were separated by a small strip of land. One of the lakes was higher than the other, roughly five meters of land difference between the two. The land that separated the lakes appeared to be a human-made dam. The lower lake was fed by water from the higher lake, which then fed the moat through a channel that also appeared artificial in its appearance.

A large wall ran along the outer edge of the city, and unlike Safdin, the city did not expand beyond the wall and instead was wholly contained within. The stone structure was roughly ten meters high, with towers every hundred meters. The towers, each topped with a parapet, had crossbowmen with their weapons leaning against the stone walls. Guards patrolled the top of the wall, from tower to tower and back. A pair of guards walked between each tower, as they patrolled in opposite directions. They carried lances with the points polished and a red pennant attached to the tops. On the red pennant was a golden griffin, rampant with its mouth opened, fangs showing. The wings of the griffin were spread behind it, folded in slightly.

Inside the wall, the city was divided into sections. One housed a large open marketplace, much like the one Michael saw in his dreams. The market bustled with thousands of people buying and selling goods. Wagons littered the market, likely vendors that lived outside the city and came into the city to sell their wares. One large road let to and from the market, laid out from northwest to southeast. A gate in the wall, set between two of the towers, led to a drawbridge that allowed people and wagons to cross the moat into the city. For a city that was supposedly a shell of its former glory, Shemont appeared quite lively. Perhaps enough time had passed to allow the city to finally recover from the devastation of the wars.

In the north section of the city stood the castle, which rose high above the city, and the separate wall that surrounded it. Pennants flew from towers throughout the castle, the same symbol as seen on the guards' pikes earlier. The white stone of the castle shone brilliantly in the sunlight, reflecting the magnificent rays of golden light. The entire structure appeared like a beacon, guiding the lost to this city. Michael wondered how easily this city welcomed visitors.

South of the castle and west of the market stood an arena; inside the arena, a fight raged. A massive crowd gathered in most of the seats, where they roiled as the fighters tangled with each other. In one of the seats was the king and beside him sat the queen, both looking regal in their stately attire. The king wore an elegant robe, the golden griffin embroidered on the front, with high stockings and black suede slippers, a gold buckle adorning the tops of his feet. Atop his head, the king wore a golden crown made of a simple band decorated with crossed eagle's wings on the front. The wings rose with their tips just touching above his auburn hair, the faintest hint of grey showing in the sunlight. The temples of his hair boasted more grey hairs than any of the rest of his hair. The king's wings of grey seemed to support the crown atop his head.

The queen appeared to be with child, her belly swollen under her loose, bright yellow gown. Her hair, brown in color, was braided twice on each side of her head before it formed one singular braid that she pulled forward over her left shoulder. Her crown, a simple silver band, showed three gems on the front. Two emeralds and a sapphire were set within the silver. The band of her crown rose to a point over her forehead, the gems set in the crest with the sapphire in the middle and the emeralds lower on the sides.

A highly decorated officer stood behind the king and queen, his eyes never resting on the same spot twice. His tabard was the same as the other guards, though his helmet bore a golden crest that stood several hands over the top of his helmet. The officer was armed with a sword, which hung at his left hip, a knife was placed in his belt on his right hip, and a kite shield hung on his back. His face was rough from an unknown number of years of war and fighting. This officer possessed the look of a seasoned military man. His back was straight as an iron rod, his feet spread slightly wider than shoulder-width apart. His hands were clasped in front of him, just below his belt buckle, gold in color.

"Whoever that is, he looks as dangerous as Bruce," Michael said.

"I agree. It makes sense to have the man closest to royalty be so deadly. Likely there were threats against the king and queen with the conflicts that have plagued Drendil," Týr responded.

"Have we seen enough?" Joshua asked, sweat beading on his forehead.

"I think we have seen everything we need," Týr replied.

The orb closed immediately, and Joshua started panting heavily, catching his breath. Casting this spell clearly took more work than the previous orb spell, and he needed a few moments to collect himself before they moved on. Joshua finally climbed into his saddle, ready to leave. The travelers then goaded the horses and continued their journey toward Shemont.

Chapter Thirteen

or'Kath tested his shoulder by moving his arm in circles of various sizes and speeds to ensure the wound healed enough. His shoulder would never be the same again, but he could at least get it close to its previous condition. A dull pain stabbed as he rolled his arm back and forth. *That was a lucky stab,* he thought to himself, thinking back to when the knife plunged into his arm. He had gone a great many years without a mortal wounding him, and this time he was wounded by a *woman* of all the combatants he faced. To avoid being wounded by mortals, he chose to spend very little time in their realms, and the time he did spend in their world made him feel physically sick. He resisted the urge to retch all over the floor. It would be a shame to make a mess on such a nice floor in the Mage's tower.

The tower was magnificent and quite secluded. The previous resident had been a Dark Mage from the Sorcerer's College who met his demise in the dungeon of that wretched school for children. To Vor'Kath, any mortal Mage was a child who yearned for knowledge that was far beyond what they could comprehend. The Assembly of Mages, as they had called themselves, sought out knowledge and power of which they possessed little understanding. Despite that, they made the effort to gain more knowledge in the world of Magic. They even, somehow, learned of the existence of the Vor *and* found a way to contact not one, but two of his clansmen. *Perhaps some mortals hold the potential to be a* real *Mage*, he wondered. That Mage who cast an observing orb showed much potential, even withstanding an attack from a Vor's sword. *That* alone was more than impressive in several ways.

The commandeered tower stood nearly thirty meters high, the tallest structure in the surrounding area. Only the mountains a few kilometers to the north and west were taller. A room at the top housed various plants scattered throughout the room. Despite the owner dying almost four hundred years before, the tower maintained a cleanliness that would be expected of most Mages. This was almost entirely because of the undead servants the Mage employed throughout the tower and its sprawling grounds.

Vor'Kath used his own spells to take over the tower's staff. The poor minions tried to attack him the first time he arrived at the tower, drawn by the spells he could sense within its walls. After he slew a small handful of the servants and claimed the remaining as his own, they ceased their resistance. The remaining servants obeyed dutifully, just as they were ordered to. Funny how they worked for him without question. Now if only he could get the goblins to do the same thing. He was giving the little cretins some freedoms though. Goblins were expendable assets, but the undead? They were much harder to come by in the mortal world. Their stupid bans on the full strength of Magic would prohibit them from experiencing such utilities as these.

Each of the plants growing throughout the tower's laboratory served a purpose. Some bright-colored and flowering plants attracted insects, which would then become food for other insects attracted by other plants. The insects themselves, Vor'Kath believed they were called bees, produced their food, and would sting if they felt threatened. Such interesting creatures they were. These bees were much smaller than the ones he was used to in his own world which were nearly the size of his hand. Some plants were poisonous and could be combined with others to make powerful, deadly poisons. Some cured disease, some healed wounds, others were good sources of food. One plant, dull green in color could be made into a salve that would reduce the aches left over after an injury. This he found odd since the plant's leaves boasted ridges of spikes that stung to the touch, but it was the juice inside their leaves that made the salve useful. After mixing the green plant with a few others into a paste, Vor'Kath made the salve and rubbed that on his shoulder. The salve cooled and tingled as he applied it. The soothing effects continued even after the salve dried on his skin.

Finished dressing his wound, Vor'Kath stepped out onto the balcony that adjoined the laboratory at the top of the tower and quickly surveyed the mortals' realm from his vantage point. He could see a scarce cluster of hills in the distance that turned into the foothills of the Hepmis Mountains that stretched east to west between Erith Bay to the other side of Drendil, effectively cutting the kingdom into pieces. A strand of the mountain range broke off and ran south far to the east of the tower. On the other side of that strand, not that he could see it from his current perch, stretched a vast, dense forest where the hordes of his goblin servants lived when they weren't busy doing his bidding. Those woods belonged to Audro now. Snow covered the peaks of the distant mountains and clouds cascaded over their tops. The clouds brought with them a promise of poor weather. *How delightful*, Vor'Kath thought to himself. Far to the west, the sun was beginning its descent beyond the horizon, throwing streaks of vibrant colors into the sky. Pastels filled the sky and reflected from the clouds over the mountains. *Such a disgusting view.* He despised the colors, not because of his alignment with the evilest force in the universe but because the colors simply sickened him.

Where are those humans? Vor'Kath wondered as he cast a spell that created an orb that showed a view from high above the ground. He could see a vast plain sprawled out west of Shemont, one of the two cities where he sent the goblins to scout. Whether or not the goblins actually went to do any scouting work was hard for him to know for sure. Somehow, they got distracted and attacked Erith after leaving the forest. That was the only reason he joined their fight. He

215

didn't want to get make his presence known in this realm this early, but the goblins forced him to prematurely change his plans. One of the goblins changed course for reasons that he still didn't understand, and the rest simply followed. *Were they a herd of sheep running near a cliff, I would be out a year's worth of wool*, he glowered to himself. The mental faculties of a goblin differed little from those of a sheep in that respect. *What a fool I was, trusting goblins to do* my *bidding*. Now he would have to find more servants to work for him. So many goblins died during that unnecessary battle. But again, they were expendable cretins. He would rather lose a couple thousand goblins to have only killed one human than lose a single werewolf, minotaur, hippogryph, or manticore for the same results. Those beasts were hard to come by even in his own world. Werewolves seemed plentiful enough here in Drendil, though. That was one benefit to the Madness coming back. They were *almost* as expendable as goblins. Almost.

He went back to watching the orb, bringing the view closer to the ground. At the edge of the plains, east of Erith, rose a small forest, much thinner than the woods that occupied the Goblin Coast, and at the edge of the woods, he could see a fire. Someone had set up camp. He moved the orb to get a closer view. There were horses. Three of them. One brown, one grey, one black. As the view came closer to the camp, allowing him to see the faces of these campers, a white sheen appeared, and he suddenly lost his view of the site. *This has to be them. The Mage is quickly learning spells.* What a disappointment that his knowledge was barely going beyond what a child would know in the Vor's homeland.

Vor'Kath stared into the orb a few moments longer, hoping the Mage would drop his protective dome spell as he fell asleep. Since it remained, it clearly showed he learned to anchor his spells, that way he didn't have to hold them in place. *Perhaps this isn't a child Mage I will be dealing with,* Vor'Kath pondered while he continued to watch the camp until the sun finished setting and the sky grew dark. He wondered if this was the older Mage or the bald one who stood up to him in Erith. Soon he would know. Soon.

Chapter Fourteen

arly morning hints of sunlight gently sifted through the trunks of the trees as the sun began its ascent over the horizon far to the east. A gentle breeze rustled the tops of the trees and a few leaves floated away from their branches. Birds sang their trilling songs as the light of morning spread through the trees. Some of the songs were cheerful, as they lilted through the air. Others were gloomy, cawing songs that echoed through the forest. One bird, its feathers the colors of fire, perched itself in the tree above a camp where a pile of smoldering embers in the middle of a clearing surrounded by three men and their horses. The bird, its magnificent coloring that appeared to rival the colors of the sunrise, watched the men as they slept, its head tilting from one side to the other.

To the north and east of the camp rose the human city of Shemont. The tree branches covered much of the view of the city from the camp. Despite this, the white and grey stones of the city's wall could be seen between the trees, but the exact shape was blurred through the branches. A nearby road ran north to Shemont and south toward a range of mountains. This road showed signs of heavy travel, yet there was no one walking or riding down the road this early in the morning. A thick, dark forest stretched for leagues beyond the mountains to the south; it was an old forest with many secrets. It was a forest men feared to traverse.

As one of the men in the camp stirred, the fiery-colored bird perked up and flew away, its wings beating rapidly as it turned south toward the mountains. The man who stirred rubbed the sleep from his eyes, then watched the bird grow smaller as it flew away. Týr was the first of the travelers to rise this morning, and he stretched as he stood up. A series of popping sounds came from his back as he leaned back to stretch. The popping was a welcome, desired sensation. Sleeping on the ground, even with some type of bedroll, was always unbelievably rough on his back. One thing he missed about the thief's camp he lived in most of his life was the cot in his tent. It wasn't much of a bed since it could be disassembled and carried on his back within a matter of moments, but it was more comfortable than the ground. Soon they would be in a city again and that meant, he hoped, having access to a comfortable bed. The less he slept on the ground as he grew older, the better. The inn he and

Svenka stayed in their only night together in Erith had comfortable beds, and Týr missed sleeping in a comfortable bed instead of a cot or on the ground.

Partially sliding them from their sheathes and returning them, Týr checked his knives to ensure they were clear in their scabbards and walked into the trees. They would need some food for breakfast, and something other than songbirds was bound to live among the giants surrounding him. He checked for signs of life and found relatively fresh tracks left by a rabbit. They were less than an hour old, so there was something nearby they could eat. He followed the tracks briefly before he removed one of his throwing knives from his belt. It was a sharp, lightweight knife with a perfectly balanced weight. The blacksmith he stole the knives from was an exceptionally skilled smith. Being a thief didn't mean Týr was entirely devoid of morals, and he wanted to ensure that someday the blacksmith would be repaid for what the knives were worth. They were nice blades and in rare moments like this, he felt a tinge of guilt that such an artisan wasn't paid for such work. The blade of the throwing knife was sharpened on both sides, and the handle had no wood or leather wrappings. There was no need for a wrapped handle when you were throwing a knife. The additional material would throw off the weight of the weapon.

The rabbit circled a tree and crossed its tracks a few times, making the task of tracking the sporadic, furry creature that much harder. It wasn't an impossible task, but it was certainly difficult, and the rabbit was making him work for his food this morning. Týr examined the plethora of tracks left behind and followed the freshest set, perhaps ten minutes old. The rabbit was close, and it would make a good breakfast if he could get it.

Týr crouched and followed the footprints, watching them and the surrounding area at the same time. He twirled the knife in his hands and readied it for flight. The tracks rounded a large oak tree, one of the largest he could see around him. *The rabbit has to be on the other side of the tree*, he thought to himself. *Carefully*. He crept around the tree and watched the ground to ensure he didn't step on any sticks or loose stones that might make sounds and alert his prey. He had skipped putting on his shoes before setting off, and the ground was cool under his bare feet. Dirt slipped between his toes as he moved his feet. He planted a heel, rolled the outside of his foot down onto the ground carefully. Then the ball of his foot. His movement was slow and precise.

On the other side of the tree, Týr saw it. A rabbit. It sat in a small clearing between a few trees as it nibbled on a plant. The stem stuck out from its mouth and slid up as it chewed. Its back faced him, its ears folded down against the back of its neck. It bent down and grabbed another plant, which it promptly pulled from the ground. Some of the roots left the dirt with the rest of the plant. The fur around the rabbit's neck rippled as it ate, the movement of its jaw shaking the rest of its still body.

Týr pulled his right hand back and let the knife fly; the blade rotated in the air and finally pointed toward the rabbit's neck. Its ears flitted as the knife approached and the rabbit began to turn, but the blade planted before it could see the source of the faint noise it detected. The rabbit's body went limp and crumpled onto the ground. Its back legs kicked a few times before they finally settled. *Breakfast*, Týr thought when he grabbed the rabbit's still-warm corpse and removed his knife from the base of its skull. Joshua and Michael would be happy to have something other than dried meat for a change. It wouldn't be so hard to eat as that peppered boar stew the innkeeper served them in Erith. The tubby man used far too much pepper to season the boar, especially when the meat was good quality and would have been fine on its own without any seasoning. Týr wondered how there was any pepper left in the whole city after that man cooked. Back at the camp, Joshua stirred and sat up, wiping his eyes. He blinked repeatedly and looked questioningly at Týr, who proudly held his trophy up by its back feet.

"How did you...actually, never mind. I don't want to know," Joshua began to ask, then dropped his question.

"Can you light the fire while I prepare the rabbit?" Týr asked, removing a knife from his belt, and cutting the feet off the rabbit. Before he could get two feet removed, the fire roared to life. The feet came off the rabbit easily enough, then the rest of the skin had to come off. Tyr made a small incision in the rabbit's pelt and began ripping the flesh as he removed it from the meat underneath. His mouth already watered as he finished skinning the rabbit. With the skin removed, he cleaned the entrails out, which he promptly tossed into the fire. There was little use for rabbit intestines, at least while they were at a camp about to head into a city. The pelt though, he would save. A trader in the city might give him some coin for such a prize. He would have to wash the blood out of the fur, but that was a minor inconvenience. Michael stirred with the warmth of the fire

222

and watched as Týr prepared the rabbit. The flayed carcass was set over the fire to cook, and the meat become crispy on the outside as the flames lapped at the meat.

They left the camp and made their way to the city not long after Týr cooked the rabbit, and everyone got some food in their bellies. There were some potatoes left over from the food he and Svenka purchased in Erith, which went quite well with the roasted rabbit. Rather than riding around the woods, Joshua suggested traveling to the nearby road on foot while they guided the horses, then riding the rest of the way to the city. The trees were too densely packed to ride between them, but not so much that it made it difficult for the horses to navigate behind the humans. The walk through the woods was quick; the road was less than half a kilometer from the camp, and they were out of the woods within an hour. Finally, back to riding, the horses appeared happy as their hooves rang out a quick cadence.

Shemont loomed before them, a large, magnificent-looking city. The wall around the city was imposing but not threatening. Anxiety built in each of the travelers as they approached the drawbridge on the west side of the city, leading into the market area. The men didn't have much time to learn their way around this new city, and they needed to meet with someone important to discuss Michael's premonitions. Joshua hoped that whomever they met with would be perceptive to their mission. The last thing they needed at this point was another obstacle. There had been enough of those along this quest.

As they approached the drawbridge, the halves dropped together to cross the moat, and they joined a line of wagons waiting to cross.

Unlike Dennison's guards outside Erith, the Shemont guards neither searched wagons nor questioned visitors, something for which Týr was thankful. Joshua led the group through the city toward the castle, as each of them hoped they could find whoever would listen to their quest and provide them aid.

Inside the city's wall, the marketplace bustled with hundreds of people who swarmed the vendors for their wares. Shouting and mayhem governed the entire area like in any large city's market. Merchants stood behind their stalls and listened to the cries of their customers. People shouted for fish, vegetables, grains, cloth, and anything else that could be imagined. Prices were negotiated just as loudly as goods were requested. From an outsider's perspective, the market seemed to be pure chaos with no sense of order to any of the madness, yet somehow the vendors and customers found harmony within the pandemonium.

After they worked their way through the city, the group found a stable near the castle where they left the horses. Joshua talked to the stable hand about keeping the horses there temporarily, and they were able to avoid paying a fee for the time being. From the stable they walked to the castle, running into a military officer who directed them to speak with the Master General for a meeting with the king. According to the officer, the men would know him when they saw him. Týr speculated that this was the decorated man they saw through the orb. It was likely this Master General they were on their way to see was the man who was guarding the king and the Queen of Drendil.

An expansive courtyard stretched out before the castle. Pairs of guards stood in various strategic places throughout the courtyard and other pairs patrolled throughout. A column of soldiers, their pikes all shined and polished to reflect the sunlight, marched into the courtyard, and blocked the path of the travelers for a few moments. An officer trailed behind the soldiers, a moderate crest rising from his helmet. He barked movement orders and a cadence to which the soldiers marched. Each of the soldiers in the formation wore leather boots with thick soles and metal plates on the front of their legs. Their heavy shoes created a heavy droning sound as the formation marched along. Once the column of soldiers was in the courtyard, the officer called a halt and the formation took one step, then stopped moving as one unit.

"We should be careful going into a castle as armed as we are," Týr commented, watching the guards cautiously. "Especially if we are requesting an audience with the king."

"If you are this worried, you can leave your weapons in the stable with your horse, Týr," Joshua replied.

"I'll die before parting with any of my weapons," the former thief said.

The travelers moved through the courtyard and toward the stairs which lead into the castle. Six guards stood at the sides of the stairs near the door at the front of the castle. The lances they held, with the points tilted inward toward the center of the wide staircase, created a tunnel of sorts. The guards, eyeing Joshua as the group approached, ignored the travelers as they approached and amazingly none of the guards wavered on their feet. Michael would have thought they were statues except he saw some of them blink. Once inside the castle, a servant ran up to the group, and as he neared them, he bowed deeply.

"Greetings master priest. How may I be of service to you this morning?" the servant inquired as he rose from his bow.

This knowing a priest thing is convenient, Týr thought, admiring the fact he didn't have to sneak into this castle.

"We need to meet with the king at once about an urgent matter," Joshua replied.

"Very well, sir. I would imagine he has some time before heading to the arena for today's festivities," the servant replied, turning around, and guiding the group of travelers toward the king's study. "There is a tournament for the knights this week. The winner of the tournament will win a hunting trip in the Readsoll Forest with the king. It is quite an honor that the knights should be fortunate enough to fight, let alone have a chance to win. Every combatant in the tournament is extremely skilled, and it made for great entertainment so far."

The servant continued talking about the knightly tournament as they walked. The entry hall of the castle where they currently walked was roughly thirty meters from the portcullis to the stairs at the back of the hall, fifteen meters wide, and twelve meters high. The ceiling high above was vaulted like a cathedral with arches that rose to points in the ceiling. Windows of colored glass marked the walls, casting rays of tinted light onto the hall's floor. In the center of the floor, under the travelers' feet, was a plush red carpet marked with golden griffins every few meters. Joshua stepped carefully to

226

avoid treading on the griffins, while Michael and Týr simply walked and looked around the extravagant hall. Pillars rose from the floor to the ceiling at five-meter intervals. Between the pillars were plinths for statues, of which there were three on each side of the carpet. The men and women depicted in stone were regal, powerful people, judging by their depictions, their bodies shown in heroic poses. The men all held swords in various positions, while only one woman held a sword and shield, her face contorted as if she were forever fighting a war with no one else at her side. The servant entered the staircase at the end of the main hall.

After they went up the stairs at the end of the hall, they turned left and walked down another hall, to another spiraling staircase on the right-hand side. The servant walked quickly while still maintaining a comfortable gait. They walked up several flights of spiraling stairs before they arrived in another hallway. This hallway was more subdued than the castle's main hall. The carpet, while still bearing golden griffins—they were every ten meters here—was a more subdued crimson than in the main hall. There also were no windows in this particular passage, the only light being provided by sconces and oil lamps. Several doors stood along the sides of the corridor which were simple without being plain.

At the end of the hallway, the servant entered another spiral staircase and went up one more level before exiting into another hallway where he turned right instead of left. Michael tried to keep track of their movements from what he remembered of the view of the castle as they came through the courtyard, but the twists and turns left him with no idea of where they might be. As far as he was concerned, the group was lost. The current floor seemed to match the previous one with the subdued coloring, light only from sconces and lamps, and carpet that was more plush than in the castle's main hall. The only difference between the two levels was the presence of many additional guards. The previous floor had guards standing to the side of a couple of doors, but here, on this level, guards stood outside most doors with their lances held upright. The guards also carried swords that were sheathed on their left hips. One guard wore his sword on his right hip, which Michael found odd, but not something worth questioning.

The servant guided them to the end of the hall and turned down a conjoining hallway to the left. He stopped outside a door halfway down the hall where two guards waited, as well as a third man, the same man who Joshua, Michael, and Týr saw in the orb a couple of days prior. The servant bowed and presented the guests to the officer. The servant introduced the Master General of Drendil to the guests and promptly left when waved away.

"What business do you have with the king? He is about to leave to watch today's portion of the knights' tournament," the Master General said. He looked the guests up and down and scrutinized their appearance thoroughly.

"We are on an urgent quest, and we have an immediate need to see the king to discuss a matter of grave importance," Joshua explained.

"I get dozens of people coming here every week who claim to have a quest the king must hear. Please tell me why—" the Master General started before the door to his right opened.

"Alwin, are we ready to leave for the arena?" the king asked.

"Your Highness, these men wish to speak with you about an urgent quest. I was just questioning how truly urgent their mission is. We are ready to leave for the tournament unless you want to hear what these men have to say," the Master General said.

"Who are these men and what is their quest, Master General?" the king asked.

"I was in the middle of asking them, sire. I haven't heard any of their stories."

"Well, then let's hear it and *I* shall determine what comes next," the king said.

Joshua very quickly explained everything that had happened to him and Michael since their meeting in Feldring, making sure to give only the necessary details for the king so he could understand their urgency. When talking about the goblins attacking Erith, the king, and the Master General both grew visibly concerned, sharing looks back and forth. The guards standing beside the king's door blinked in concern, though they never reacted beyond that.

"Erith was attacked? This is news to us," Alwin said.

"This sounds like a credible threat, don't you agree, Alwin?" the king asked.

"It does, Highness. I just wonder why this is the first we are hearing of this. Do you have an idea of when this Vor might attack?" the Master General asked.

"Honestly, we have no way of knowing when the attack will happen," Joshua replied.

"What do you need from us?" the king asked.

"As Joshua mentioned before, the premonitions show us all being soldiers guarding the city. I know this may be unorthodox, but maybe we could join the guard to further the timeline of events. I don't even know if that is how any of this works, but it could be worth trying, right?" Michael suggested.

"I didn't sign up for this journey the two of you dragged me on to join the army and guard a city," Týr protested.

"Young man, destiny is often a weight and a series of tasks in which we do not want to partake. Please consider that," the king responded, eyeing Týr. "If the premonition shows that you are soldiers wearing my livery, that may be the only solution for us to defeat this Vor. At least then it would be the entire army fighting at your side instead of a ragtag group of three fighters against such a powerful foe. This may also be the best way to ensure you're all equally and properly trained for using weapons."

"Your Highness, are you sure about this decision? We know so very little of these men. They have suddenly appeared claiming to be on a quest guided by destiny. There is no way for us to know that they aren't agents of Madness here to topple the city or resume the wars. We have come so far, and I would hate to see that progress thrown away on a hunch," Master General Alwin protested.

"Master General, please allow these men to join the army. I will give you until the end of the week to get them enrolled in the required training," the king countered. "Now, if there is nothing else, there is a tournament that is awaiting my arrival."

"As you command, sire," the Master General responded with his fist clapped to his chest as the king departed with the guards in tow.

The Master General motioned for the group to follow him, and they went into one of the rooms not far from where the king exited. The room was a spacious office with shelves, a desk, and two chairs that sat before the desk. The General sat behind the desk and removed a large ledger from the shelf beside him and dipped his quill into a small vial of ink. In the ledger, he recorded the names of his visitors.

"If you truly wish to join the army, your training will begin tomorrow morning at the first bell after sunrise. You will hear six chimes. We will meet in the courtyard here and I will start your evaluation and training process. After that, I will ensure that you get fitted for uniforms and settled into the barracks. The soldiers stay in the northwest quarter of the city, north of the market. Do you have any questions?" Alwin asked, sprinkling very fine sand on the fresh ink to ensure it wouldn't smear.

"General, I have been told that your army employs Mages. Is there any way I can be included or evaluated for that unit?" Joshua asked.

"It's *Master* General, priest," Alwin responded. "And yes, the army has a battalion of Battlemages. You are more than welcome to join their ranks if you qualify for such an undertaking. If there are no other questions, you are dismissed. I will see you bright and early tomorrow to start your training. I will have the Battlemages send the equivalent of a captain for your evaluation tomorrow, priest. I hope this is all to your satisfaction. The Kingdom of Drendil thanks you for your service. I can guide you back out of the castle if you would like."

Together, guided by the Master General, the travelers left the castle, going down the same staircases they went up, and out through the main hall. Once in the main hall, the Master General departed, and the travelers made their way back outside on their own. The formation of soldiers was no longer in the courtyard, having likely marched off somewhere or been sent out on their patrols. After leaving the courtyard, the group found an inn near the stables, ate food, and rested, as they waited for their training to start the next morning.

Chapter Fifteen

The next morning Master General Alwin walked into the courtyard early as he waited for the three newest recruits in his army to arrive for their evaluations. They weren't late, he simply arrived early any chance he got. He made it a point to be early to his engagements. An added bonus for being in the courtyard early was he could watch the officers who conducted their inspections and assignments for the day. As a General, especially as the Master General of the Drendil Army, he was rarely required or expected to interact with brigades of soldiers. A career soldier, Alwin spent the majority of his life serving in the army. As a junior officer, he ran divisions and platoons. Drendil had known peace since the Second Mages' War, but even his grandfather wasn't alive for that engagement. Life as a career soldier who had fought in no wars was different, but thankfully, no one else in the army fought in any wars, so there was no room for judgment from the rest of the troops. Short of all-out wars, there were conflicts and skirmishes soldiers participated in, but those were mostly against monsters or rowdy local lords.

It was rare for him to interact with a junior officer, as his role now was more political and administrative as the head of the military under the king. He was an overseer for the military, the highest-ranking officer in the army. Only two other men in the kingdom held equal rank and they were the Supreme Warlock from the army's Battlemage Legion and Superior Admiral of the Navy. He only dealt with the Army's cadre of Generals, and that was only when they needed something from him that they could not get themselves. Generals were almost always able to get anything they wanted such as equipment or assignments. He could think of a very limited number of times when he needed to get involved in something a General could not handle on their own.

After the formation of soldiers left the courtyard, Alwin removed his sword from its scabbard and practiced against one of the wooden dummies set up in the courtyard. In addition to the dummies, several target bosses were set up for archery practice. The largest boss was roughly a meter in width, made from tightly bound straw backed by thin wood panels that would slow the arrows without breaking them. One of the bosses was a quarter meter in size, placed twenty meters from where the archers were designated to stand.

234

In preparation for the training day, Alwin sharpened and oiled his sword the evening before. He was proud that that was something he still did himself. Some of the Generals had their aides care for their swords, but Alwin still preferred to do some things himself, especially as a career soldier. As the Master General, he didn't often have to worry about things as trivial as fighting with a sword, but he still cared for, trained with, and maintained his weapons as any soldier should. This was something he learned early in his career as a lowly private. His sergeant at the time was adamant about a soldier needing to maintain his weapons.

The blade of his sword struck the dummy repeatedly, and the sharpened edge sliced through the soft wood held together by strands of rope. The dummy moved, to a degree, much like a person would; the arms and legs writhed under the constant attacks. The sword flashed left then right, up then down. It never stabbed, always slashed. Air rushed past the blade, which sounded like a soft, high-pitched whistle, as it swept through the air toward the dummy. Alwin's feet moved gracefully, as if in a dance, left foot here, right foot there. He stepped with grace and speed; He still remembered the forms and routines he learned many years ago as a private in the army. These were things that would be impossible for a career soldier to forget, even after retirement.

As the blade of the sword sunk into the head of the dummy, Alwin noticed the arrival of his newest recruits. They stood a few meters away and watched in varying levels of amazement; the hardened mercenary was impressed, based solely on the briefest glint in his eyes, though no emotions showed on his face. The priest's face was covered by his cowl though visible enough to show he was also awestruck. The third, the former carpenter, stood and gaped at the sight of the performance. Alwin removed his sword from the dummy and returned it to its scabbard. He still thoroughly enjoyed the feeling when his blade slammed home. A Warlock walked out of the castle as the Master General welcomed his recruits. This was the Mage who would test the priest's skills.

"Let's begin your training. Michael, would you like to go first or last?" Alwin asked, returning the Warlock's salute.

"Second, Master General," Michael replied.

"Very well. Týr, please step forward," Alwin called.

*   *   *

Týr stepped forward and clapped his fist to his chest as he saw other soldiers do. The Master General returned the salute and immediately barked orders at the former thief. His voice was rough after a few words as someone like the Master General likely didn't yell orders often.

"Draw your weapons!" he called. Týr removed two knives from his belt.

"Engage the target."

Týr faced the dummy with his knives readied. He had left his cloak in their room at the inn and no longer worried about the lightweight garment getting in his way during the exercise. Some of his other knives were also left behind as well. He only carried two knives and his short sword. Svenka's knife felt comfortable in his hands. The handle was formed to her hand after years of use, but it still felt like it belonged in his own. The leather, now smooth from the long periods of use creaked as he tightened his grip on the knife. He waited for the next order to be called.

"Attack!" the Master General called.

Týr flew into a whirlwind as his blades struck the dummy in the stomach, arms, legs, and what would have been its neck. The knives flashed, struck, and moved quickly. His feet danced about, nearly as graceful as the Master General. They both spent their entire lives in a combative state, but Týr felt he had more kills under his belt than the General. After a quick strike to the stomach, he ducked, spun, and planted his other knife in the dummy's left leg. The blade sank a few centimeters into the wood, the tip of the blade wholly hidden inside the dummy.

"Well done. Now, what can you do with a sword?"

Týr removed his knives from the dummy, sheathed them, then drew his sword and stood at the ready for the command to strike. Once the call came, Týr again flashed at the dummy, as he made sure his sword targeted key areas. Strikes landed on the head, arms, chest, and legs, just as with the knives. Týr danced from side to side, dodged imaginary strikes, and attacked enthusiastically. He ended his dance with an uppercut slice that stuck the blade of his sword in the right armpit of the dummy, just below the rope that connected the arm to the torso.

"You're aggressive, but decent," the Master General called. "We can use soldiers with your fighting skills, especially if we are to take down this Vor. Well done."

*   *   *

Joshua waited for his trials to begin and wondered what spells would be tested. The Warlock revealed a metal ball roughly hand-sized from behind his back and tossed it into the air. As it traveled upward, he called out 'lightning' and Joshua threw a bolt of lightning which struck the orb. Another appeared as the first fell, and the captain called out "ice". As the second orb fell, it was coated in a thick, unnatural frost and the orb shattered when it landed. The original orb flew into the air again, propelled by a simple spell made of air, and the captain called out 'fire' and watched as Joshua cast a fire spell that threw fire that moved as a liquid which cut the orb into two pieces, each piece burning away as it landed on the ground.

"Where did you learn *that* spell?" the Warlock asked.

"I received a book of spells from one of the Heron Priests and this was one of the spells in that book," Joshua answered.

"Bring me the book later," the captain replied. "I am very interested in learning that last spell in particular."

"You're not concerned about the nature of this book? The priests seemed concerned about my possessing it," Joshua said.

"We are less concerned with the zealous priests and their prohibitions. So long as the College is fine with spells, we are as well," the Warlock answered.

"Very well," Joshua said. "I've never encountered a test like this. How does my ability to strike a ball determine aptitude for your unit?"

"It's rather simple," the Warlock replied. "We can talk about that after the last of the evaluations today if you would like."

*   *   *

Michael stepped up to the examination area when the order came. His heart, beating like a timpani drum, sounding like it was in his ears. His hands shook and his knees trembled slightly. His breathing was shallow and fast, and he tried to take deep breaths to calm himself. He thought back to his time training on the boat and the stances and motions he learned from the sailors. *Be the sword*, he thought to himself, *the sword is an extension of your arm.* The sailors' voices echoed in his head between the heavy pounding of his heart. Everything in his life that happened up to this point now rested on this test and his ability to fight a fake, wooden man with the sword in his hands. His breaths came faster now. Waiting for the Master General to start calling commands felt like an entire lifetime passed. Everything around him slowed down. The dummy, which still wiggled from Týr's test, moved slower. The sound of his heart thumping in his ears slowed to where it felt like minutes passed between each beat. Even his breathing felt slower somehow, even though he knew he breathed faster than normal.

He heard the first call. Even though the Master General barked the orders as he had for Týr, the words slowed, leaving the Master General's mouth so slowly that it felt like each letter was being sent to Michael's ears individually. He emptied his mind and felt his right hand grasp the handle of his sword, drawing it from the scabbard that hung at his left hip. The blade slid from its sheath with ease, the scrape of the sword against the metal gate at the end of the scabbard rang in his ears as time slowed down. He knew the next command was coming, but there was no telling when it would—

"Strike!" the Master General called.

Michael moved his left foot forward and to the left slightly; the sword came down, swinging from the left to the right, the tip of the sword whistled as it sliced through the air on its path toward the dummy. He felt resistance as the blade contacted the wood and slid through the outside of the dummy's chest. His right foot slid toward his left foot and brought the sword back to his target. He missed the chest and struck the right arm. Michael winced as he saw that he missed a strike. He felt like he could see the sword moving as if time suddenly crawled.

Michael's right foot, planted shoulder-width apart, moved toward the dummy. He brought the sword back, pointing the blade to the ground, and threw his shoulder into his wooden enemy, which made the whole wooden man bounce before Michael spun to his left. His sword swung with him, and the blade became lodged in the dummy's back, midway up. The dummy jolted as the blade connected and stopped.

*   *   *

"That's plenty, Michael," Alwin said, ending the test. "You are more skilled than I expected, given your background. Warlock, have you concluded your testing?"

"I have, Master General. Joshua will make a wonderful addition to the Battlemage Legion," the Warlock replied.

"Very well. You may go with him to assign him any necessary equipment. Týr," Alwin said, as the Warlock saluted once more before leaving, "I can have you assigned to a special unit that I will discuss further with you, behind closed doors, if you are interested. You will still be in the army, but there aren't uniforms involved, and you would not be on patrol duty. What do you think about this possibility?"

"I would have to hear more details but, I'm interested already," Týr replied.

"Very well. Michael, your skills are adequate to be successful in the army. Unfortunately, because of your rudimentary skills and other opportunities not being available, I cannot offer you anything more than a standard guard position for the time being. This does mean you can get all of the training you'll need if you're going to fight something as dangerous as a Vor. I've not fought one myself,

241

but I read the history texts from the First Mages' War when Vors fought alongside the Dark Mages. What do you say?"

"I accept, Master General. When do I start training?" Michael asked.

"Training will start tomorrow here in the courtyard. Now, I need both of you to come with me, please," Alwin replied as he led the two to his office to discuss details about their assignments.

*   *   *

"Týr, I have an unofficial unit that handles…*special* assignments that the king does not want to be attributed to the kingdom or our military that I think you would be a good fit for, for now. They could use someone with your fighting style, and your taste in weaponry," the Master General said as he pulled his chair out from under his desk and sat down. He opened a small, plain wooden box on his desk and removed a pipe and a small leather pouch with tobacco.

"What types of missions are involved with this special unit?" Týr asked, breathing in the sweet smell of the pipe smoke.

"The missions range from disrupting supplies to assassinating a myriad of targets who threaten the kingdom."

"When I'm not actively on a mission doing those things, what will I be doing for you?" Týr asked. His interest had certainly been piqued.

"You will spend time in Shemont or the surrounding areas, looking for threats to our kingdom. You will report to me once a week with your findings, or more frequently if you find something drastic."

"What dangers would require more frequent meetings?"

"Recently we discovered a den of werewolves living in one of the forests not far from here. Supply wagons go through that forest, so that was a threat that needed to be dealt with immediately. This unit can arm its soldiers with specialty weapons when the need dictates," the Master General replied flatly.

"I accept this assignment. When do I start?" Týr asked.

"I can have you meet with the unit's captain tomorrow morning. Be here, this time tomorrow outside my office. We will discuss your assignments further at that time."

"What will my assignment entail, Master General?" Michael asked.

"You will be part of the regular army, patrolling as a guard while you are in garrison. And unless we go to war or have someone attack the city, you will be in garrison. Your sergeant will be able to provide you with the specifics about your assignment. You will meet him tomorrow morning in the courtyard when you start your training," the Master General replied, puffing on his pipe.

Chapter Sixteen

…Nearly a year later…

Michael woke up in his barracks room, just the same as he had for quite a while now. It was a simple but cozy room, large enough for sleeping and enjoying a day off when one of those came along, but little else. The room contained a bed and a desk, in addition to an armor stand, a weapon rack, and a wardrobe. The furniture was spartan at best, covered in a dark wood-tone varnish so it shone slightly in the light of the single oil lamp he was permitted to have in the room. A crimson rug covered most of the wooden floor, the golden griffin centered in the rug. Every guard living in the barracks had the same furnishings. This ensured that life felt equal to everyone.

The rug felt soft against Michael's bare feet. Despite looking old and worn, the rug was still plush. He stood beside his bed, stretched, then started putting on his armor. A cotton shirt and thick pants first, then the chainmail. Over the chainmail went the tabard, crimson with the king's golden griffin, just as everything else he wore. Stiff leather greaves covered his legs and matching pauldrons covered his shoulders. He then put on the leather bracers and finally his helmet. After enough practice, Michael smoothed the process of putting on his armor down to about half an hour. Now, the only things missing from his uniform were his sword and belt. Those always went on last with the leather belt cinching the tabard close to his waist.

With his uniform on, Michael left his room and walked down the narrow hallway to the stairs at the end of the hall. To leave the building, he went down two flights of stairs then doubled back down two hallways. Plain wood doors that matched the quality of the furniture lined both sides of each hallway. On Michael's floor the doors were painted green, on the next floor up they were blue, and the floor below had gold doors.

For the most part, Michael enjoyed his time in the army. Within six months of completing training, the captain promoted him to corporal and immediately assigned Michael a squad of guards to watch over. Leadership, while rewarding, came with its own heavy price. Michael had noticed, some time ago, the presence of more grey hairs, and his face showed creases on the sides of his mouth and around his eyes. The grey in his hair existed before, but the subtlety of that color faded as he led his soldiers. After another few months, he was ready to be promoted to sergeant, something that

245

was not expected for anyone so new to the army. His promotion ceremony was scheduled for that afternoon. With the promotion would come a new assignment, a whole platoon. Michael felt excited for the new assignment, but also some anxiety about having so many guards to look after. The next step would be lieutenant, though that would require serious dedication and experience. Not every sergeant was promoted to the officer ranks, and for good reason.

Neither Týr nor Michael saw much of Joshua since he was assigned to the Battlemages. They kept to themselves in a tower on the other side of the castle and rarely did anyone visit them. Even though they were in the same army, soldiers seemed wary, to say the least, of the Battlemages. Something about Magic was still unnerving to the Drendillians as a whole. A letter arrived the day before, under Michael's door, saying that, if at all possible, Joshua would be at the ceremony today. It would be nice to see the priest again. Michael wasn't sure if they could even call him a priest anymore, as he had little involvement with anything to do with the priesthood since the goblin attack in Erith.

Týr was now within the guard regiment instead of the special unit that didn't exist. When Michael asked, Týr said it was something about an assignment that went wrong but learned nothing more. Michael didn't press the subject, as he could tell that Týr was upset about losing his special assignment. The reassignment only happened a few weeks before, so the hurt was still incredibly fresh. Now that he was in the regular army, Týr patrolled the streets like other garrisoned soldiers. He was also being promoted to sergeant in the afternoon alongside Michael, though Týr's was more of a formality than Michael's promotion. While serving with the special mission unit, he was paid as a sergeant at the same time that Michael was promoted to corporal. Now the ceremony was simply to ensure he wore the correct uniform. Týr would also have a platoon assigned to him that afternoon, though rumors said he would be getting an evening shift platoon. Týr seemed to be a person that preferred nights to the day, anyway.

Michael opened the door and stepped outside. The day was already bright and sunny, an omen for a hot day. The cooler autumn weather started a week earlier, but then it warmed up again as summer fought to cling to the world. This was something Michael found strange. Back in Feldring, as winter approached and the cold was once again offered a chance to cling to the world like a wet shirt, nothing seemed capable of breaking its grasp. On top of the sudden shift in the weather, any day spent wearing armor and walking the streets was warm, but today would be especially hot. Only a few clouds floated in the sky; shade would only come from the buildings in the city. Thankfully, Michael would only have to stay in the guardhouse for the day and report any findings the patrols found to the shift captain. It would be a slow day while he waited for the promotion ceremony.

*   *   *

Michael walked up to the guardhouse to relieve the previous guard. He was early getting here, by a little less than a half hour, but he made it a point to relieve guards early. This was a principle that many guards didn't hold. Even with as early as he was, it would still take at least ten minutes for the turnover with the previous guard. Walking in, Michael saw the man asleep at the desk. He lounged in the chair with his arms folded over his chest, and feet propped up on the desk, one crossed over the other. Careful not to wake the man prematurely, Michael examined the ledger that sat under the guard's right heel. He failed to log three hours of activity! *This will be fun.*

Michael looked at the guard again, making sure nothing was behind him that would injure the man, and placed some extra weight on the back of the leaning chair. The fact that the guard could sleep in a chair that was leaning without falling over was impressive, but not nearly as much as staying awake while on duty. The extra weight on the back of the chair was just enough to hurtle the chair toward the ground. Michael hoped that the fall startled the guard in the process. A little fright might teach him to stay awake during his shifts.

"Are you *fucking* mental?" the guard shouted, darting to his feet. "You almost killed me."

"You were sleeping on duty, *and* you failed to log the last three hours of patrol notices. I should report you to the lieutenant," Michael stated. *Let's see what he thinks of that.*

"You report me for sleeping and I will report you for almost killing me. You aren't promoted yet, Michael," the guard protested.

"And how, exactly, did he almost kill you, private?" a gruff voice called from the back room of the guardhouse.

Michael and the guard snapped their feet together and clapped their fists to their chests as the Captain of the Guard walked out from the back room. The captain was a bull of a man who easily weighed over one hundred kilograms, mostly from muscle. Being a captain, he warranted more protection than most guards, and as such wore iron plate armor instead of the leather and chainmail that those at the rank of sergeant or below wore.

"I'm waiting for an answer, private," the captain snapped.

"Sir, I'm a corporal. I don't understand why you're—" the guard replied, his voice creaking as he spoke as if he were still maturing and too young to be in the army. Michael chuckled to himself about that.

"No, you're not. This is the third time you have been caught sleeping on duty in the past month, and I've had enough of it! If this were up to me, you would be out of the army. Turn over your watch to the corporal and then come with me, *Private*," the captain snarled.

The door slammed behind the captain as he stormed out of the guardhouse, which left Michael alone with the guard. An initially heated glance shot from the guard before the realization that it wasn't Michael's fault set in. They quickly went through everything that happened so far that day, excluding the three hours missing in the ledger, and Michael soon assumed responsibility for the guardhouse.

Within fifteen minutes of the other guard leaving, another pair entered the guardhouse and reported that everything was normal on the streets. This required a simple entry to be made in the ledger. 'Patrol seven reports a normal status.' Michael suspected the next four hours would go exactly like this. Most days in Shemont were quiet, but Michael wouldn't change that for anything. Especially knowing the abnormal day that would eventually strike the city. The city would hurt enough whenever the Vor attacked. Michael wanted to talk with Joshua about that today after the ceremony. *Hopefully, he can make it*, Michael thought to himself as he continued to read through the previous day's entries in the guardhouse ledger.

* * *

"And by the authority granted to me by the King of Drendil, I hereby promote you to the rank of sergeant," the Captain of the Guard called out, his gravelly voice loud enough for those gathered to hear the proclamation. All the promotions were done in the castle's courtyard. This allowed the king the opportunity to appear if he wished, despite how uncommon an occurrence that happened to be. The king was quite busy, after all, and there were a lot of guards and promotions. It would be unrealistic for anyone to expect one man, let alone the ruler of a kingdom, to show up for thousands of promotion ceremonies. Even were the promotions held in the king's study, no one would be upset if he were unable to attend.

The small group of assembled guards clapped at the end of the ceremony. Michael and Týr turned to each other and clapped their hands together with a brief embrace. The captain called the group of soldiers to attention, and the men all snapped tall with their hands at their sides. He then dismissed the gathered soldiers who appeared more thankful to be done standing around the courtyard than anything else. Once the crowd dispersed, the captain turned to Michael and Týr and smiled and shook their hands individually. His hands were large enough he could shake both simultaneously, but he wanted his congratulations to be unique.

"You are both very deserving of this. Continue what you are doing, and you will surely be lieutenants in no time," the captain said. "I haven't seen anyone make sergeant with only a year in the army in quite some time. And the way you surprised that guard earlier was quite well-done."

"Thank you, captain. It's not that hard to stay awake while on duty. I was just outraged that it happened, more than anything," Michael said.

"What happened?" Týr asked, his curiosity piqued. Michael filled him in on what had happened in the guardhouse and Týr laughed raucously at the private's expense.

"I heard the Master General say he wished to speak with both of you today. Stop by his office when you leave here."

"Yes, sir," Michael and Týr answered in unison as they clapped their fists to their chests.

The captain turned and left the two sergeants alone. A doorway opened in the air behind them, and they turned, Týr with his hand on his knife, ready in case it was bad news coming through the door. Joshua stepped through the doorway, his Mage's robes flowing in the air as he walked. He clasped their hands, Michael first, then Týr, congratulating both on their promotion.

"I know I haven't spoken to you both much since we received our first assignments. I have some news that we need to discuss with the Master General," Joshua said.

"We actually need to see the Master General apparently," Týr said.

"Yes, I spoke with him yesterday and told him I have findings that involve all three of us. We shouldn't discuss more until we are in his office. Let's go," Joshua said, heading toward the gate of the castle.

*   *   *

Joshua knocked on the Master General's door and opened it when prompted. The Master General sat at his desk, smoke rising from the pipe in his hand, and read a small book. The cover of the book was dark leather with gold lettering and decorations. The lettering mentioned something about the tactics involved in war, but Michael wasn't able to clearly read the cover fast enough. The Master General set the book and his pipe down as he leaned forward to give his guests his full attention.

"You wanted to speak with me, Mage?"

"Yes, sir. I have made a discovery about the Vor. We believe he is recruiting monsters into an army, though I don't know where he is amassing this force. They aren't in our world that much I do know," Joshua said.

"What kinds of monsters?"

"What I've seen includes goblins, minotaurs, at least one manticore, and a few dozen werewolves. I saw other creatures, but their descriptions aren't within the records that we maintain among the priesthood or the Battlemages. I do know they are dark creatures that have no purpose or reason for living beyond death and destruction," Joshua replied.

"So, the Vor is amassing an army of monsters. What do you assume comes next? I would assume the only reason to gather an army is to attack," the Master General said.

"That is my assumption as well. Since he is gathering his forces, I would say there are two options: draw him out and attempt to defeat him before he gets his full army amassed or wait for him to attack when he is ready, whenever that may actually end up taking place. Personally, I don't think waiting for him is the best solution as he will be able to gather enough strength to level the city, or whatever action achieves his ultimate goal," Joshua replied.

"How would you draw him out without bringing his army with him? I don't want to leave an army of monsters alive, nor do I want to threaten the citizens' lives at the hand of monsters. Could we get our forces together and go after him before he has the chance to attack us?"

"Without knowing which world the monsters are in, it's hard to tell whether we would even survive in that realm," Joshua replied.

"So, what do you suggest, Mage?" the Master General asked, taking a deep drag from his pipe, and blowing the smoke toward the ceiling.

"There is something we can do to try to draw the Vor out of his hiding place, but those spells are dangerous and volatile. Do you remember hearing about the goblins attacking Erith about a year ago? We, well I, cast a spell where we could observe the Vor and that drew his attention to us, and he sent his goblins to attack Erith, rather than doing whatever else they were supposed to be doing. I would hate to put Shemont under such risk."

"It seems like we can't do anything but let him amass more of an army while we do nothing," the Master General countered, once again blowing wispy blue-grey clouds into the ceiling where they roiled and dissipated.

"I'm not suggesting we do nothing; I'm simply saying that we can't do anything without Shemont being ready for an attack. How quickly can the army be readied?" Joshua asked.

"The army should be ready and briefed on their assignments, if necessary, within a day. This time tomorrow the city would be able to withstand any assault the Vor can throw our way," the Master General replied.

"Sir, can you make that call?" Týr asked.

The Master General sat at his desk and thought while he continued to smoke his pipe for a few moments. He leaned back into his chair and puffed thoughtfully at his pipe. He closed his eyes and inhaled deeply, clearly thinking of alternatives to the situation Joshua had laid out for him. There must be a possibility other than drawing an army of monsters into one of the kingdom's capital cities and risking an unnecessary loss of life. Something that wouldn't put thousands of innocent people in danger. Erith was still recovering, and being independent from the Kingdom of Drendil, their army was already weaker. Their constant dealings with Lord Dennison, who went rogue from the king's authority, wore their soldiers down to the point of inability. Unfortunately, the goblin attack came too soon after Dennison was dispatched for Erith to recover their garrison.

"What are you going to do?" he asked finally.

"This isn't the only Vor out there. There is an entire world full of them, and I wish to summon another of his clansmen, trap it, and find out where our adversary resides, and what his mission is," Joshua replied.

"You want to do *what*? Have you gone mad?" the Master General asked, sitting up straighter, if that were at all possible.

"I believe that getting another Vor to talk with us is going to give us enough insight to set traps for our target so we can control him and his forces, rather than being surprised by his assault and losing the city. We have to plan for what he will do, rather than simply react to what he is already doing when he attacks," Joshua suggested.

"This doesn't sound like something I can approve, Mage. The king will have to make the final say on something this *obtuse*," the Master General mocked, his face contorted.

"Sir, you have to believe that I wouldn't have suggested this if there were any other options. But I have a plan that involves other

Mages. We can trap the summoned Vor and ensure it can't do anything while in our realm," Joshua asserted.

"This still has to go before the king. This is his city, not mine. Who knows, perhaps the king will be more easily convinced that this isn't a completely asinine idea. This would never be allowed if I could make that decision. I don't care how large of an army the Vor is pulling together," the Master General stated. "I will go see if the king has time to hear this ridiculous plan of yours, Mage."

*   *   *

"Mage, what *exactly* is it you plan to do after summoning another Shadow Knight to our world? Do we not have enough problems with the one that you have to defeat? I am having a hard time seeing how this plan is going to save the world," the king articulated.

"From my understanding, not everyone in the Vor Clan is a Shadow Knight in the same sense as the ones who are chaotic in their missions. But to ensure that we don't bring another chaotic Vor into our world without restrictions, I will cast a spell that turns the summoned Vor into a statue. Once I have done that, we can remove some of that effect and talk with our summoned captive. This is the only solution I can think of to find further information for our quest," Joshua appealed.

"How many Mages do you need to accomplish this? And how many soldiers do you need on standby?" the king inquired.

"I only need five other Mages, and perhaps a platoon of soldiers. Any more than that would be unnecessary for our purposes," Joshua clarified.

The king was silent for several moments before deciding. "Fine."

Chapter Seventeen

The next day a platoon of soldiers and six Mages gathered in the castle's courtyard. Joshua spoke with the Mages. He decided not to walk them through his plan until right before it happened. While Joshua did that, Michael and Týr briefed the soldiers of their role in the process. The soldiers would form a protective ring around the Mages, their pikes and lances pointed toward the center of the circle. The Mages would join their spells together and summon the Vor under Joshua's direction. If anything went south, the soldiers would intervene while the Mages were busy with their casting.

Both the king and the Master General stood in the courtyard, surrounded by an entourage of guards between them and the ritual site. The Master General lectured the guards on strictly protecting the king at all costs. At least three times he reminded them that their lives hinged on the king not being harmed if anything went wrong with the spellcasters. Obviously, the king's guard would protect the king with their lives, but Alwin still felt it was still necessary to clarify the point. Heads would roll if anything happened to the king.

Joshua verified with the Mages that they were ready and next checked with Michael and Týr regarding the soldiers. Finally, he spoke with the king to ensure they were ready for everything to commence. With everyone ready, the ritual began. The Mages cast spells together, joining their casting with Joshua, who took control of the ritual. As he cast the spell, a dark doorway opened in the middle of the circle; the edges of the doorway were jagged and shimmering, unlike the one Joshua used the day before. The entrance to another world shone like a mirror, the front, facing the group and showing nothing on the other side. A face appeared in the doorway. The face was beyond pleasant to gaze upon, gentle in its appearance.

"Why have you summoned me?" the face demanded, its voice booming as it spoke.

Joshua cast another spell and the face shrieked as it and a body were pulled through the surface of the portal. It closed immediately upon the Vor exiting. The instant the Vor touched the ground, removed from her realm, she instantly started turning to stone. The transformation stopped at the back of her head and just below the jaw, leaving her face clear of the stone.

The Vor was tall and slender, almost willowy. Her face was no less gentle outside of the mirror-like doorway, though her hair was visible now, flowing freely. Her hair was long, reaching nearly to her thin waist. Despite her soft appearance, something about the Vor seemed lethal. Were she not encased in stone, this situation would likely have been a disaster.

"Clearly, you are stronger than we anticipated, chaining your spells as you have. What do you seek from me? Do you wish for power you cannot begin to fathom? Perhaps it is riches you seek. I can satisfy all of your deepest desires. Release me from this prison you have created, and whatever you desire is yours," the Vor appealed. With her body outside of the doorway, her voice still boomed, but less distorted. An echo came from somewhere, sounding like she spoke with two voices instead of just one.

"We actually only require information from you," Joshua clarified.

"I will give you five questions. Ask carefully, as I am under no obligation to tell you anything, let alone the truth," the Vor cautioned.

"There is a Vor in our realm who threatens to descend our world into chaos. What is his purpose here?"

"You have both asked and answered your question. You have four questions remaining."

"What is his name?" Joshua inquired.

"Vor'Kath, though that information changes nothing of your mission to destroy him, I believe."

"Where is he hiding the army that he has formed?"

"He is hiding them in our plane of existence, though again I believe that doesn't help you," the Vor replied. "You have two questions remaining."

"When will he send his army against our plane?"

"It will be in the future. I know not enough of his plans to say more specifically," the Vor claimed. "There is one question left."

"If we cannot kill him, is there a way to prevent him from being a problem?" Joshua asked after a pause.

"What you are doing to me seems effective. I would rather be dead than a statue, though I imagine you would rather not have a statue of Vor'Kath standing in the middle of your city. There is an island northwest of your city where dark rituals take place. That island is the source of what you call 'Madness' and would be a fitting prison for him. Study the book you received in Erith, and you shall find the spell needed to snare him to that island if you should so desire that outcome," the Vor stated.

Joshua opened the doorway once again and began withdrawing the stone from the Vor's body slowly. When the creature's arms were freed from the stone Joshua put the Vor back in the doorway, returning her once more to her own world.

"I wish you well against Vor'Kath. He is a force of destruction, even within our realm. Please, ensure he does not return to us," the Vor pleaded; her voice boomed once again from beyond the mirrored portal.

"Before you go, allow me to ask one final question."

"Since you returned me promptly, yes, you may ask one final question," the Vor granted.

"Is Vor'Kath stronger or weaker than you?" Joshua inquired.

"He had grown strong with the power from his ally. His nature as part of the Vor clan is not this chaotic. He has aligned himself with a power that is unknown to us. Be wary facing off against Vor'Kath, as his fall might draw his ally from the shadows," the Vor cautioned.

"Thank you for answering our questions."

"We will be watching your progress. Farewell, traveler."

The Vor left the view of the doorway which promptly disappeared. As the mirrored door closed, the Mages unlinked their spells from each other. With the threat removed, the guards relaxed, raising their pikes, and leaving their ring formation. The Master General dismissed the guards around the king, who approached Joshua to discuss the ritual. The king had a curious look on his face.

"It sounds like we learned nothing from that ritual. What will you do with what little information you gained from this, Mage?" the king inquired.

"Now that we know the Vor's name, I can begin reading through texts to see what, if anything, is known about him specifically. Also, the Vor said his powers came from a powerful entity, and I can research his powers to try and find who gave him those powers. If we can find the source of the power, we can learn his weakness and how to defeat him," Joshua reasoned.

"What if his powerful ally comes after us for disrupting whatever plans might be in place?"

"Your Highness, I believe that is a risk we must take in this instance. Whatever Vor'Kath is planning must be countered or we could lose the world to Madness, as I've explained to nearly everyone throughout this quest. I mean no disrespect, saying this, Highness," Joshua explained.

"Mage, I sense urgency, not disrespect. Be cautious of your tone in the future," the king said. "So, you have to research more now? Will you need any additional resources for that?"

"No, sire, I will be fine researching on my own," Joshua reassured.

"How much time will you need for the research?"

"It's difficult to put an exact time on this, but it will take at least a few months, if not longer."

"I will grant you the time you need for this, provided you can find what is necessary to stop this threat. I want you to report directly to me and the Master General in three months with an update. All three of you," the king demanded.

"Thank you, your Majesty. I will get to work on this right away," Joshua assured.

*   *   *

After the king, Master General, Mages, and soldiers left the courtyard, Joshua stayed behind to speak with Týr and Michael about their findings. Because of the promotion ceremony, Michael and Týr earned this day and the next day off to rest and get their new uniforms situated. This meant they would have plenty of time to catch up with Joshua, something all three wanted a chance to do.

The group headed to a pub not far from the castle. The Dwarven Cave was relatively new and was primarily used by soldiers to have a place to unwind after their shifts. Morale among the soldiers had risen drastically since the pub opened a few months prior, something the Master General appreciated. Concerns of morale issues always ended in large stacks on his desk.

Inside the pub was dim, even in the middle of the afternoon. A few oil lamps provided enough light to see the menu the owner brought them, notice when drinks ran low enough to get more, and not much else. Few ever actually wanted to see the food they were eating at a pub, as it was only appealing to an ale-soaked stomach. The soldiers didn't complain about the food, out of fear that the food would go away. Despite grumbling about the quality of the food, no one wanted to patronize a pub that served only drinks, and it was nice to have something other than their typical rations every so often.

Týr sat against the wall, which gave him the best view of the whole pub. Michael sat to the right and Joshua sat to the left. One of the pub maidens brought three tankards filled with lager to the table, already sure of what the two sergeants wanted. She correctly assumed the Mage would drink the same thing. After downing the first tankard quickly, the group finally started talking. Before long, they filled the table with empty tankards, and the light coming in through the front windows of the pub diminished severely as night fell upon the world.

Shortly after their fifth lager, the same barmaid brought over trays of fried fish and potatoes, one of the staples on the menu. The three soldiers wolfed down the greasy fish and potatoes, feeling weariness setting in as they started another round of drinks. The beer was good, cold, and frothy, something they were all thankful for as nothing could ruin quite a day like a warm, flat beer.

When the group finally left the pub, they staggered into the street. Michael stopped walking and, wavering, looked around to get his bearings. He knew he lived in the barracks, which should be…west…of the pub, though he didn't remember which way was west. Or east. Right as he started stumbling toward a building, he hoped was his barracks, Joshua had an idea.

"Why don't I make a portal for you to get to your barracks?" Joshua suggested.

"That would be great," Michael replied through hiccups.

"Describe your room for me," Joshua requested.

Michael described his room, but because every barracks room looked the same, Joshua couldn't picture the specific room enough to create a portal. Finally, Týr said he could make sure Michael got home safely, guiding Michael toward the correct building. Michael staggered behind Týr, following his guide as best he could before finally reach his room and falling into his bed with his armor still on. He groaned, feeling his sword hilt jammed into his stomach underneath him. Sitting up awkwardly, he removed his sword and belt, placing them on the floor and lying back in bed. Darkness descended as his eyes snapped shut now that he was in the comfort of his bed. Just as he had every night for so long, Michael slept with the same nightmare that haunted his sleep, wishing that someday soon the nightmares would fade away.

Chapter Eighteen

...About six months later...

Joshua, Michael, and Týr stood outside the king's office for their upcoming quarterly update. Inside his office, the king shouted at someone, the sound of screaming bleeding through the door. The guards to either side of the door shared a sidelong glance between themselves, their eyes wider than normal. What the king was yelling about couldn't be heard, but his voice carried a heat and fury that none standing in the hallway wished to receive themselves.

The Master General's door cracked open, and the man stuck his head into the hallway. He whispered down to the trio standing outside the king's office and told them to wait inside his office while the king continued his tirade. Clearly, they didn't need to know the identity of whomever was the target of the king's ire. The trio quickly made their way to the Master General's office. Michael and Joshua sat while Týr stood beside the closed door.

"I didn't think it appropriate to have you listen to the king yelling at anyone. Do you have an update for His Highness?" the Master General inquired.

"I do have an update, but I feel it best to wait before we are in front of the king to only relay the news once. I apologize, Master General," Joshua stated.

"There's no reason to apologize, Mage," the Master General reassured, tapping the ashes from his pipe.

"Thank you, Master General."

*   *   *

"I understand you have an update for me," the king stated, his voice a touch raspy from the yelling earlier.

"Yes, Highness. From my reading, I believe that Vor'Kath has aligned himself, more than likely, with a being of the Shadows known as Kalathan. The power of dark lightning, teleportation without the use of portals, and several other powers he acquired all are tied to Kalathan in one way or another," Joshua averred.

"What does this mean to us?" the Master General inquired.

"It potentially means two things: Vor'Kath is much stronger than I anticipated, and he might also be capable of resurrecting himself from the Shadow Realm. If he *can* resurrect himself, that means killing him is not an option for removing him as a threat."

"How can that be possible?" the king asked.

"I thought the same thing when I originally stumbled across this information, but it seems that Vor'Kath has been encountered in the past, though I don't know exactly when. I speculate it might have been part of the First Mages' War. From everything that I've read, his body was destroyed, but later he returned as if having never been wounded. There is concerningly little documentation available on this topic beyond that, I'm afraid," Joshua clarified. "The only documents available are wildly speculative but this is something they all seem to agree on."

"How do we combat the potential for resurrection? I need to make sure my kingdom and her citizens remain safe."

"I completely understand your concerns, Highness. I have found a series of spells that will help us to bind Vor'Kath to an island, as recommended by the Vor we questioned. As she told me, there is an island north and west of here that has been overrun by the Madness that, I believe, Kalathan started in this world. It shouldn't be a problem for us to trap him on that island and imprison him there. From that point, we would just have to maintain the prison spell to prevent his escape. Now, the hard part is actually casting the spell. This is not a spell that one Mage alone can cast no matter how strong they may be with Magic. It requires ten Mages casting in unison, or it will fail," Joshua mentioned.

269

"I knew you would try to find a way to not kill the bastard," Týr scoffed mostly under his breath.

"What's that, sergeant?" the king inquired.

"Sorry, Highness. I just don't think that we should show mercy to this monster. He and his goblins decimated Erith in an afternoon. He killed my sister. He is amassing an army the size of which only the Allfather alone knows. Now instead of killing him, we are looking at letting him live," Týr replied.

"I agree that death would be the best solution, but if he can bring himself back from the dead—" the king started to say when he was cut off.

"We don't know that he can do that, Highness. This is all speculation," Týr said.

"Cut me off again, and you will see what else is speculation, sergeant. Do not test my patience again," the king growled.

"I'm sorry, Highness. I just am not fully on board with this plan," Týr explained.

"This plan sounds risky. What would you need from us?" the Master General inquired.

"I simply need nine strong Mages who will need to learn the spell with me, and a squad of Mages to keep us safe when this battle happens. Also…" Joshua started, then trailed off.

"Out with it, Mage," the king demanded.

"I have been examining a map of Shemont in search for the safest place to fight Vor'Kath when he actually attacks. According to Michael's premonition, the initial attack happens in the market after the south wall falls. But it's also possible that other mines will be dug under strategic points to overtake the city and surround our soldiers. I think the best place for our defense against Vor'Kath is in the courtyard, where his spells will be less lethal to the remainder of the city compared to if we fight in the market or anywhere else in the city. Now, I know this presents a grave amount of danger to you and your family—"

"You're *damn* right it presents a danger to my family, Mage!" the king shouted and slammed his fist on the top of his desk. He stood, walked to his window, and paused to peer down into the courtyard to calm down before he continued. "That being said, you are right. The risk of fighting Vor'Kath in the market or anywhere else in the city is too great to my people for me to allow that to happen."

"So, will you permit us to use the courtyard for our battle, Highness?" Joshua asked.

"Provided my family and I can be out of the castle before it starts, yes. If we aren't out of the castle, I need you to stall him elsewhere, until we can escape," the king replied.

"We will control the situation and can do that for you, Highness," Joshua said.

"Do you have anything else for me, Mage?" the king asked.

"I have nothing else at the moment, sire," Joshua replied.

"Anyone else have anything for me?"

"No, Highness," Michael and Týr replied in unison.

"Then go back to your assignments. Mage, I want you to continue looking for information on how we can defeat Vor'Kath, even if it involves not killing him. I have never dealt with an adversary that could withstand death. Now, before you say anything, Sergeant Týr, I know that is only a possibility and not a promise of powers he possesses."

The trio clapped their fists to their chests, then filed out of the king's office with the Master General following closely behind them. With the door closed, they discussed the plan of moving forward and everything else that Joshua thought he could find on the subject without asking the Sorcerer's College or the Anselin Mages for any further information.

"If you need to reach out to anyone else, let me know first so I can inform the king. Reaching out to Anselin or the Sorcerer's College may be disliked by the king as our relations with those entities have been strained in recent years. If needed, I will take the brunt of his ire if we must contact either place. There's no reason for you to be the target of that man's wrath. If I know we need to reach out, I can convince the king to agree to such arrangements. He trusts my counsel," the Master General stated. The look on his face implied he wanted to say something else about the College, though he simply left it alone.

"The College did not create the Madness, Master General. That was caused by unsanctioned sects of Mages that started practicing rituals there," Joshua clarified.

"True as that might be, the king may be wary about asking them for help getting rid of a malignant Vor working for Kalathan. That is a bridge we will cross when it's needed."

With nothing further to speak about, the trio left the castle and returned to their assignments. Týr wasn't scheduled to be on duty until later that evening, and Michael already finished his day's assignment before the midday meeting with the king. Both headed to the Dwarven Cave near the market for a few drinks and some food they might regret later. Týr decided not to drink as he would be on duty later, and that was frowned upon. As sergeants, they needed to set the example for the other guards; otherwise, their authority could be compromised or questioned at the very least.

Chapter Nineteen

...Sometime later...

or'Kath stood on the balcony of his appropriated tower. He enjoyed the grounds, as they grew to his liking. The servants maintained the tower much better now that a master oversaw them, and with that alone, the already tower felt very significantly more accommodating. Perhaps when all of this was over, he would take up permanent residence here. Perhaps. It was secluded, unknown, and incredibly remote, three qualities he preferred in choosing a home. But it was still in the mortal's world, and he hated their world so much. Their world was far too fragile for his liking, too delicate. Their world reminded him of the shell of an egg. When considering the tower as a home, he already knew the forest where he assigned Audro, his behemoth of a minotaur, was close enough that teleporting there and back was not overly demanding on him. He could even use a portal instead of teleporting.

Of all the things that Vor'Kath found in the tower, perhaps the most useful was a trinket that allowed him to communicate with others, using Magic, without the need to actively cast spells. The trinkets, there was a pair of them when he found them, proved incredibly useful. The other half of the pair went to Kalathan, the nightmarish monster who bestowed upon Vor'Kath his enhanced powers. Granter of powers that he was, Kalathan was far from an agreeable being. Vor'Kath only dealt with him when it was absolutely necessary.

Regardless, when either of them wanted to communicate, they simply needed to grab the stone, and the other would begin to vibrate. The vibration would continue until the other stone was touched. This made it convenient to talk to Dark Lord Kalathan. Vor'Kath really preferred not speaking with him at all, but this was his life. He also assumed Kalathan preferred not to speak with him. The World Eater was very much a behind-the-scenes manipulator.

Vor'Kath felt his stone vibrate as he found himself thinking about the trinkets. The vibration was gentle, enough that one would notice the vibration but not enough to be a nuisance. Vor'Kath grabbed the stone that hung from a small necklace he wore tucked under his robes to keep the trinket safe. Almost immediately, Kalathan began speaking, not waiting for Vor'Kath to acknowledge the desire to speak.

"You're stalling," the dark voice that came through the stone growled. It was times like this that Vor'Kath was thankful for Kalathan not wanting to meet face to face. His wrath was greater than anything Vor'Kath experienced before, and it was not something he wished to face again.

"My lord, I promise we are ahead of schedule. The army is growing as we speak—" Vor'Kath started to say.

"You're stalling, *and* you make excuses for your lack of progress," Kalathan continued, his voice growing loud enough to shake a tapestry that hung on the nearby wall.

"I apologize, my lord. I am working as fast as I can. Progress has slowed because—" he was cut off again.

"I don't care why your progress has slowed. You need to fix that deficiency now." With that, the stone, which vibrated throughout the conversation, grew still.

Once again, Vor'Kath found himself thankful that the stone only communicated voices. He dreaded seeing the facial expressions that came along with this conversation. *I cannot wait until this endeavor is over,* Vor'Kath thought to himself, as he worked his way down the spiral staircase within the tower. The stairs went around the outer edge of the tower, so at points where the tower narrowed, there was less space for two people to walk side by side going up or down. This was an oddity that Vor'Kath liked as it meant the tower was easily defendable from above, and fewer people could funnel their way up the stairs at a single time. It was further proof that the tower was meant to be occupied by someone who enjoyed a certain lack of visitors.

At the base of the stairs, there was a circular room that opened up to the double doors that led out of the tower. Currently, one of those double doors was open. They should be closed, as Vor'Kath kept them locked, for his privacy. However, one of the goblins Vor'Kath chose as his marshals stood in the doorway, appearing pitiful and frightened. Goblins rarely looked anything but frightened and pitiful. They were incapable of much beyond those two qualities. *Such woeful beasts. I will be happy to leave them behind when all of this is finished.* A horrid odor filled the entryway with the presence of the goblin. Such disgusting beasts they could be. It would be hard to believe that they bathed more than once in their lives.

"What is the status of the army? Are we ready to attack?" Vor'Kath asked.

"We cannot," the goblin hissed, its nasal voice a result of having such a shortened nasal passage.

Vor'Kath, standing on the bottom step, listened as the goblin prattled on about some incomprehensible reason why the army couldn't attack yet. The wretched goblin made excuses for the army's shortcomings. Finally having enough, Vor'Kath cast a spell and struck the goblin with the darkened lightning, a wonderful power granted to him through his arrangement with Kalathan. The goblin's body flashed as the dark bolt struck it. After a few moments, all that remained was a small pile of ash that soiled the pristine, tiled floor. One of the undead servants hobbled over— accompanied by the sound of thousand-year-old joints creaking as it moved—cleared the ashes from the doorway and bowed deeply as its master walked through the door. Vor'Kath thanked his servant, a resurrected body, or rather, mostly a skeleton held together with some rotting flesh, and opened a portal to the plane of existence where his army gathered. He would see the shortcomings the goblin spoke of for himself. Perhaps they were actually ready to attack now, but the goblins were afraid of the consequences of assuming something so bold.

Before he stepped through the portal, Vor'Kath stopped and considered the situation that played out at the bottom of the tower. Was he really any different than Kalathan? He struck down a soldier doing his bidding because of a failure. Kalathan could have easily done that, though he chose not to. Did that mean that Vor'Kath was worse than his dark master? *What a preposterous notion,* he thought to himself. Perhaps he was blinded to reality, being so closely involved with the goblin. He shook the thought from his mind and stepped through his portal.

Stretched before him in a vast valley was an army of thousands of goblins, dozens of minotaurs, hundreds of werewolves incapable of reverting to their previous forms, ogres that stood over four meters tall and nearly two meters wide at the shoulders, half a dozen manticore, a small handful of hippogryphs, and a smattering of other monsters he dreaded only because they were so ferocious. He wasn't even sure of their proper names, but he knew that many goblins paid with their lives to get the beasts caged for their master. The manticore and hippogryphs were caged and muzzled for fear they would eat more of the goblins.

Those precautions prevented only a portion of the possible deaths, especially with the manticore, but things went better than expected. Talons and tails were vicious on beasts like the manticore, and for that reason alone, Vor'Kath was beyond willing to lose a few goblins to them if it meant having such ferocious monsters as them in his army. And monsters they were. They had no apparent sense of what was going on. They only knew that the goblins were the ones to cage and muzzle them and that the goblins would be the main target of their revenge when they were uncaged. That could be solved with a simple spell, though the death of some goblins to the manticore, instead of the humans, was not going to impact his results at all. The goblins were, he reminded himself again, expendable assets.

I need a larger army to truly devastate the humans, but if Kalathan wants me to attack, so be it, Vor'Kath thought to himself as he gazed down upon his army from his perch that overlooked the valley. The army filled the valley below him and writhed like a group of cockroaches under a bed. Most of the movement came from the goblins, their sheer numbers forming the largest part of the army. Poor, wretched creatures, they had no idea they would be the manual labor for this whole expedition. The other monsters would form most of the attacking party. The ogres and the manticore alone would rain havoc upon Shemont. Of this, he had no doubt.

Vor'Kath cast a spell which created a funnel in front of him; he could speak into the funnel and inform his whole army, in whatever tongue they spoke, of his intentions. Even from his vantage point, a large rock that jutted out above the valley, the entire mass of monsters would be able to hear him. The rock Vor'Kath stood on was only twenty meters above the bottom of the valley. With the spell cast, he spoke into the funnel, drawing the attention of the whole mass of monsters. The writhing soon stopped as he started speaking.

"Our time is at hand, my brethren! The digging party will depart ahead of the rest of the army to prepare their tunnels to bring the city's walls crumbling down. Your time to slaughter the filth that is the human city of Shemont, the humans who are responsible for your twisted existences, your demented creators, is nigh! We will descend on them as they have on us, as we slaughter every last one of those sorry bastards!"

The monsters in the valley below roared, grunted, and squealed; the cacophony of bestial yells echoed through the valley. Vor'Kath closed the funnel spell and turned to the remaining goblin marshal, who he forgot was standing with him and gave his orders for digging tunnels under the moat and into the city. They would place specially crafted devices in key, strategic points under the walls to bring the stone barrier crumbling down. Vor'Kath smiled with the thought of his plan's success, and the promised reward of immortality. Kalathan could be an utter bastard at times, but a promise was a promise.

Chapter Twenty

...A few days later...

The moon rose toward its apex. Dark, dense clouds mostly hid it from the sky above the city of Shemont. Without lamps, such little light would exist that no one would be able to see more than a few meters away. A stiff, cold wind howled through the city as it sliced through the layers of wool that Michael wore in anticipation of the night's chill. Winter was still a few weeks away, and according to everyone in the guard unit, there was less than a month before the first anticipated snowfall. It would likely melt away quickly for the first couple of storms. The city was beautiful when it was covered in snow. The white powder gave the stone a softer, homier feel.

Michael walked the streets, something that was odd for a lieutenant, though instead of patrolling, he spent his time tracing the steps of a patrol that failed to check in. That too was odd in its own right. Thankfully as an officer, his days of patrolling the streets were far behind him. Now, he occasionally tracked down wayward patrols or drunk soldiers and put them on a corrective path. Since being promoted to lieutenant, Týr and Michael both received assignments to the same unit, partially because they needed two lieutenants in the night regiment, and partly because the Master General wanted Týr and Michael together in case Vor'Kath attacked. Joshua was also assigned to their unit, one of the few Mages assigned anywhere outside their mystical tower. The guards were wary of the Battlemages, especially so having one in the regiment with them. Joshua tried repeatedly to reassure the guards, to no avail.

As he walked down the main street toward the market district, Michael sensed something wrong. Something about tonight seemed too...*familiar*. In fairness, most nights felt the same after being assigned to the night regiment for any time longer than two months. This was a sensation that the day regiments didn't have to deal with as they were able to maintain the proper diurnal schedule. Michael returned to the guardhouse to check with the sentry there to see if the patrol checked in during his time out looking for them. Týr was already in the guardhouse, inspecting the ledger for any hints of where the missing patrol could be. This was work that could have been delegated to the sergeants, but the captain seemed adamant about them finding the missing patrol immediately. He made it *very* clear that the lieutenants were not allowed to punish the guards. *That* would be the captain's entertainment for the evening. This captain either had too little to do or too much time to complete his tasks. Either way, it was an issue that Michael chose to ignore as his main concern was finding the missing soldiers. Alive but in trouble was better than the alternative.

Michael decided to examine the ledger, as it could help him in his search for the patrol. The last relevant entry he found before pointed him toward the market, but he could have missed something among the other entries. Another guardhouse, just south of the market, could also contain a clue to their whereabouts. The patrol should have checked in hours ago. Something about the night was certainly wrong. If only he could pick out what that was. He ran toward the market's guardhouse. The heels of his boots clicked against the stone street as he jogged. Breaths came in and went out quickly as he picked up speed. It was a quick run, maybe five minutes, to the market, especially at this time of night with no one on the streets to get in the way.

Michael burst through the door and the guard sitting at the desk shot out of his chair, startled by the interruption, especially from an officer. He stood as if there was a steel rod in his back instead of bones and muscles. The guard was young, perhaps twenty years old at the most, judging by the smoothness of the skin under his eyes, his lack of grey hairs, and the slight chubbiness in his cheeks that said he was still maturing. Green eyes looked expectantly at Michael under thin eyebrows. His hair was blonde, and his eyebrows were only a touch darker than his hair.

"Sir, what can I do for you?" the guard inquired.

"Has this missing patrol checked in with you?" Michael asked in turn. He hated answering a question with another question, but the situation demanded it.

"There's a patrol missing?" the guard gasped.

"I need to see the ledger, immediately," Michael replied. The guard slid the chair away from the desk and stood up so Michael could look at the ledger.

It showed no signs of the patrol, much like the other guardhouse. Michael checked the ledger once more to be sure, then left, heading back to check in with Týr. The city was only so big; the patrol must be somewhere. They met in the street halfway between both guardhouses. Týr had a grim look on his face, but it was rare for him *not* to have a grim look on his face. Even when they were promoted to lieutenant together, his face looked grim. It was possible the man still hadn't gotten over the loss of his sister and likely wouldn't until Vor'Kath was dead.

"Still haven't found the missing patrol?" Týr inquired.

"Not yet. The market guardhouse didn't know we even have a patrol missing. This whole situation is not good, Týr," Michael said. Týr looked at Michael, clearly deep in thought. After a few moments, his eyes went wide.

"Is tonight the night?" Týr wondered aloud.

"No, it can't be to—" Michael started, then had a flash of the dream that had haunted him for years. "*Shit!* I think it *is* tonight! We have to find Joshua. Now!"

The pair sprinted to the guardhouse where they knew Joshua would be. It was only a few hundred meters, but Michael felt a burning stitch in his side just as they reached the guardhouse. The instant Týr's hand touched the doorknob, the dreaded underground ringing began. It was a hollow, sinister ringing, like a bell placed underground, but was clearly the sound of metal clashing against stone. Before Týr could even turn the handle on the door, Joshua yanked open the door.

"If that sound is what I think it is, the king must get out of the city now! Someone needs to inform the Master General and have him escort the king, queen, and prince from the castle," Joshua said.

Týr ran off, saying he would inform the Master General and make sure the king was out of the castle. Joshua and Michael rallied the guards nearby, wanting to get as many people in their positions as possible. Joshua sent Michael off to the market guardhouse to spread the word, forming a portal to get the Mages.

Michael ran back to the guardhouse, his heart throbbing in his ears as he ran. His breath came in bursts along with the sharp pain in his side. No matter how many times Michael ran with the guards, he always felt like he was going to die. Still, he was on a mission: get to the guardhouse. That was the only thing that mattered right now. Instead of focusing on the pain or his pounding heart, Michael focused on his breathing and his stride. In, out, in, out.

Reaching the guardhouse, Michael again burst through the door, the guard behind the desk yanked his feet from the top of the desk and nearly fell backward. Catching himself, he snapped upright and clapped his hand to his chest as Michael told him there was no time for that.

"Get the guards into their defensive positions. The attack is happening tonight!" Michael shouted.

"What attack, sir?" the guard questioned.

"Just get everyone in their defensive positions. I pray for the safety of the prince that you are competent enough for that at least," Michael snapped.

His mission accomplished, he turned and jogged back out of the guardhouse. He got three meters from the guardhouse before a portal opened before him and he stumbled through and fell face-first into the plush carpet of the castle's main hall. The portal behind him closed the moment his face touched the velvety carpet.

Joshua, Týr, the Master General, and the royal family all stood on the other end of the portal, looking at Michael as he got himself up off the floor, straightened his uniform, and clapped his fist to his chest. Joshua helped him get to his feet, and both turned their attention to the royal family. The queen, her dark green nightgown drawing some sidelong glances from the men, save the Master General and the king, both of whom still showed heavy amounts of sleep on their faces. The Master General, despite looking like he just woke up, still happened to be fully dressed. The king wrestled with getting the last of his armor cinched properly.

"Lieutenant Týr tells me tonight is the night. Are you ready, men?" the king asked, looking at all three with a slightly judging glance for looking at his wife in her nightgown.

"Yes, sire," the trio responded.

"The Mages are already in position, working to find and stop the tunnels as fast as they can," Joshua added.

"Good. I don't want to lose any more of the city than is absolutely necessary tonight. Take this bastard down. I don't care what it takes," the king ordered.

"Your wish is our command, sire," Joshua replied.

"I want him dead as much as anyone, sire. As you know that murderous asshole killed my sister. Pardon my language, your Majesty," Týr added, looking to the queen.

"Lieutenant, you don't have to apologize for such dull obscenities. My husband often has a sharper tongue than you," the queen replied, smiling at the eye roll the king gave her.

"Right, let's get going, your Majesties," the Master General reminded. "Mage, please summon a portal for us. We are heading to Anselin. King Erkan III arranged shelter there for the time being. The Elves are being extremely hospitable at the moment. It's quite fortunate given our past experiences with them."

"Good luck, men," the king said, clasping hands with the trio before stepping through the portal that Joshua created. Once the royal family and the Master General were through the portal, the shimmering doorway in the air closed.

Joshua opened another portal into the courtyard, saving them a few steps. Once in the courtyard, another Magic doorway opened, and fifteen Battlemages stepped through led by an older Mage Joshua knew was named Respen. The older Mage boasted a gnarly scar going from his mouth to his right earlobe, a milky right eye, and thin, wispy hair that waved as he walked. They all greeted Joshua as they stepped into the courtyard. The leader of the group, a Grand Warlock, was easily identified by his more extravagant robes, clasped hands with Joshua, telling him that two groups of Mages were on their way to disrupt the two mine locations they knew about. One was coming under the market, hoping to bring down the southern wall, and the other was coming from the north, attempting to burrow directly under the castle. Fortunately, the Mages' scouts found indicators that these were the only two mines burrowing under the city. This would allow the soldiers and Battlemages to focus their efforts in the correct places.

"We are at your command, Joshua," Respen said.

"Very well. There won't be time for further explanation so let's make sure everyone understands the plan the first time," Joshua replied.

As Joshua explained his battle plan to the Mages, a shriek sounded above the courtyard. Piercing and shrill, it came from the top of the castle and sounded like an eagle. A monstrous beast, with an eagle's wings, head, and legs, attached to the back half of a horse, came flying into the courtyard, its talons ready. It grabbed one of the Mages by the chest and as the beast flew away, the Mage screamed loudly. It was the only way anyone could tell where the monster was in the darkness of the overcast night. Responding to the threat, the other Mages flashed multiple spells at the creature before finally a bolt of lightning connected with one of its wings. The monster faltered, dropped the Mage, and flew off, its right wing flapping gingerly.

"And so, it begins," Joshua stated. "Surely there is worse to come this night."

*   *   *

The ringing echoed throughout the city and came from the south and also sounded like it was right under the courtyard. Suddenly the sound under the courtyard stopped, which left only the sound from the south which continued to echo through the city. A portal opened and a squad of two Battlemages emerged, a mine showing through the doorway behind them. Blood splattered two of their robes, and another held his arm, his hand glowing white as he healed the wounds he sustained.

"The northern mine is stopped, and we sealed the entrance with a spell the goblins won't get through no matter how hard they try," the female Mage said, gasping for breath.

"Wonderful. Any news from the south?" Joshua asked.

The clang of metal against stone continuing from the south provided the answer to the question before anyone else could speak. *Ting. Ting. Ting.* The echo filled the still calmness that enveloped the city. With the second squad of Mages still missing, the commander ordered the first squad to assist them in getting the mine stopped, save the wounded Mage, who cast another healing spell then protested that he could still fight. Respen acquiesced, seeing this. The Mages opened a portal and stepped through. The doorway snapped shut an instant later.

Not long after the Mages left, a deep rumbling sound resounded through the city and the ground trembled briefly. To the west, crashing sounded from the gate. Joshua opened an orb, to look at the area outside the gate. Hundreds of goblins and dozens of other creatures gathered outside the city's gate, spanning across a bridge that led to the entrance. A minotaur and a handful of werewolves could be seen on the land side of the bridge as they waited for the goblins to break through.

A monstrous beast, shaped like a man but several meters tall and a few wide stood on the outside of the gate, swinging what appeared to be a dead tree ripped from the ground. The monster sported a hunched back and a head that appeared to have been smashed a few times, as deformations and crevices formed in the top of its skull. It had knobby knees and elbows, and massive hands, nearly a meter across at their widest. The creature wore a loincloth that left very little to the imagination, a horror on its own since the ragged, threadbare cloth covered the monster, but only just. Each time the tree contacted the gate, the *thud* could be heard in the courtyard. After a few attempts at breaking down the gate with the tree, the beast dropped the tree on a handful of goblins gathered at its feet and started throwing its beefy shoulder into the thick wood of the gate.

"Why was the drawbridge not raised?" Respen growled.

"That isn't a drawbridge, sir. That bridge is the only way in or out of the city at night," Michael clarified. It was clear that the

Mages ventured so infrequently from their tower that they didn't know enough about their city.

"We need to do something about that bridge," the white-haired Mage growled. "We cannot let the monsters get into the city."

"Send us, sir. We'll take care of them," one of the Mages offered.

"Look!" Joshua said, pointing to the orb. The image inside the orb pulled back, showing the thick hordes of goblins stretching far to the west.

"There have to be at least thirty thousand goblins alone. What's that coming through the horde?" Týr asked, pointing at the orb.

Coming through the sea of goblins, with enough breadth around for a clear visual, Vor'Kath walked toward the bridge. His hood was raised as it always had been, but it was clear he looked into the orb as if he looked into the souls of those in the courtyard.

"You are too late. Your precious city has already fallen. I will not stop until every man, woman, and child has been killed in the streets and your city drowns in its own blood," he threatened. Once he finished speaking, he waved his hand and vanished without opening a portal.

"Damn," Joshua swore.

Chapter Twenty-One

Yor'Kath disappeared and left no clues as to where he went. Joshua closed the orb and growled to himself, wishing that hadn't just happened. This was not going to be pleasant for anyone involved. Especially if he could resurrect himself if they ended up killing him.

"What do we do now?" Týr inquired. He chomped at the bits like a stallion, anxious to get his blades wet with goblin blood.

"We don't know where he went. He could be in any number of realms, and my Magic can't reach beyond this one." Joshua replied.

"What if we combine our spells? Could we pull him into our world?" one of the Battlemages asked.

It was a fair question. A lot could be done when Mages cast their spells together that normally couldn't be done singlehandedly without tiring out a Mage too quickly to get anything else done. Unfortunately, casting spells together did tire out the Mages, just to a degree less than if they cast alone.

"How many Mages do we have here?" Joshua asked.

"There are twenty Mages here in the courtyard. Everyone except us is either at a gate, ready for an attack, or working to take out the mines. Speaking of, we should have heard back from the squad at the mine," Respen stated flatly.

"We haven't heard from the Mages. This falls on us now. But how do we find Vor'Kath if he is beyond this realm?" Joshua thought aloud.

"Could you use the bond?" Michael asked. Joshua's eyes widened as he realized the simplicity of the suggestion.

"The bond! He has to be able to find us every time using the bond! Why have I not thought about that? Dammit, I'm an idiot! We could have been tracking him this whole time," Joshua exclaimed.

He removed the raven trinket from around his neck and described the spell to the Mages in the courtyard. They started the spell, casting together. Joshua joined them after he set the raven on the ground amid the Mages.

A large cloud of light formed overhead, just as Michael saw in Erith's temple with the Heron Priests, but this light cloud was larger and denser. The cloud showed a strange land with jagged rocks and red soil. The few plants that could be seen all looked dead, their stems and leaves brown and crispy. Vor'Kath stood in the middle of an open expanse of red soil, occasionally marred by stones that jutted out of the ground like teeth.

The Vor, an orb floating before him, watched the slow progress his army made into the city. What could barely be seen was a group of Mages fighting through a small army of goblins and other monstrous creatures at the opening of the market mine shaft. Fire and lightning flashed in all directions as two Mages struggled to fight through the horde. This was why the Mages had not heard from their counterparts at the southern mine yet. For every goblin slain, another four seemed to appear. Other monsters, werewolves among them, rushed at the Mages and Michael and Týr watched as first the fire, then the lightning, stopped abruptly.

Joshua cast another spell, and the light from the cloud overhead began swirling in a funnel toward the raven stone that lay on the ground. Just before the light could touch the smooth stone of the trinket, a manticore flew overhead and shrieked as it landed in the courtyard. The beast roared, its lion face snarled and flashed its teeth as the beast reared on its hind legs. Týr and Michael rushed toward the monster, their weapons drawing as they moved. Respen stopped casting the spell, and the cloud of light flashed briefly as he left the group of spell casters and turned toward the creature. As he prepared to throw a fireball, the scorpion tail pierced his chest and raised him off his feet before it immediately slammed him into the cobblestone of the courtyard. A sickening crunch accompanied his body slamming to the ground.

Týr threw a knife toward the creature which struck its right wing and punched through the fleshy skin of its bat-like wings before it clattered against the stone not far from the beast. The monster roared again and charged at the soldiers who rushed toward it. The beast's massive paw flashed at Michael, who barely ducked under the four razor-sharp claws. Týr squared up to the monster, a knife in one hand and his sword in the other. Once more a furious paw reached toward the soldiers and Týr swung his sword, slicing one toe and claw from the creature's paw. Another blood-curdling shriek came from the monster.

The scorpion tail snapped toward Týr, revenge its only desire, though Týr had a different outcome in mind. Time appeared to slow down as Michael saw the tail race toward Týr's chest, the pointed, scaly tip of the scorpion tail reflected light from the cloud spell. As Týr was about to bring his knife up to stab the tail, Michael's sword flashed upward in front of Týr and sliced through the tip of the tail. Týr was splashed with a thick, greenish fluid. His face and neck were wet and sticky, now covered in the hot liquid. He could only imagine how his tabard looked.

The beast shrieked once more and finally flew off, heading toward the top of the castle. Michael could only see where it went because of the Mages and their cloud spell which provided some light for the courtyard. At least there was something else helpful about the spell, beyond being able to track Vor'Kath. The manticore disappeared into the darkness of the cloudy, moonless night, its pained shrieking heard even after the beast couldn't be seen.

Returning to the Mages, Michael and Týr saw the light absorbing into the raven, which now was the dull stone color it was before. Joshua picked up the raven and rubbed the surface with his thumb, which caused the stone to light up as he touched it. Suddenly the raven lit up brightly, the brightest amount of light appeared at the beak, which pointed to the west, toward the bridge with the monster and the horde of goblins.

Crashing and splintering sounded from the west, along with the shouts of guards and screeches of goblins. Even from this distance, it sounded like the monstrosity had broken through the gate and likely tore through the lines of soldiers gathered inside the gate. Something so large would make quick work of the soldiers who were not trained to fight such a large creature. They were trained to fight men, or Elves, who were not much larger than they were.

A group of soldiers ran into the courtyard, coming from the south. They gasped, out of breath, and removed their helmets as the visors did sometimes make it difficult to breathe, especially after running. That was one of the reasons Michael stuck with wearing his leather patrol armor instead of the battle armor he was issued after his promotion to lieutenant. The plate armor was also rather bulky and made it rather difficult to move. And tonight, of all nights, he needed to be able to move freely.

One of the soldiers in the group, there were only seven, told the lieutenants that they were overrun in the market and moved back to the courtyard. The sergeant told them that hordes of goblins, werewolves, and minotaurs swarmed the market after the southern wall collapsed. They fought as long as they could and managed to bring down two minotaurs and a werewolf, along with untold numbers of goblins. Sadly, they were the only survivors of the ordeal. If things went according to plan, there should have been two hundred guards in the market. Týr wanted to question why they had left the courtyard to leave the city vulnerable, but a portal opened in the courtyard and cut him off.

Through the portal came a group of three dozen Mages, though not Mages from Shemont or even Anselin judging by their pristinely white robes with colored stripes at the cuffs of their sleeves. Joshua, seeing them, told Michael and Týr that they were from the Sorcerers' College. The group of newly arrived Mages was made up of Elves and humans alike, though far fewer humans than Elves. One of the Mages, who looked to be in command of the newly-arrived group, stepped forward and began talking to Joshua.

"We sensed a dark presence in the world and have come to help you dispatch it. I know your king is wary of the College, and we understand this unnecessary cautiousness, but we will help you to eradicate this menace. What help do you need from us?" the Mage asked.

"The presence you sensed is a Vor who is assaulting the city with an army of goblins and other monsters. If you can help us keep the monsters from the courtyard, we can get his attention and fight him here. There is a breach in the southern wall at the market where the goblins are flooding in. Take our soldiers with you," Joshua said, presenting the seven soldiers who just arrived from the market, "and they will help you hold off the goblins in the market. We will get the Vor to come to us here in the courtyard."

"It's a Vor? Allfather curse this night," one of the other Mages in the group called out.

"He doesn't need to curse this night, just those fools who opened our world to the Vor in the first place," another Mage added.

"How do you expect to take down a Vor with only a handful of Mages? One Vor is easily stronger than fifty Mages," yet another Mage interjected,

"Very well. We will hold off the horde from getting to the courtyard," the first Mage said, motioning with his hand to the other Mages who appeared to get the hint and followed the soldiers out of the courtyard.

Joshua talked with the other Battlemages and planned their trap for Vor'Kath. They would cast a spell that would attract him and then cast a protective dome over the courtyard. This would prevent his lightning spell from raining down on them, and it would keep him stuck in the courtyard. The dome would have to be cast the instant he set foot in the courtyard, as casting it too soon would prevent him from walking into the trap, and it would tip their hand that they were prepared for him. The worse he thought of the humans the better. The trap should catch him by surprise and make him angry enough to not think clearly.

The Mages began casting their spell, a pillar of light that shot into the sky and began clearing away the clouds overhead. The night sky overhead was filled with stars, though the light that came from the pillar drowned out any sign of them; the moon was still hidden behind the thick, unnatural clouds that flooded the night sky.

As they anticipated, a dark portal opened at the edge of the courtyard and Vor'Kath stepped through. He reached his left hand into the air and made his curve-bladed sword appear from nowhere.

His doorway closed behind him, and he walked toward the group of Mages, Týr, and Michael at a menacingly slow pace. The screams and battle sounds that came from behind him only added to his sinister approach. Lightning sizzled in the sky above, bouncing here and there through the clouds overhead.

The moment his foot touched the cobblestone of the courtyard, a white dome formed overhead and snapped down to the ground, covering every portion of the courtyard save where the Mages clustered as they cast the spell. The protective dome formed quickly with multiple Mages casting together. Vor'Kath convulsed briefly once the bubble touched the ground, appearing to be hurt by it. He looked to Joshua, Michael, and Týr and spoke, his gruff voice booming within the bubble.

"You are children meddling in matters that are beyond your understanding. Priest, *you* are strong but are still a child. Leave the spellcasting to those who hold a better understanding of consequences. The Vor gifted the humans so much of what you know today. You owe us a debt."

"This you claim, trapped without all of your powers," Joshua stated.

"You killed my sister, you piece of shit. I will laugh as your last breath leaves your lungs," Týr growled.

"It pleases me that you have such hatred roiling at the surface. It will make you careless, you petulant cur." Vor'Kath said.

"Keep talking. I'll still gut you like a fish," Týr replied.

"Why take time talking if you came to fight, Vor'Kath?" Joshua asked, wanting to step in before Týr got himself into trouble.

The Vor stopped mid-step and turned his attention from Týr to Joshua. "Where did you learn my name?"

"I summoned another Vor right where you stand," Joshua replied.

"Perhaps you are not a child, priest—" he was cut off by Týr.

Týr lunged at Vor'Kath, his late sister's knife in his left hand, his own in his right. One knife flashed to the right, the next to the left. A knife came up as Vor'Kath reacted, bringing his sword around. The knife and the dark, slightly curved sword met in a shower of sparks, the sword bouncing away quickly from the knife. Týr closed the distance between him and Vor'Kath so the sword would become less effective, but not so close that Týr would be touched by his evil hands. It was an art for Týr, as he found the perfect combat distance in any fight.

Michael, reacting slower, finally joined Týr. Joshua and the other Mages started casting their spells. With the two soldiers fighting the Vor, his focus was split, and Týr was able to land a strike with Svenka's knife, cutting into the Vor's right thigh. Vor'Kath shrieked, a piercing sound that knocked Týr and Michael backward a couple of steps. The wound was only deep enough to cut into the muscle but not to leave any lasting damage. There was blood. Black blood oozed through the ashen skin beneath the dark, motionless robes. Týr used the opportunity to plant Svenka's knife between their adversary's ribs. The shriek from Vor'Kath grew louder and sharper.

At the same moment that the Mages finished their spell, which captured Vor'Kath in the same petrifying trap they used on the other

Vor. As the stone consumed Vor'Kath, his left hand lit up as he attempted to cast a bolt of lightning toward the top of the dome. As the lightning shot from his hand, the stone enveloped the Vor and his bolt of lightning. The stone captured the whole aggressive display as a statue, lightning bolts, knife, and all. Michael and Týr panted, the fight over and their bodies in the rhythm but nothing else happening to keep the adrenaline flowing. Michael sheathed his sword and put his hands on his knees, breathing deeply.

"Why did you do that? Do you not see the knife in his side? I had him right where we want him: dead or dying. Joshua you complete—" Týr shouted before he was cut off.

"I know you want revenge for Svenka, but this is the best way to ensure he doesn't resurrect," Joshua argued.

"We don't even know if he can do that! You bungled this whole thing. I joined the army and have spent the past two years traveling with you only for you to dash any hopes I had of putting Iona's killer in the ground, asshole!" Týr yelled then stormed off to the edge of the bubble.

"I understand how you feel. You aren't the only person who made sacrifices tonight or any other time along this journey. Michael and I can *never* return to our homeland because the people of Prikea fear the Madness here. You think you're alone in this, Týr, but you're not. You think that, because you're angry, you get to be right automatically. Everyone else must bend to your will so that you can rigidly stand there and say what *must* happen within the world. Well, you can't!" Joshua shouted back. This was one of only a few times that Michael saw Joshua actually raise his voice.

301

"Joshua, do you need us any longer?" one of the Mages asked. "We can go help the soldiers clear the city if you don't need us."

"No, we don't need you here. Go, help clear the city. Thank you for the assistance with this," Joshua replied. He kept his eyes locked on Týr.

"Just because you lost your priesthood, you think that means you can control the lives of others?" Týr shouted once more, getting in Joshua's face. Týr was slightly taller than Joshua, his nose sat at Joshua's eye level. The two glared at each other.

"I didn't *lose* my priesthood. I am still a priest but became a Battlemage for the king so that we could save the world from this monster that we have trapped in stone! You—" Joshua started when Michael cut them off.

"Why are we fighting each other? We won this battle, right?" Michael asked, stepping between his comrades.

"Except we haven't. This *thing* is still alive, and we still aren't going to do anything about it, are we? We're just going to leave a monster that aligned himself with one of the most dangerous beings in any world alive, simply encased in stone to prevent me or anyone else here from seeing such a monster die. And why? Because the thing *might* be able to come back to life if we kill it. What a stupid *fucking* reason not to kill such a powerful enemy," Týr growled.

"The risk of resurrection is incredibly high, dealing with Kalathan. I don't know what could happen if Vor'Kath were to resurrect. He could become so powerful that none of us could possibly hope to take him down. At the very least with him encased in stone, we know where he is and how powerful he remains. Please try to understand why I might be a little hesitant to kill something that could come back to life. I don't know what powers Kalathan promised Vor'Kath. I don't know what arrangements they have made in their alignment," Joshua countered.

"Um, Joshua, is Vor'Kath supposed to be able to move his hand with this spell?" Michael asked, staring at the statue.

Joshua and Týr stopped their argument and immediately turned to inspect the statue of Vor'Kath. What had just a moment before been solid was now starting to move. The stone crust around the Vor started to crumble and fall away, the stone pieces dissipating like pipe smoke as they fell. Bits of Vor'Kath started breaking free. His hands and fingers wriggled as the stone came free. Joshua rushed to the statue immediately and cast a spell pushing a gust of wind at the bolts of lightning, breaking them free from the rest of the Vor. The bolts of lightning, still encased in stone, broke on the cobblestone ground of the courtyard, fizzling completely.

Týr, seeing the statue coming back to life, hurried over and waited for the knife he buried into Vor'Kath's side to thaw from the stone. When the knife was eventually free from the stone, Týr yanked out the blade, inspected it for any damage or remnants of stone then stood at the ready for the next battle that would surely start once the Vor was free from the stone. As the stone finished peeling away from the Vor, he wavered on his feet and his sword hand fell to his side. The slightly curved blade of his sword scraped against the stone. He appeared much as Michael felt after drinking too many ales in the tavern. Finally, he shook his head and seemed

303

to remember where he was, the sound of battles nearby seeming to jog his memory.

Vor'Kath swung his sword and its wicked edge struck only air in front of Joshua and Michael. Týr, his knives already in hand, circled around behind the Vor like a wolf closing in on a wounded deer. Michael drew his sword and squared up to Vor'Kath. He imagined what would happen next would be a traditional duel between the two of them. Michael raised his sword and assumed a stance that would be appropriate for a duel. Michael prepared to move his feet swiftly and strike like a serpent. Týr, now fully behind the Vor, locked eyes with Michael and nodded slowly. Joshua, off to Michael's right, had two spells ready, one a ball of fire that floated in his hand, the other looked like a ball of clouds roiling in a tumultuous storm, similar to the storm that *Queller* found herself stuck in off the coast of Drendil what felt like a lifetime ago.

Vor'Kath raised his sword, ready to attack when a portal opened over his head and a giant hand reached out and grasped the Shadow Knight. The hand, meters in size, held the Vor like a small doll and left him incapacitated. Týr, Michael, and Joshua stepped back, fearing what else might emerge from the portal.

"Vor'Kath you failed me! You haven't met your end of our arrangement and I shall not meet mine," a foul voice echoed through the portal and filled the courtyard with immense darkness. The hand started to withdraw into the portal, taking the Shadow Knight into the mysterious land beyond the doorway.

"No!" Týr shouted and jumped toward Vor'Kath, grabbing on to one of the fingers of the hand as it disappeared beyond the portal.

The doorway to whatever land lay beyond closed immediately, leaving no sign of Týr or the Vor. Michael and Joshua stood in the courtyard, looking at where the portal was only a moment before. Týr was *gone*! As was Vor'Kath. Several moments passed before either Michael or Joshua spoke, confused about what had transpired.

"We should help the others clear the monsters and goblins from the city," Michael suggested.

It was not a bad suggestion, though neither he nor Joshua moved toward the sounds of fighting, which grew closer to the courtyard. Overhead the clouds that once blocked out the stars and covered the city in the impenetrable darkness started to fade, revealing the first hints of morning time as the sky grew a few shades lighter. Sunrise remained two hours away at the least, but there was a sign that light was coming to this world again. As the clouds peeled back from the city, Michael felt a wave of hope crash over himself. They had done it. The world was saved.

Epilogue

Michael and Joshua stood together in the courtyard on a portable dais used for ceremonies at the castle, wearing their best uniforms. On the dais was also the royal family, the Master General, and the Supreme Warlock, the leader of the Battlemages. She was the equivalent of the Master General, but specifically for the Battlemage Legion. Michael was being promoted to captain for his efforts in defending the city and the Kingdom of Drendil. Joshua was also being promoted to Warlock, the equivalent of a captain in the Battlemages Legion. A posthumous promotion was also given to Týr. The king and Master General, both usually stoic in their manner, appeared visibly upset during the ceremony for Týr. Despite the promotions, the king had a different idea of what kind of reward would be fitting for Michael and Joshua, given their service, though he kept his idea secret from them. The Master General tried to protest, saying that meritorious promotion should be plenty for their efforts. The king listened to none of it. It was one of the few times Michael and Joshua were privileged enough to see an argument between the two.

Throughout the courtyard stood ranks of soldiers and Battlemages formed in columns with an aisle leaving the dais. Their metal armor glinted in the sunlight. The soldiers all stood rigidly, their arms at their sides and their feet together. As he gazed into the sea of armor, Michael saw the faces of battle-hardened soldiers. Soldiers who lost their comrades during the battle for the city. Soldiers who also deserved so much for their efforts. Hundreds of lives had been lost defending the city, a price that no one ever wanted to pay.

On the dais was a bench where Michael and Joshua sat with the Supreme Warlock, the Master General, the queen, and the prince. The king stood at the front of the dais and addressed the sea of armor-clad soldiers. Instead of his regular long sword, the king wore a rapier at his left hip, its scabbard highly decorated with strips of gold and jewels. The sword was obviously more ceremonial than anything else. Perhaps this was the most ceremonial sword the king owned, which would also make it one of the least useful swords in his personal armory. *What does he have planned for us?* Michael wondered to himself.

"Every one of you fought valiantly to protect our city and our kingdom. You are all beyond deserving of every award that will be bestowed upon you all, and those awards will come in due time. Today I would like to recognize the two who led the defense of the city in my absence. I cannot express enough my condolences for those we lost. Captain, Warlock, please step forward," the king called out, his voice easily reaching the back of the courtyard.

Michael and Joshua stepped forward and clapped their fist to their chest as they approached the king. He returned the salute and directed each of them to kneel as he drew the rapier from its gold-encrusted scabbard. The fine, thin blade of the sword shone radiantly in the mid-afternoon sunlight. The king took his sword and touched the point of the blade on Joshua's right then left shoulder in quick succession.

"I name you Sir Joshua the Ravenous, Knight-Captain of the Royal Order of Drendil. Rise, Sir Joshua," the king proclaimed.

Joshua rose and clasped arms with the king then was brought in for a deep embrace, a proud smile beaming on his face. While the king embraced him, he whispered in Joshua's ear, though Michael could not make out what was said. Joshua, after being released from the king, stepped back, and stood behind Michael. The king side-stepped so he was standing before Michael, and the rapier flashed from his right shoulder to the left. As the sword touched Michael's left shoulder it rested there briefly as the king made another proclamation.

"I name you Sir Michael the Valiant, Knight-Captain of the Royal Order of Drendil. Rise, Sir Michael," the king's voice rang out clearly from the dais to the far edges of the courtyard. Just as with Joshua, Michael and the king clasped arms then embraced.

Once again, the king whispered to his newest Knight, "You have done a great service to Drendil. I know this land is not your home, but please accept an estate in the city that shall be yours and your family's for generations. You have more than earned it, Sir Michael."

The courtyard resounded with the thunder of applause and cheers as the soldiers clapped their armor-clad hands together. The queen stood, holding the hand of the little prince, who came to just above her knee, with her left hand and approached Michael and Joshua. She embraced both and gave them each a kiss on the right cheek. As the applause from the soldiers continued, the Master General and the Supreme Warlock both clasped hands with the new knights, showing their acceptance of them within the order.

*　　*　　*

Michael received the key to his new estate. It was a comfortable house on a stately plot of land that would be suitable for him and his family, should he ever have one. A squire waited inside the estate for him and bowed deeply as Sir Michael walked through the doorway, introducing himself. The man was a bit jittery but seemed nice enough with his first impression.

"Good evening, Sir Michael. I am George, your squire. I shall attend to any needs that you have. Congratulations on the achievement of knighthood today, Sir."

"Thank you, George. You don't have to call me Sir constantly. Michael is fine."

"Sir Michael, you should get some rest. I have readied a bath for you, as well, if you would like to wash up. Shall I help you to remove your armor?"

"A bath sounds wonderful. And I can manage to remove my own armor, thank you, George. If you are wanting to help me with something, I have a few of my belongings in the captains' barracks building that you could fetch for me," Michael replied already thinking about the hot water of the bath and how nice that would be after such a long journey.

"Yes, Sir. I will retrieve your belongings right away. Please, make yourself at home. This is your estate, after all," George commented.

George bowed deeply once more before he left the house. Michael explored the manor for a few minutes and found his bedroom, much bigger than any of the barracks rooms he occupied in the past year and a half since joining the army. He had a study with empty bookshelves that begged to be filled. Some books were already provided, likely by George or perhaps even from the king himself. Tactical guides for battles, a book with detailed maps of the surrounding area, and a thick, leather-bound book with pictures and descriptions of various fauna found in the wilderness of Drendil, including some of the monsters they fought during the Siege of Shemont. The beast that looked like a horse and eagle forced together was called a hippogryph. A rare monster not found in

Drendil until the night of the battle. *Hippogryph*, Michael thought to himself, *I wonder who comes up with the names for these beasts.*

Across the hall from the study was the bathing room. A mirror hung above the chimney, where a welcome fire burned. The nights were growing colder, and as it was already evening time, Michael could feel a touch of the night chill setting in. In the middle of the floor was a large bathtub, made of metal that was formed to look like a large, oblong bowl. Steam rose from the water in the tub and bubbles were already floating atop the water. Michael found an armor rack in his bedroom and removed his armor and the linen clothing that went under the plate and chainmail armor.

He slowly lowered himself into the hot water filled tub, large enough for him to stretch out his legs and still be mostly under the water. The water's temperature was perfect. Warm but slightly on the side of hot. Just enough that Michael noticed his skin began to turn pink, but not hot enough to hurt. He leaned back in the tub and closed his eyes. He breathed in the warm air in the bathing room and felt himself drifting to sleep. It was the first time in many years that he found himself sleeping without a haunting nightmare or any dream of things to come.

...To be continued...

Excerpt from *Downfall*

Far to the east of the great human city of Shemont rose a mountain range that ran north and south. To the east of the mountains spread a vast desert with many hills of golden sand but very little else. To the west of the mountains, a great and mighty forest bounded toward the sky. Pine, beech, oak, and maple trees comprised the large part of the forest. Groups of like trees gathered together in the forest. There were pockets of oaks clustered together in various areas, with a few singular oak trees rising where long ago a squirrel had buried an acorn for later in the year.

Speculation from travelers, mostly merchants and the occasional bard, said this was likely one of the oldest forests on the continent of Drendil. Rumors spoke of great evils lurking deep in those forests, unseen and unknown. These types of rumors always surrounded strange places in the land that once teemed with Madness caused by dark experiments.

The mightiest trees rose so high that standing at their bases, one could hardly see the tops. Half a dozen men together could barely reach their arms around the bases of some trees. The forest was thickest further from the mountains; the trees thinned then altogether stopped as they grew close to the mountain range. Amid the grand mountains was a crater, which replaced what had once been the greatest of the peaks. This was a remaining scar in the world from the devastating eruption of a star found by a Dwarf in the former mines of Madira nearly three hundred years before. The reaction had been so great that the very mountain collapsed into the ground, something not helped by how deeply the Dwarves delved into the earth. Many speculated they had attempted to dig into the very center of the planet in search of ore, gems, and other valuables. Vegetation had started to grow close to the collapsed mountain, but the crater still remained with only a bridge that spanned the gap. The bridge was rickety and old, so travelers seldom crossed it, especially since there was only a desert on the other side of the mountains. Some claimed the desert was haunted, though that was likely just myths stretched and complicated over time. Within every rumor was a nugget of reality that became twisted until the truth became a hardly recognizable shell of its former self.

Sir Michael the Valiant, a Knight-Captain of the Royal Order of Drendil walked through the forest with his bow at the ready. He had spent the last few days in these woods, hunting down one of the hippogryphs that attacked Shemont during the battle that took place a few years prior. Reports stated that the hippogryph was one of the evils rumored to live in this forest, and he was determined to find

313

and kill the monster. This monstrosity was a mixture of an eagle and a horse. The front half was the eagle, with talons, wings, and a beak. The back half was the horse, with a tail and hooves. The beast was elusive and had given him a hard chase, but he followed its tracks. It had terrorized the land for quite some time, and Michael took up the call to slay the hippogryph. The king offered a bounty for anyone who brought him the monster's head. Michael wanted the bounty. George, Michael's squire, had some ideas for improving the knightly estate, none of which would be cheap.

Michael was not of average height in Drendil, though during his time living in Prikea, many considered him tall. His face had once been young, but with years of experience in the army, and more recently as a hunter, his boyish features had weathered. Lately, he hardly recognized the face that gazed back at him in the mirror. He wore leather armor which gave him protection but didn't hurt his mobility or his stealth. Plate armor would have made too much noise to sneak up on any kind of beast, let alone the hippogryph. At his waist he wore a steel longsword of perfect mediocrity. His status as a Knight-Captain meant he could have picked any weapon he wanted from the king's armory in Shemont, but his own sword had suited him fine after he took it to the castle's blacksmith for an adjustment. The army's blacksmiths focused, out of necessity, on quantity of materials rather than quality, and while Michael understood the need for a surplus of weaponry, he preferred craftsmanship he could trust. The castle's blacksmith imbued his very soul into his wares and ensured that he returned any weapon in significantly better condition than when they came to him. The price had been steep, and Michael had to wait two months to get his sword back, but he considered the effort to be worthwhile.

On the back of his belt, mounted sideways for easy access to the contents, Michael wore a quiver which contained a few dozen arrows. They were special arrows he had received from the armory. Designed for hunting beasts with tough hides, the arrows had thick shafts with a fiercely pointed arrowhead attached to the front and stiff feathers on the back. The heads had a single point with many barbs. Looking at the point head-on, it looked like a cross. The arrow's sharpened edges meant he had to use them cautiously; he sported more than a few scars on his hands from using them without wearing a gauntlet.

The forest was too quiet. Birds and squirrels should have chirped and chattered in the tree branches overhead. Something was gravely wrong. The silence hung in the air like a thick fog. This likely meant the hippogryph was close. Now it was just a matter of finding the beast and slaying it. Michael read as many books as possible that he could find about the hippogryph, but not many existed in Shemont's libraries, even among the multitude of shelves the Battlemages owned. Fewer than half a dozen books in total told anything about hippogryphs, but those books had been helpful enough in tracking the beast. The Mages had tried for so long to get the king to cancel his bounty so they could capture and study the beast, but His Highness ignored their wish after the beast destroyed a village. The king had specifically said they could study it after it was dead if they so desired. This hadn't made the Mages happy, but the king cared not for their happiness in this matter.

Michael walked through the trees, remaining mindful of his footing. According to the documentation, the hippogryph was supposedly able to hear and smell better than a dog, so if it were nearby, it likely already knew of his presence. With senses like those, the creature didn't need any more advantages, and Michael did his best to step as silently as he could, taking care to avoid stepping on sticks and twigs buried in the underbrush.

A pile of freshly broken maple branches lay on the forest floor a few meters ahead. Michael stopped and inspected the branches. They had broken off from high above, likely because of the hippogryph. Perhaps it had tried to perch on the branches, and they had broken under its weight. Perhaps they had fallen as it flew through the forest while it hunted. It was hard to say for sure. Another small pile of oak branches was about ten meters away, so Michael at least had clues he could follow. He was getting closer to his prey; he just knew it.

Hunting the hippogryph was not hard. When it was near people, one simply had to follow the cries of those seeing such an unnatural beast. In the forest, seeing these piles of branches, hearing the sound of animals dying, or the flapping of its great wings was a good sign. With the front of an eagle, the beast ate what an eagle would eat: rabbits, small varmints, fish, and other such creatures.

Not far ahead, Michael spotted a clearing through the trees; it was a perfect place where the monster could have landed deep in the forest. He ensured his bow was ready, drawing the arrow back and riding it all the way forward. He didn't have to check his bow, but it had become a habit for him to do so over the few years that he had been hunting and fighting following the Siege of Shemont.

Michael approached the clearing behind a few trees that would offer him concealment and protection from his quarry. The beast could fly quickly, and its talons were astonishingly sharp. They had, in fact, torn through at least a dozen soldiers during the Siege of Shemont those few years ago. The army had succeeded that night, but not in the ways they had desired. They had lost Týr beyond all possible searching, and the Battlemages had tried everything they could think of to bring him back. From what Joshua and the others said, the bond with him simply didn't exist anymore. It was difficult to tell whether this meant he was dead or alive, and that was something Michael wished not to think about. His loss, along with the countless other soldiers killed by the goblins, ogres, Minotaurs, werewolves, and other monsters that Vor'Kath had accumulated, had been steep, especially since they had neither captured nor killed the Shadow Knight which had been the goal of the entire affair.

Despite all the losses, the city was safe, and the Royal Family had survived, staying in Anselin, through the collective effort of the soldiers involved. Some of the soldiers that had fought that night still saw the king as cowardly for fleeing the city with his wife and son instead of fighting. These years had been an unpleasant time for the king since the Siege. The Master General had also taken some heat for accompanying the king, which Michael thought was fair. The Supreme Warlock of the Battlemages had avoided getting any of the backlash as many people in Drendil, especially the soldiers, still feared Mages and their uncertain powers.

Michael knelt behind a massive oak tree, listening for anything moving in the clearing on the other side of the tree. He heard nothing, but that didn't mean anything. He had made that mistake before and had earned the scars to forever remind him of that. He doubted his face would ever fully recover from that mountain lion. That had been an embarrassing way to nearly die. It took months for Joshua to stop bringing up that incident.

Michael crept around the tree, his bow up and ready to draw. The clearing was empty. He scanned the trees high above looking for any sign of the white feathers and fur of the elusive hippogryph but saw no signs it had even been here. He dropped his bow and sighed briefly. It was starting to look like this would not be his day to claim the bounty…

Made in the USA
Middletown, DE
05 November 2023

41915479R00201